SUNSET BOULEVARD

A-LIST NOVELS BY ZOEY DEAN:

THE A-LIST

GIRLS ON FILM

BLONDE AMBITION

TALL COOL ONE

BACK IN BLACK

SOME LIKE IT HOT

AMERICAN BEAUTY

HEART OF GLASS

BEAUTIFUL STRANGER

CALIFORNIA DREAMING

HOLLYWOOD ROYALTY

SUNSET BOULEVARD

If you like THE A-LIST, you may also enjoy:

The **Poseur** series by Rachel Maude
The **Secrets of My Hollywood Life** series by Jen Calonita
Footfree and Fancyloose by Elizabeth Craft and Sarah Fain
Haters by Alisa Valdes-Rodriguez
Betwixt by Tara Bray Smith

SUNSET BOULEVARD

THE A-LIST
HOLLYWOOD ROYALTY

ZOEY DEAN

poppy

LITTLE, BROWN AND COMPANY
New York   Boston

Poppy

Hachette Book Group
237 Park Avenue, New York, NY 10017
For more of your favorite series, go to www.pickapoppy.com

First Edition: August 2009

Poppy is an imprint of Little, Brown Books for Young Readers.
The Poppy name and logo are trademarks of Hachette Book Group, Inc.

alloyentertainment
Produced by Alloy Entertainment
151 West 26th Street, New York, NY 10001

Cover design by Andrea C. Uva
Cover model photography by Roger Moenks
Cover background photography by George Doyle/Getty Images

ISBN-978-0-316-03182-0

10 9 8 7 6 5 4 3 2 1
CWO
Printed in the United States of America

To my parents, Debra and William, for never making my epic dreams feel too big for me and for helping me feel like the star of my own life. Oh, and for genetically gifting me with good looks and a quick wit.

All right, Mr. DeMille, I'm ready for my close-up.

—Gloria Swanson as Norma Desmond, *Sunset Boulevard*

I'LL GRANT YOU THAT

Myla Everhart's black SUV pulled up in front of Beverly Hills High, and immediately, her driver, Charlie, came around to open the door. Myla sighed and stepped out onto the school's front walkway. At least she'd gotten to come in late. After a terrible, sleepless weekend, she'd gotten her mom, megastar Lailah Barton, to call the attendance office and tell them Myla would be missing her first few classes, citing "female troubles." Worked every time.

Myla walked toward the front doors, faking a bounce in her step. She could almost hear the whispers of the students gathered on the front lawn between their second- and third-period classes. Normally, Myla loved when people talked about her. Relished it, in fact.

As long as what they were discussing fell along the lines of:

• How she'd snagged a limited edition pair of Louis Vuitton peep-toe pumps.

• How her long ebony hair maintained its shimmer.

• How she'd rocked Gucci on the red carpet for one of her parents' new movies.

• What an impossibly beautiful and perfect couple she and Ash Gilmour made.

But she and Ash were officially broken up. She strode down the path at the center of the front lawn, staring down the curious eyes of the student body. She knew exactly what today's Myla Fun Fact was.

Myla Everhart, caught making out with Lewis Buford, the biggest slimeball asshole at BHH. Caught by Ash, that is. Ash, who was mortal enemies with Lewis.

Myla held her head high, gliding across the BHH grounds in her new Miss Dior silver stilettos. Yesterday she and Ash had called a truce, vowing to be civil to one another. True, it was better than him hating her forever. But it wasn't exactly the outcome she'd been looking for.

But at least she had her girlfriends. She was on her way to meet them now. Billie Bollman, Talia Montgomery, and Fortune Weathers could be counted on to take her mind off things. Myla usually chose retail therapy over "Why doesn't he like me?" wailfests, but today, she needed to unload some baggage, and knew her besties would be there to carry it for her.

Her friends were waiting for her in their usual spot, a sunny corner just outside the main entrance to BHH. A light breeze drifted by, and the white Moonstone rose-bushes lining the paver-stone pathway swayed, their dancing, curvaceous shadows flickering over the girls. They were huddled in a circle, like a football team with great taste in couture, but looked up and gave gleeful shrieks as Myla approached.

"Omigod, omigod, omigod," Talia cried, bouncing

on her strappy mulberry Fendi platforms. Myla couldn't wait for her glossy brown hair to reach shoulder length again after an ill-fated bob. "Did you hear?" She tightly wrapped her thin, tan arms around her buxom chest, as if her petite frame couldn't contain her excitement.

Myla shook her head. She wondered briefly if some new rumor about her and Lewis had surfaced, but decided to play it cool. "No, what's going on?"

"Two words . . ." Fortune Weathers chimed in purposefully. She stepped between Talia and Myla, adjusting her black satin Chanel headband so that it rested over her canopy of blond hair. "Grant. Isaacson." She arched one slightly overwaxed brow to punctuate the news, looking like the star of a 1950s commercial for dish soap.

Billie Bollman tapped her bubble-gum pink ballet flat against the brick wall, her smile two sizes too big for her long, horsey face. "He's *here*," she squealed, twirling a strand of her fine, white blond hair. "Somewhere. This is so much better than the time JT performed at your birthday party."

Myla suppressed the urge to roll her eyes. Grant Isaacson was all the current hotness if you were a girl between ages twelve and eighteen who couldn't find a real boyfriend. He'd only acted in two movies. Lucky for him, a beyond-hot love scene with Kristen Bell in Martin Scorsese's *Cocked*, a crime drama about a suburban pizza delivery boy who outwits the mob, had made the film a categorical success with the unlikely teen girl demographic. Grant—a pale, high-cheekboned hipster with permanently mussed dark brown hair—was master of the glower, a sleepy-eyed, purse-lipped glare that most teen girls believed could only be improved if he took off his shirt. Personally, Myla thought his famous look was just a lame attempt at Derek Zoolander's Blue Steel—without the comedic timing.

"Oh-kay," Myla said finally. She was so not in the mood to feign giddiness over a random celebrity sighting. She could eat breakfast with the world's hottest on- and off-screen couple, Lailah Barton and Barkley Everhart, every day if she wanted to. Nicknamed Barbar by the press, her adoptive parents reigned supreme in Hollywood. There were no celebrity sightings to outrank them—except maybe their unspoken rivals, Brangelina—and no news more coveted than that of whatever they did next: charity in the third-world, adopting another malnourished child as a souvenir from an impoverished country, or even something as minor as sitting next to one of their old flames at the Oscars. Of course, nothing beat the news that they were bringing home their sole biological child after sixteen years of separation. They'd done just that two weeks ago, when Myla returned home from Paris to find Jojo Milford sitting at her dinner table. Jojo was Barbar's *real* kid, and Myla, who'd been adopted from Thailand years ago, had instantly detested her. Probably because their parents just couldn't get enough of their bio-kid. After a few weeks of putting Jojo through the wringer, Myla was finally coming to terms with Jojo being here, even liking her a little. Maybe because, for all the attention Jojo was getting, at BHH Myla was still the queen. And that was what counted. "So what about him? He goes here now?"

Talia's eyes widened. "I can't believe you haven't

heard," she whispered, as though ashamed Myla would be so out of the loop. "He just got cast as the best friend in *Class Angel*. They're reshooting a lot of it here this week. I guess they want it all to feel like a real high school." Myla, Billie, and Fortune all turned to Talia, surprised. Her attention span was often so short she didn't finish reading text messages. Talia shrugged. "I read *Variety*."

Myla shook her head, her golden Alex Monroe dragonfly earrings swinging. *Class Angel* was a lame teen movie that she wouldn't have been caught dead seeing even when she was eight years old. And if it was being reshot, it was probably a solid bomb. "Why would I bother reading up on a movie with Fairy Princess in it? Do I look like I spend free time arranging my Bratz doll collection?" The only reason anyone her age knew about *Class Angel* was its A-list collection of stars: Kady Parker was the industry's newest wild child, even if she had never gone full Lohan. Hunter Sparks was the tabloids' latest favorite player, and cover reports of his conquests sold almost as many mags as new baby rumors about her parents. And Amelie Adams was the ultimate good girl. She had a loyal little-kid following from her long-running TV show *Fairy Princess*, and the entire world seemed to be awaiting her eventual fall with sick, rapt attention. Myla had been lying when she pretended to be ignorant of the movie. Her little sisters, Ajani and Indigo, were *Fairy Princess*–obsessed and Myla had promised to take them to *Class Angel* when it came out. Though she'd definitely wear a disguise.

"You would know because Grant Isaacson is the

hottest guy on earth," Fortune said, a little bitchily. "You don't *look* like you live in a cave."

"Yeah, I get it. He's filming a movie here," Myla said hastily, making a mental note to reprimand Fortune later for her impudent tone. But right now, she was impatient to move on. They needed to address a more important topic: how Myla could wish Ash a happy birthday next week, in a heartfelt but not desperate way. "So what?"

"We have the perfect plan is what," Billie chirped.

"You're looking at Amelie Adams's and Kady Parker's new BFFs," said Fortune, drawing out pauses between the letters. "We get close, and we get Grant."

Myla gave Fortune her most sympathetic half-smile. The plan was so lightweight, it would barely qualify for an item on Myla's to-do list. "But why go to all that trouble just to land an actor? Just have one of our parents phone in a favor."

Talia's jaw set in a hard line. She and Myla had been friends long before Fortune and Billie because Talia's mother, Peg Montgomery, owned Montague's, a high-concept brasserie that was a Barbar favorite. In fact, it had been the famed locale of Barbar's hush-hush wedding ceremony and reception. "Who would phone in the favor? You? Just like all those times you've helped when your parents are shooting?"

"I've called in favors," Myla fired back, instantly feeling defensive. It was the truth: Freshman year, her girlfriends had requested bit roles in Barbar's remake of *It's a Wonderful Life*. Hunter Sparks had had a supporting role, and at the time, they'd been into *him*. So maybe it hadn't really worked—Myla had forgotten to ask until the last minute, and they'd only gotten to visit the set, on a day that Hunter wasn't even there. But the fact that she'd gone out of her way for them was what mattered. Where was the loyalty?

"Anyway, Grant will see right through that, Myla," Billie scolded. "It has to be real. And the Lacey twins are off filming their stupid show, so they're out." Moira and Deven Lacey were the school's acting double-threat, and had just announced a junior-year hiatus as they left to film their hit CW show, *School for Scandal*, on location at a Connecticut boarding school. After bragging nonstop about their minor roles in *Class Angel*, they apparently didn't think the parts were worth sticking around for.

"Okay," Myla said, feeling like she might shrink into the pleats of her Marc Jacobs dress. She was used to the occasional snippiness from Fortune and Talia, but Billie was unfalteringly loyal. She'd trade couture for Walmart separates if Myla insisted. What the hell was going on today? Myla lifted her chin proudly, trying to pretend this mini revolution didn't bother her.

The bell chimed, signaling that class was about to start.

"It's okay, Billie," Talia whispered, leaning her petite frame into Billie's athletic one. "She'll see."

Myla's friends fell into step together, forming a previously unheard-of line ahead of her. Two paces behind, Myla felt like the left-behind caboose on the runaway train of her life.

THE PUKE HEARD ROUND THE WORLD

"*That fucking bitch just puked in my mouth!*"

"*Can you say BarfBarf?*"

Barnsley Toole's nasal voice rang in Jojo Milford's ears—and not because she was imagining things. BHH's halls were alive with the sound of retching. Her retching. The video of her yakking on that tool Barnsley was on all her classmates' cell phones, and the interest hadn't waned. She'd hidden in the nurse's office during homeroom, and even kindly old Nurse Jannings had asked, "You're not going to get sick again, are you, dear?" Jojo couldn't believe Nurse Jannings even knew what You-Tube was.

Pulling the hood of her Roxy sweatshirt over her shoulder-length walnut-colored hair, Jojo zipped through the crowded halls to her locker, avoiding eye contact with everyone she passed and praying she wouldn't walk into a wall or something. Not that she could really make her situation much worse.

Which wasn't to say that her situation couldn't get any worse on its own. Her gray metal locker was painted with bright red letters: *BarfBarf Spew Zone—Beware!*

For what felt like the billionth time that week, Jojo found herself thinking, *If only I'd gone to Greenland*. Her adoptive fathers, Fred and Bradley—the only parents she'd ever known—were spending the year there on sabbatical. She'd almost gone with them, until her dads received a call from her *biological* parents, Barkley Everhart and Lailah Barton—aka Barbar, the world's most famous and adored couple. They'd finally found Jojo and invited her to stay with them. Within a few days, she'd said goodbye to Sacramento and her two professor dads and hello to Hollywood. So far it had been with disastrous results.

Jojo licked her finger and attempted to wipe away the cruel words on her locker. But her spit had no impact, and the nasty scrawled letters swam before her eyes. She spun the dial on her combination lock, trying to focus on the click of the numbers instead of the murmurs surrounding her in the hallway. Even the tabloids had been nicer to her in her "time of heave" than her fellow BHH students. *Us Weekly* had mentioned the video, but chalked up Jojo's retching to food poisoning. People said her inability to hold a drink was proof she was too sweet and innocent for the Hollywood life. Even the usually scandal-hungry *Star* said that Jojo's drink had been drugged. But at BHH, everyone knew and relished the facts: Here she was, a Sacramento imposter in their beautiful world, who'd drunk wayyy past her limit and fallen victim to Barnsley Toole's lame come-ons, all of which had been captured on tape at Lewis's party and would later air on Barnsley's MTV show, *Barnsley's Babes*. If she were her sister Myla Everhart, her fellow students wouldn't dare be so overt in mocking her. She knew rumors about Myla kissing the equally douchey Lewis Buford were circling, but only in hushed, deferential tones. Apparently, it took more than being the child of the world's most famous couple to earn your wings at this place.

"Aw, poor BarfBarf got a wittle note on her locker." Rod Stegerson, surrounded by some of his BHH football teammates, sauntered past. His meaty red face, close-cropped brass-colored hair, and short, thick neck made him look like a less handsome version of the orange brick guy from *Fantastic Four*. Jojo glared toward him.

"Why the dirty look?" Rod paused. "'Cause you'll never get a piece of the Rod? Sorry, BarfBarf, I like to kiss with tongue, not chunks."

"So it's true that steroids shrink your brain," Jojo mumbled, annoyed that a jock's lame dis could prompt an instant stress knot to form beneath her shoulder blades. Rod waved her off. "I'm not even going to dignify that with a response." He turned his hulking shoulders away from her, and he and his crew strutted down the hall. Jojo shrank toward her locker, making one more attempt to wipe away the offending words with her sleeve, to no avail.

Feeling powerless, she hefted her backpack onto her shoulder, almost glad the class would be kept busy with a pig dissection in biology, and spotted Jacob Porter-Goldsmith and his friend Miles Abelson rolling an AV cart down the hall. She'd met Jacob, who, she remembered, preferred to be called Jake, in the computer lab on her second day here, and so far he was the only person who'd been nice to her. Jojo moved in front of her locker, wishing she'd worn heels so her head would hide the writing at the very top of her locker.

Jake smiled and gestured to Miles to wait as he moved toward Jojo through the emptying hallway. A few students in distressed denim shot Jake derisive looks with each *swoosh-swoosh* of his brown cords. Third period was about to start.

"Hey, how are you doing?" he asked shyly, self-consciously running a hand through his messy curls.

Jojo gestured to her locker, smiling a little at his sweet concern. "Oh, I'm awesome. Who knew you could be instantly well-known around here just by losing your lunch on a D-list wannabe?" Jojo grimaced at the idea of just how "famous" she was. Her best friend from Sacramento, Willa Barnes, had texted her shortly after Barnsley's video was leaked online, to say that she and the soccer team had seen the whole awful event and were pulling for her. Jake grinned. "Like I said before, this will pass. Give it a few days." It was the same advice he'd given Jojo a few weeks ago, when Myla had been spreading lies about her. Unfortunately, this time what everyone was saying was true. "Trust me, BHH will move on to something else. Maybe even me."

Jojo smirked a little at this. Even though he was adorable, with his ruffled curls and lean, muscular body, Jake was mostly invisible to the BHH student body. Probably because he had no idea how cute he was. The key to popularity, if Myla was any indication, was confidence—even cockiness. "Maybe, but it seems like the gossip wheel keeps landing on me." In her first weeks here, Myla had made Jojo's life a living hell with one nasty rumor after another. The focus had shifted briefly when Myla turned her fury on her ex, Ash Gilmour, telling people that he was a chronic bed-wetter. Now the wheel of misfortune was back on Jojo, but it wasn't Myla's doing. After Saturday's terrible party, Jojo and Myla had a bond, if a tenuous one. "This is so not like JFK—my old high school, in Sacramento. I swear, you can't even graduate from here without mastering the art of gossip."

"I'm flunking out, then," Jake said, his hazel eyes dancing. "Was JFK some kind of clique-free utopia?"

"I don't know. Kids could be mean, I guess. But they weren't so organized about it. Let's put it this way, Justin Klatch, who is basically the coolest, hottest guy ever to walk the halls of JFK, would be crucified at this place." Jojo flashed to an image of Justin's all-American boy face. He'd be eaten alive here. In fact, at BHH, Jojo would probably have a shot with him.

Jacob patted Jojo's arm awkwardly. "I doubt my classmates would ever elect me their spokesperson, but for what it's worth, I'm sorry people are such assholes around here. Miles, too."

Miles, hearing his name, gave a mock salute. "Aye, aye, sir." He pushed his glasses back up the bridge of his long nose. The kids at BHH called him McNothin' because he resembled McLovin' from *Superbad*. Jojo thought he looked more like a stretched-out, preteen Paul Rudd.

Jojo let loose a chuckle, for what felt like the first time in days. She felt her mood lighten from pitch-black to foggy gray. "Thanks, Jake. You too, Miles."

Miles nodded dutifully. "I'm working on an asshole

cure," he said, rubbing his hands together like a mad scientist. "I'll let you know when it's ready."

Jake rolled his eyes at Miles's joke, nodding his head toward Jojo's locker. "I see people are leaving you notes."

Jojo blushed. "It's nothing."

"Everything's spelled correctly," he said. "So at least we know Rod's not a suspect." He paused. "Hold on a sec." He jogged to the cart and opened a plastic Tupperware container, grabbing some kind of cloth and a spray bottle.

"It won't come off, I tried." Jojo sighed. "It's permanent."

Jake shook his head. "You're talking to an expert here," he said. "Ma'am, please step aside," he commanded in a fake cop voice.

He sprayed the substance liberally over the red paint, then rubbed it vigorously with the cloth. The letters instantly faded, leaving just a faint ghost behind. "I had 'I Want My Mommy' written on mine for a whole day before I realized it was just pep club wax pencil," Jake explained, admiring his work. "Kids here don't want to risk a real vandalism charge. Some warm soapy water on a paper towel will get the residue off."

"Thanks. That's gotta go right in your high school karma bank." Jojo hugged Jake excitedly before she realized what she was doing.

Jake blushed. "Like my mom says, I'm saving for college." He shrugged, his dorky orange polo stretching across his athletic shoulders.

"For real, you're my hero," Jojo said, smiling up at

him. "You should try out for the *Class Angel* guy." Jojo could totally picture Jake in the movie as a good-natured, all-American guy, which was what the casting memo distributed in first period had said they were looking for. Tryouts were today in the library.

"I'm waiting on a call from Spielberg," he joked, backing away in Miles's direction. With a final salute, he and Miles set off down the hall.

Jojo hung back, touching the almost-invisible letters on her locker and watching Jake retreat down the hall. Before he and Miles turned the corner, Jake looked back, and—with a sweet grin—waved at Jojo.

Who knew an unlikely hero could be so likable?

CASTAWAYS AND CALCULUS

As Amelie Adams' town car pulled to a stop on the circular drive in front of Beverly Hills High, she would have sworn the sweet scent of teenage freedom was wafting up from its perfectly manicured front lawn. A courier had arrived yesterday with new script pages for her movie, *Class Angel*, and instructions to report to BHH today for a partial reshoot. They were only reshooting about half the scenes, which meant they'd only spend a week or two at BHH. But for Amelie, it meant getting to feel like a real teenager, at a *real* high school. After years of tutors instead of teachers, agents instead of friends, and scripts instead of homework, Amelie was ready for a little dose of high school reality.

She hopped out of the town car before the driver had even unhooked his seat belt. She was T-minus ten seconds from seeing Hunter Sparks again, and nothing was going to slow her down. What seemed like mere hours before, Hunter had dropped her off from a party in the Hollywood Hills, uttering words that had circled Amelie's mind all weekend: *"You need someone like me to look out for you. Because, honestly, there are a lot of guys*

*out there—guys like me, who can't resist you. And you're
too good for us."* After weeks of crushing on him—okay,
months and years—but thinking he saw her as nothing
but a little sister, the words had given her all the hope
she needed. Hope that right now pushed her toward
the school library, where they were shooting their first
scene.

She swung open the front doors of BHH, her heels
clicking against the immaculate ivory tile floor. The foyer
was filled with trophy cases, photos of star students, and
professional-looking posters advertising bake sales, fund-
raisers, and football games. It must have been just before
lunch, as some students carried doggie bags from Mr.
Chow and neat plastic boxes bearing the Zone Diet logo.
Amelie was glad she'd spent some time on her outfit,
wearing her intellectual-looking L.A.M.B. houndstooth
sweater instead of her usual set gear of jeans and a tee.
Every girl in the hall looked like her school wardrobe had
been carefully curated by a personal stylist.

Watching students fall into their cliques and laugh
with their friends just a few feet from her face, Amelie
paused to take it all in, feeling like a wildlife documentar-
ian observing teenagers in their natural habitat.

"So then he said, 'I can't date someone who wears
fur,' and I said, 'Well, I can't be with someone who
thinks minks are real animals.'" A glamorous girl with a
Rihanna haircut tapped her five-inch black patent stilettos against the marble floor, surrounded by a cluster of
lesser beauties. She turned and saw Amelie staring; her
ruby lips pursed as she scanned Amelie from head to toe.
With a sneer, she turned back to her friends. "You know,

I heard Fairy Princess is actually, like, twenty-eight, but her mom is making her pretend to be a teenager until she can get real parts."

Amelie rolled her eyes. Any other day, the remark might have stung, but today Amelie took it in stride. If she'd learned anything from teen movies, it was that bitchy girls were par for the course. Ignoring the girls, she followed the school map, part of yesterday's messenger packet, to the library. She purposefully stepped inside, swept past the circulation desk, and entered the main reading room. Gary, her director, paced back and forth along shelves of new young adult books. When she entered, his eyes fell on her like she was the Holy Grail.

"Oh, thank God," he breathed. "We thought something had happened to you."

Amelie shook her head, as the crew went back to their work. Kady Parker lounged on a love seat next to Grant Isaacson—who Amelie guessed was playing the newly written part she'd read in the revised script.

"Holy crap, I actually beat you," Kady said. "You're never late for anything. What were you up to?" Her eyes glimmered mischievously, as if she were expecting Amelie to say she'd been out all night with Hunter.

Amelie squinted doubtfully. "It's noon. Call time is twelve thirty, right?"

Gary pulled off his trademark ball cap, rubbing his head in frustration. "Did you not get the second memo? Call time moved to eleven for a cast and crew meeting. I guess you haven't heard the other news, either."

Something about the way he said it, and the doleful look in his basset-hound eyes, made Amelie shiver. She was almost grateful to Kady, who rattled off the unpleasant news before Gary could even finish his heaved sigh:

"Hunter's out. Fired," Kady said. Her sapphire eyes were like two asterisks footnoted by her tiny frown. "Not authentic enough. He looks too old for me, comes off too metrosexual, shouldn't have done those trippy Dolce & Gabbana ads for Times Square, et cetera and so on. The producers wanted real. Because nothing says down-to-earth Midwestern high school like BHH, where even the mascot wears Prada."

Amelie wanted to laugh at the joke, but felt choked by the quickening beat of her heart. *So this is a heart attack*, she thought, her brain detached from her body. She almost willed herself to faint, if only to avoid hearing one more wretched, life-ruining fact.

"I'm sorry you're finding out this way, Amelie," Gary said gently, placing a fatherly hand on her shoulder. "It happened over the weekend. The studio saw dailies and just didn't think Hunter was authentic enough." The studio had sat for a dailies session on Saturday morning and hadn't liked everything they saw. Thus, new writers—hired because they'd once served Diablo Cody at Starbucks—a reshoot of about half the scenes, and now a new *cast*? Amelie narrowed her eyes to fight the pressure of the tears mounting. She realized she hadn't spoken at all and, trying to collect herself into Amelie Adams, Child Star (Trademark), she managed to utter, "So what now?"

Gary gripped her in a half-hug, as though relieved Amelie hadn't started wailing and rampaging through the library, knocking books from their shelves. "We're casting a new Tommy Archer from the BHH student body," he said softly. "We've gotta find someone real, and a no-name. If you ask me, it's a stunt so we don't get fall-out from ditching Hunter. A casting session and a huge reshoot in two weeks. I swear they're trying to kill me."

And me, Amelie thought, folding her arms over her chest. What was wrong with her life that she could have everything and nothing at the same time? She'd last worked with Hunter when she was eleven. Would she have to wait five more years to see him again?

So much for high school being the best time of your life.

Two hours later, auditions for Hunter's replacement were in full swing. Amelie's body felt drained as she dragged herself to a black couch, where Grant Isaacson lounged, his bronze hair forming a chaotic halo over his copy of *Zen and the Art of Motorcycle Maintenance*. He pulled the book away from his face, sympathetically smiling at Amelie. "Bad, eh?"

"Way worse than bad," she monotoned, flopping back in exhaustion over the arm of the couch. She'd theorized that the real reason Hunter was let go was to afford Grant, who was currently box-office gold and was prob-ably viewed as bringing edge to the allegedly indie-fied script. Now she was trying hard not to resent him.

From her upside-down position, Amelie tried to smile at a flock of girls who hovered over the new fiction shelf, staring at Grant. The school had allowed the crew use of the library for an audition space, as long as one half stayed open for BHH students and the film didn't cause any disruptions. Apparently, BHH administration had forgotten its female population's inability to function in Grant's presence. Three pretty girls, two blondes and a brunette, were front and center, waving excitedly at Amelie. She waved back, halfheartedly.

She nodded at Grant, scratching her head beneath her new costume accoutrement: an actual halo, worn atop her red curls. Designed by Christian Siriano, the headgear was fashioned from golden lace starched into jagged points. Wearing it, Amelie looked like she'd escaped from an asylum in Colonial Williamsburg. *Insult, let me introduce you to injury,* Amelie thought.

Glancing over at his fan club, Grant smiled his *I'm probably up to no good but you're gonna love it* smile, and said, "So, where's the acting talent at this school?" The power of the Stalker Club's collective giggle could have fueled a smart car for a week.

Kady, flipping through a copy of *Spin* at one of the study carrels, hauled herself up, trudged over, and flopped on the couch across from Amelie. "We're never going to find a Tommy," she said, her slim shoulder peeking out of her wide-neck yellow tunic. "This sucks."

Amelie nodded. "Sucks" was an understatement. All the BHH guys thought they were stars in the own right. They didn't want to go by the script and play Tommy as an earnest, down-to-earth jock. Or they showed up with full makeup. Or, before auditioning, they wanted to talk to Gary about getting Tommy a few more lines.

Tucker Swanson, a surfer with a surplus of confidence, told Gary, "So you know, I surf, like, a lot, and won't need a personal trainer or anything." An Amazonian girl from the volleyball team had tried out, insisting she audition in the name of gender equality, and had even gone in for a kiss with Kady. Rod Stegerson, a truly unhandsome, beefy jock, had *succeeded* in kissing Kady, but without her consent. When Kady had left to detoxify, Amelie'd had to pick up her slack. She'd almost vomited at Geoff Schaffer's strong essence of pot and Funyuns, and had actually dry-heaved when the school's driver's ed teacher, who had to be in his thirties and had brought along headshots from his younger, better-looking years, tried out and grossly asked if she had her license yet.

Near the reference shelves, Gary paced nervously, staring down at his clipboard like it held a death threat. He sank down into one of the oversize armchairs set in a circle near the periodicals. The cast, crew, and the movie itself seemed to be dying a slow death. More than once, Gary had lamented the loss of Hunter. But Amelie knew it was no use. Gary might have wanted Hunter back, but being a director only sounded powerful. In Hollywood, unless you controlled the purse strings, your opinion didn't count.

Amelie checked the clock, hoping it was almost time for tutoring—anything to get out of here. After not returning her calls all weekend, her math tutor, Jake, had finally set a time for them to meet.

"Amelie, Kady, we need you," Gary stage-whispered from across the room. The two girls unenthusiastically pried themselves from the couches.

"See you," Amelie said to Grant, who smirked sympathetically.

Gary was pacing near the information desk, an almost

amused expression on his face. "We've got Lewis Buford over there. You know, 'MTV and *Us Weekly* follow me around because people in Middle America love two things equally: Oprah and raging assholes.' And get this: He wants to go off-book. But I have to give him a tryout or he'll cry foul and we'll be doomed. He's connected." Amelie knew Lewis Buford—well, knew of him, anyway. It was at his party where she'd seen Hunter with another girl.

"Let's just get this over with," Gary said with a sigh. "Last guy of the day, and we'll try again tomorrow. Jesus, why couldn't we be doing this somewhere where kids are actually normal?"

"Like Ohio?" Kady offered.

"Santa Clarita. Burbank. Valencia. Anywhere but Beverly Hills." He walked back to the audition area, where Lewis Buford was doing a set of breathing exercises. He rolled his head from side to side, eyes traveling back and forth between Amelie and Kady. Checking his wavy dark hair in a Clinique compact he pulled from his pocket, Lewis grinned at himself, flashing his dimples.

"Ladies, this will be the second-best threesome I've ever had." Lewis sat on the couch, close enough that Amelie could feel the smooth skin of his waxed forearm at her wrist. Ew. Lewis waved Gary, the casting director, and several assistants over. "I just want to give credit for this performance to Jeremy Piven and *Entourage*, the best show ever. Imagine, you're in a therapist's office. Red here is my wife." He pointed at Amelie. "And that little minx is our marriage counselor." He winked at Kady.

"Okay," Gary said, with forced patience. "Go ahead."

Lewis cleared his throat, posing on the couch with

his arm across the back cushion. He launched into an Ari Gold–style monologue, accusing his wife, Amelie, of being less than human, and his therapist of being an idiot. As he paced between them, he took the opportunity to look down both girls' shirts. His said everything too loudly, and finally huffed past them toward Gary, looking back for his final line. "Good day!"

Finished, Lewis took a bow, returning to the chairs. He kissed Amelie's and then Kady's hand. Amelie wasn't sure, but she thought he was wearing lip gloss. "And that, you sexy bitches, is what I call acting. Call me later for private lessons."

Shaking Gary's hand, Lewis said, "I'll leave my agent's name at the door."

He sauntered off, beyond pleased with himself. Grant looked over the top of his book, studying Lewis in amazement, like a pink unicorn had just clopped by.

"Holy shit." Grant stood, running over to Kady, Gary, and Amelie. "That was fucking awesome. Awesomely entertaining."

Gary shook his head. "Thanks for reminding me. I have to call the studio and beg them to use Hunter again." Amelie's heart leapt at his name. "Hi, Marty," Gary said into his iPhone. "Tryouts went well. Some, um, confident performers here. But no one quite like Hunter."

"Keep your fingers crossed, Amelie," Kady said, sitting down next to her. She was the only person on set who knew about Amelie's Hunter crush, since she'd practically set them up, and had been super-attentive to Amelie—at least as attentive as Kady was capable of being—all day. "We can only hope."

"So, what you're saying is, Hunter's people know we're in trouble?" Gary's voice quivered. If Hunter's agents knew they needed him, they'd ask for more money, and they were already on a shoestring budget. "Fine, but I guarantee he's worth it. I don't think there's a single kid at this school who can . . ."

His voice trailed off as he looked past Amelie to something behind her. Amelie swiveled around to see Jake standing there, his red backpack hanging limply from his shoulder, his lean frame clad in an orange polo shirt and worn brown cords.

"Hey, um, you ready for some math?" Jake croaked nervously to Amelie, blushing as he noticed her director—and now her costars—staring at him. He recognized Kady Parker, the beyond hot girl from *Die Twice*, a horror movie about girl detectives who raised murderers from the dead. The director tapped the shoulder of a plump blond woman and gestured at Jake. The blond woman approvingly clucked her tongue.

"Marty, I'll call you back," Gary said.

The casting director circled Jake in a slow walk. "We might have to take in a couple jackets but height's the same," she said cryptically.

Kady jumped up from her chair, her blue eyes twinkling. "Gary, Gary, Gary, look. . . . He's perfect."

Jake blushed. He had no idea what they were talking about, but if Kady Parker thought he was perfect . . . well, he wasn't going to argue.

"Are you here for the tryouts?" The director, apparently named Gary, asked.

"Um, I'm just here to meet Amelie. I'm her tutor,"

Jake said stupidly, running a hand through his curls. He felt uncomfortably on display. "Perfect for what, exactly?"

"Oh, um, never mind," Gary said dejectedly. "Amelie, your tutor is here."

Amelie finally got it. They'd been sizing up Jake as their new Tommy Archer. She looked Jake over impassively, like a casting director would. And Jake, well, he looked like a Tommy Archer. Like the football player with a hidden talent for writing; like the kind of guy who would be drawn to a quirky girl like Lizzie Barnett, Kady's character; like a guy who might be a star on the football field but would still feel the slightest bit awkward meeting his date's parents. Amelie grinned to herself at the memory of Jake all dressed up to meet her mom on Saturday, when he'd taken her to Lewis's party.

"Wait," Amelie said, picking up the audition pages and thrusting them at Jake. "Jake, can you do me a favor?"

"Sure," Jake said, a little too eagerly. He'd had a crush on Amelie from the moment they first met, but after their ill-fated not-a-date to Lewis Buford's party, he'd been trying to forget he'd ever liked her. When she'd tried to set up their next tutoring session, he'd resisted the temptation to call her back all weekend. But then he'd realized: A guy who *wasn't* hopelessly in love with his tutor would call her back. So now he was going to shoot for normal. Which was an improvement over awkward, love-struck freak.

"Read the lines for Tommy," Amelie said, suddenly inspired. Jake was a friend. He was no Hunter, but working with him could be . . . okay.

Jake cleared his throat and looked down at his page. "So, um, this is kind of weird. The basketball trophy is missing. And they say you took it." He lifted his hazel eyes to meet Amelie's blue ones. He looked at her like he couldn't believe she would steal, or do anything wrong. Because she wouldn't. Amelie was perfect.

"A basketball trophy?" Amelie read Kady's Lizzie Barnett lines, getting excited. Jake was a dead-on Tommy Archer. And he didn't even know it. "You jocks are all the same. Why would I take some symbol of this school's adoration of the meatheaded, patriarchal violent majority? If you hadn't noticed, I'm an artist. Brass-plated plastic isn't something I collect." Amelie was enjoying the chance to sass. At least she got to show the crew she could pull off rebellious high schooler.

Jake threw up his hands in frustration. But he didn't try to lean in, like Rod Stegerson. And he didn't cup her face in his hands, like Geoff Schaffer. "Give me a chance here, Lizzie," he said, his eyes boring into hers. "I know you didn't take it. I want to help you." He capped the line by nodding urgently, his eyes wide.

Kady and Grant were on either side of Gary, each clutching one of his shoulders. "This is the guy, Gar," Grant said. "Sign him up and let's get this thing done. I have to go shoot *A Tale of Two Cities* the third week of October."

"Come on, Gary," Kady said, squeezing Gary's arm as she grinned up at Jake. "He's perfect."

"Perfect for what?" Jake repeated, a little distracted by Kady. She was petite and sort of exotic-looking, with freckles dusting her olive skin, black hair, and inky blue eyes. "Perfect for what?" Gary repeated, sounding almost amused. "Exactly! Unassuming, yet attractive. A little bumbling, but graceful. Not overpowering, but still athletic. You just move here from Ohio, kid?"

A sound resembling a laugh escaped from Jake's throat. "No, I've lived on Bedford Drive my entire life."

"Okay, that's great. Don't change a thing," Gary said. "Go tutor, and tomorrow, come back and be our Tommy Archer."

Jake looked up toward the ceiling of the library, scanning the corners for hidden cameras. This had to be a joke, right? A reality show thing? The older man who stared at him was convincing as a director, his shirt wrinkled and untucked, a baseball cap askew on his head. Kady Parker had her arms crossed expectantly over her chest, her smirk friendly, her eyes welcoming. Grant Isaacson, the dude from *Cocked* whom all the girls couldn't shut up about, was shaking his head in amazement, like he wanted to hug Jake, but couldn't because they were two dudes, and dudes just shook their heads happily. And Amelie, her red curls fanned out behind her, stared at him with her high-definition blue eyes and mouthed, "Just say yes," a look of affectionate impatience on her face. It was a face he had a hard time saying no to.

"Um," he stuttered, cringing that he was starting a sentence with "um" for the fiftieth time that minute. "Okay, I'm in."

Jake considered himself a smart guy—at least when it came to problems with definite solutions. But he wasn't winning points right now. He'd just agreed to be Tommy Archer in *Class Angel*. Had he just solved a problem, or created one?

Amelie jumped up, hugging him, and Kady joined in, her petite frame stronger than it looked. Grant and the director clapped him on the back.

"We got our guy!" Gary shouted, completely disobeying the library's indoor-voice rule. "We. Got. Our. Guy! Yes!"

Jake caught sight of his own *Holy crap!* expression in one of the iMac monitors. This was really happening. In his head, he heard the booming voice that narrated adventure movie trailers say, "The math tutor has become . . . a leading man."

It was like something out of a teen movie. Which, Jake realized, he had better get used to.

THE GHOSTS OF GRUDGES PAST

Ash Gilmour stared at the solitary calzone on his black lacquer dinner plate. To any other guy, one of the giant meat-and-cheese-filled pockets from Frankie & Johnnie's Pizza would be a heavenly dinner, but it was his fourth this week. The kitchen was quiet, as usual, the only sounds the tiny creaks and groans of his Beverly Hills house settling. Toting his half-empty can of Rock Star across the kitchen, Ash opened the Sub-Zero fridge looking for a vegetable to complement the mountain of dough. He was greeted with nothing but his own half-filled takeout containers from the last few days.

He shuffled back to the mahogany kitchen table, setting a fork and knife down on one of the six red Egyptian cotton place mats that the maid, Zelda, washed every week, even though Ash was the only one who ate here, and he always sat in the same spot.

It hadn't always been like this.

When his mom and dad were still together, in grade school, and his older sister, Tessa, wasn't away at college, the kitchen was always buzzing. His mom and dad would playfully argue over who got the last glass of their favorite pinot noir, his mom making goofy sad puppy dog eyes and his dad pretending to pull out his short faded gold hair before finally giving in. He could almost see Tessa sitting across from him, her ash blond hair in the low pigtails she wore from seventh grade through sophomore year, flipping through a copy of *Mental Floss* and spitting out weird facts between bites of dinner.

He forced down another bite of the calzone, crumbs falling onto his faded Ben Sherman Union Jack sweatshirt. He needed to get out of this ghost house. As he watched a blob of cheese ooze onto the gleaming black plate, his iPhone sounded its familiar Jack White guitar solo. His dad's stern face appeared on the digital screen.

"Hello?" Ash answered the phone. "What's up, Dad?" He winced at the enthusiasm apparent in his voice. He sounded like a lovesick girl who'd been stood up for the prom.

"Ash, I'm in the middle of something, so let's make this quick," his dad's brisk baritone crackled over the phone.

Ash rolled his eyes. It was just like his dad to call him but then act like Ash was the one intruding. After the divorce, Gordon had become one of those harried jerks, thanks to a newfound habit of staying out late, meeting models and starlets and partying with rockers not that much older than Tessa. The mix CDs he'd so carefully made for Ash, with early cuts from the bands and artists he was working with at the time, slowed to a trickle and then disappeared altogether, and his clowning around gave way to a fog of constant grumpiness. But at least back then he was still company—grunting over the headlines in the *L.A. Times*, occasionally instructing Ash to read something about one of his musical prodigies in the Calendar section. And Tessa was still around then, choosing to finish BHH instead of attending school in Austin, where their mom lived. Then his dad met and married Moxie, an almost-supermodel from Russia, and everything changed.

"Are you listening?" Gordon snapped. "We haven't seen each other in a while, huh?"

Like you care, Ash thought, as he said, "No, I guess not."

Last April, his dad had finally married Moxie, who'd just given birth to their twins, Caesar and Julius, and moved to a fresh new house for his *new* family in Malibu. Gordon wanted Ash to move with them and go to school there, but Ash wasn't having it. He had friends at BHH, and at the time he had Myla. Not to mention her family dinners, where he was a daily guest, and never felt like an outsider. "Great decision, son, choosing a girl over your family," Gordon had said. "You can just live here, by yourself, but don't come crawling to me when she dumps you." Ash had hated his dad for saying it, and from that moment on wanted to prove he didn't need Gordon for anything. But then Myla went on a three-month trip over the summer and Ash, with nothing to do, realized how lonely the house could be.

Her trip, at least, was temporary. But now he and Myla were truly over, and the cold reality of eating takeout alone at a table for six had really started to sink in. He still couldn't sleep right. Every night, the vision of Myla kissing Lewis fucking Buford refreshed itself in his head.

"Meet me at Spago, at eight, okay?" Gordon said.

Ash toyed with the corner of the stiff place mat. His dad hadn't said, "Meet us," just "Meet me." Did he really want to have dinner, just the two of them? Ash wondered if his dad had some kind of birthday surprise in mind, even though he didn't turn eighteen until next week.

"Yeah, sure," Ash said. "Any special reason?"

"We'll talk when you get there," Gordon said. "See you then." Gordon hung up without a goodbye.

Ash jumped up and tossed his calzone in the trash. He was having a father-son dinner. As he placed his empty plate in the dishwasher he felt oddly cheered. His dad would never come out and say he wanted them to be close again. But if Gordon Gilmour was capable of even a minor reconciliation, then maybe Ash had it in him to forgive and forget.

A few hours later, Ash pulled his 1969 black Camaro up to the front door of Spago, the incessant beat of The Ooh La Las, his dad's latest musical find, thumping over the sound of passing cars on Canon Drive. Clicking his iPod off, he checked his hair in the rearview mirror. Using more gel than he ever had in his entire life, he'd managed to tame his hair off his face, so it looked a little more dignified. The last time he'd been out with his dad, for a Grammys pre-party at the Museum of Modern Art, Ash had worn his hair in its usual floppy style only to have Gordon chide, right in front of Bruce Springsteen, "Ash, I may work with musicians, but remember, you're the son of a businessman, not a rock star. Try a little professionalism."

Tonight, he'd made every effort not to let his old man down. He wore a dove gray fitted Hugo Boss shirt, a gift from Myla that had never left the box, tucked into a pair of charcoal slim-fit Armani trousers. He slung his jacket, a black narrow blazer with a slight sheen, over his arm as the valet opened his door and Ash made his way out and into the restaurant.

Spago's interior looked like a geometry lesson gone horribly awry. An obsessive-compulsive guest could spend hours trying to find all the trapezoids, diamonds, and parallelograms hidden in the paintings, the furniture, even the ceiling. The décor was mostly unchanged since the restaurant, historic by L.A. standards, had opened in 1982.

Ash walked directly to the hostess stand, even though he was early. It was seven forty-five, but he wanted to be here before his father, just to show how important this night was to him.

The hostess, a tall, sharp-featured woman with short, spiky black hair, greeted Ash with a purr. "May I help you, sir?"

Ash, noticing many men were wearing jackets, slid his on as he answered. "I'm meeting my father, Gordon Gilmour," he said. "I'm early, though."

The woman checked the giant reservation book spread open atop the hostess stand. "Mr. Gilmour's party has already been seated, in the private dining area," she corrected him. Ash nervously checked the time on his phone. He was definitely early. And what was this about "Mr. Gilmour's party"? She waved one hand for Ash to follow her, and they cut through the dining room, past a table of harried-looking agent types all tapping e-mails into their BlackBerries.

The private room was painted the same bright yellow, but the lights were dimmer, and candles flickered on each of the dozen tables. A long red felt banquette ran along one wall, and Ash found Gordon sitting here, surrounded by his minions from his label, More Records. Gordon was laughing at something his lead A&R guy, Lee Winters, was saying. His bellow seemed to suck all of the air from the room. Gordon's eyes flickered in Ash's direction, but the way his father's gaze swept right over him, Ash could have been a busboy.

He stood there dumbly. His dad had said, "Meet *me*." Not "Come to some boring business dinner so I can ignore you in front of my staff."

Ash saw his dad's high forehead crinkle above his raised eyebrows. His eyes, a harder brown than Ash's, scanned his son's neat hair, jacket, and pressed pants. "Everyone, I think you know my son, Ash," he said, and immediately, the whole table was at attention, the half-dozen guys in suits rising to clasp Ash's hand tightly and slap him on the back. The two women competed with their male counterparts for firmer handshakes. Ash sat down, water and a glass of red wine materializing before him. Next to him was an empty place setting, the wine drained, traces of red lipstick smudging the rim of the glass. Maybe Moxie *was* here. He thought he smelled her heavy rose perfume still swirling in the air.

"How's the car?" Gordon asked, leaning across the table. When he'd moved to Malibu, he'd left several of his pet cars at the Beverly Hills house, and told Ash he could have one. Ash had chosen the 1969 Camaro SS not only because its turbo engine took full advantage of rare openings on Sunset Boulevard but also because his dad used to take him for drives up the PCH in it. But ever since Ash started driving the Camaro, Gordon had taken a newfound interest in its health and well-being, as if expecting Ash to total it within months.

"Good, drove it here today," Ash said, taking a gulp of the dry wine, letting its warmth course through his chest.

Waiters came to the table, adding seared tuna, panroasted chicken, and braised veal to each plate, alongside baby artichokes, fresh cavatelli pasta with pine nuts, and oversize mushrooms bursting with goat cheese. Once everyone had food, Gordon clinked his glass with his fork.

"You all know why we're here," he boomed, as his staff clung to every word. *Not me*, Ash thought. Gordon rarely mixed family and business. "We have an auspicious new addition to the talent roster at More Records, even if she has been in the bathroom an awfully long time."

Light giggles burst out around the table.

"Honestly, I hate the work that goes into scouting England for the States' next pop stars, but More Records has built a legacy of finding the best of those and bringing them across the pond." He chuckled before his staff caught on that he expected them to laugh. "She's, as you know, a bit of a handful. We haven't had someone like this on our hands since our little role in Keith Richards's solo career. But I'm daring to say that . . ."

Gordon's voice trailed off as all eyes turned toward

the far corner of the room. Daisy Morton, Britain's latest sensation and Gordon's newest client, stumbled in, toting a half-drunk bottle of wine in one fist.

Applause broke out around the table, and Gordon's flock stood with wineglasses raised. Ash gulped down his stuffed mushroom in surprise. Daisy Morton? *Crazy* Daisy Morton? With the boyfriend she'd met through a prison pen pal program? Who'd drunkenly pushed down one of the stoic guards at Buckingham Palace? What was his dad *thinking*?

The words *hot mess* weren't quite strong enough to describe her. Daisy's hair, dyed violet with roots the color of wet sand, was clasped to the sides of her head in two sagging buns. Her pretty face had been attacked by her makeup bag with a faint line of fuchsia lipstick running across her cheek, Joker style. Her eyes, twinkling mischievously under the dim lights, resembled two full silvery moons, but her ravaged black and blue eye makeup bruised the effect. She was all chaos and drama with—Ash had to admit—a few really catchy woe-is-me songs. But even the occasional good song wasn't enough to convince Ash that fans followed Daisy for her great music, and not for her train wreck of a life.

"Oi, Mr. Gilmour," Daisy shouted, in a nasal voice too loud for the room. "What're you banging on about?"

"Just toasting you, Daisy," Gordon said, beaming at his new find like she didn't resemble someone who'd just survived nuclear Armageddon. A thick layer of powder made Daisy's face look pasty, but healthy-looking olive skin peeked out from the straps of her long black American Apparel tank top, which she wore over a fluffy purple tutu, a trademark of hers, and a pair of red Converse high-tops.

"Love a toast, love," she said, in her Cockney slur. She raised the wine bottle victoriously as she ambled to the table. She caught Ash staring and smiled, displaying a set of surprisingly white and nearly straight English teeth. Her left incisor overlapped her front teeth by a centimeter, which Ash might have found cute if not for the rest of her. She tipped the wine bottle back, swigging greedily, as she fumbled her way toward the table. Slamming the nearly empty bottle down at the seat next to Ash, she asked, "And who's this bloke?"

"Ah, someone finally asks," Gordon said, gesturing for everyone to sit again. Daisy plopped down in her chair, her hand flopping lazily onto Ash's leg. "This is my son, Ash. He's about your age and, since I'm in Malibu most of the time, we thought he could be your right-hand man while you're in Beverly Hills," Gordon said, winking at Daisy.

"I'd prefer if he used both hands on me, if you don't mind," Daisy teased, her hand sliding dangerously close to Ash's zipper.

Ash felt his jaw turn to stone, his teeth fighting each other in their involuntary grinding. *What. The. Fuck.* His dad wanted him to play assistant to some crazy-train English broad who thought he was man meat? His eyes cut to the emergency exit, and he imagined darting for the door, jumping into the car, and driving to Mexico. He'd change his identity, start fresh. His new name could be Quentin McQueen. Or Jack Plant Page.

Gordon laughed, his mouth still full of veal. The rest

of the table followed suit, except for Ash, who was still in shock. Shouldn't they be horrified? His dad had basically sold him off to some wrecked, horny freak.

"Don't worry, birdie. We're going to have some fun," Daisy whispered wetly in his ear, her breath warm and winey against his neck.

Gordon rose, nodding to Ash. "Come with me to the bar for a second? I need something stronger."

Ash followed his dad to the bar in the main restaurant area. The other patrons stole glances at them, knowing the back room of Spago was sure to conceal boldface-name types. The bartender, an Amazonian girl with mahogany hair that swished like it was animated by Disney, purred, "What would you like?" Her velvety brown eyes never left Ash's dad.

Gordon squared his shoulders, leaning against the bar. "Surprise me."

Watching as she poured several shots of Grey Goose into a silver cocktail shaker, Gordon muttered to Ash, "So, I noticed you looked upset back there."

Relief washed over Ash. So his dad wasn't so dense, after all. "Yeah, I was just a little surprised, is all," Ash said, pushing back a lock of hair that had somehow escaped the gel's death grip. "But honestly, so much is going on in my life, with school and this whole Myla thing—we broke up, Dad—that I think Daisy would just be awfully hard to swallow right now. I bet Lee would love to do it," Ash suggested, naming his dad's number one lackey.

The bartender set a martini glass with a curvy blue stem in front of Gordon, her maroon lips curved in a smile. "Grey Goose martini with lemon peel. Hope you like it," she said, swishing away to take another order. Gordon took a long, slow sip and turned to look at Ash.

"You're right. Lee would love to do it. Guy would sell his left nut for the chance to move higher on the totem pole. But look at Lee. He's thirty-two. Totally out of touch. Still thinks *American Idol* is hip. Daisy is a special case. She's . . . fragile. I need someone who she can see as a friend, as a peer. So of course I thought of you."

Ash knew his dad's salesman mode. Smooth patter, *you're my guy* pep talks. He'd heard it all before. But he'd never been on the receiving end. He couldn't remember the last time his dad had complimented him, and even if it was with an ulterior motive, it felt . . . good. A hell of a lot better than criticism and derision. As his dad's hand closed tightly around his shoulder, Ash knew he'd say yes.

He nodded. "I'll do it."

Gordon's eyes went from serious to alight, like a slot machine hitting diamond sevens. "I knew I could count on you," he said, patting Ash's shoulder once more before turning to head back into the dining room.

Ash closed his eyes, hating that his father's tiny gesture made him feel like a grateful, freshly trained puppy. Inhaling, he concentrated on sound: silverware chiming against plates. Wine being poured into glasses. Voices mingling in the air.

Just as he was convincing himself this was a good thing, that Gordon would appreciate him for a change, he heard it: Daisy's loud voice, somehow traveling from Spago's back room to the main floor. "Where's that dishy son of yours, Mr. Gilmour? We're gonna have a right time."

Ash sincerely doubted that.

RODS AND MONSTERS

Jojo slunk into her American history class and found her seat, three desks back in the center of Mr. Castorman's classroom. She nodded a hello to Myla, who sat two rows away. Myla half-smiled, examining her freshly painted deep red nails. Jojo looked down at her own hands, her short, squared nails done in a similar color but chipping already. On Sunday Myla had taken her to Elle, one of the poshest manicure salons in the city, as a sort of peace offering after their rocky start. Ever since the Barnsley incident Myla had been really sweet, and seemed to have accepted the fact that Jojo was in her life for the foreseeable future. But Jojo wasn't counting her chickens yet. As grateful as she was for a friend in her sister, Jojo still didn't trust Myla. Who knew when she would change her mind?

Rod Stegerson was holding court with a few of his buddies, talking about the San Diego Chargers' poor performance on *Monday Night Football*. Jojo flipped open her massive textbook and pretended to read about the Lincoln-Douglas debates.

"Hey, dudes, look who's here." Rod leered in Jojo's

direction, his ruddy face orange under the fluorescent bulbs. She shrank in her chair, dread colliding in her stomach with the roast-turkey-and-Brie wrap she'd downed for lunch in a little-trafficked corner of the BHH library, which had quieted down since the *Class Angel* film crew had moved on to a different location on the grounds.

"She looks so sweet and innocent, right? But check this out." Rod pulled his iPhone from the pocket of his Abercrombie sweatshirt, flourishing it like he had something new to show them. Jojo felt queasy at the tinny sound of her digital hurling.

Just then, Lewis Buford strode in, his handsome face smiling widely to show off his deeply dimpled cheeks. His rugby shirt, emblazoned with his initials, L.B., in huge Old English type, was unbuttoned, revealing a tanned, waxed chest. He immediately found Myla's desk, girlishly perching on the corner. "Myla, where've you been, baby?" he purred, seemingly oblivious to Myla's hateful expression.

"Everywhere you're not, Lewis," Myla said coolly, looking directly at him with her catlike green eyes. Since the party, Lewis had been calling her nonstop. After his billionth call, Myla had changed her outgoing message to, "This is Myla Everhart. Leave a message and I'll call you back. Unless this is Lewis Buford. Two and a half words for you: Not. F-in. Interested."

Lewis clucked lewdly, sliding off the desk. "I'll catch you after class, babe. Trust me, you want me." He squeezed Myla's shoulder as he passed.

Myla shrugged him off, rolling her eyes. Jojo watched as Lewis stopped next by Rod, watching the video play yet again. "Didn't that fucking kick ass?" Lewis said. "Barnsley got, like, two hundred e-mails on the MTV website and the episode hasn't even aired yet."

Their teacher, Mr. Castorman, walked in, and Jojo felt relief wash over her. Once class started she could at least listen and try to forget their teasing.

"Class, give me ten minutes," he said instead. "I have to go finish an important phone call in the teachers' lounge." It was common knowledge that ancient Mr. Castorman, who had exactly seventeen hairs left on his liver-spotted head, did the *New York Times* crossword during lunch. Everyone in his sixth-period class got lucky about once a week when Mr. Castorman couldn't finish the puzzle before the bell and left his students unattended as he got the last few words.

Jojo glared at him angrily as he left. How dare he leave her here with these vultures?

"Sweet," she heard Rod say, feeling her insides shrivel. "Let's go talk to our little BarfBarf."

He swaggered over, his jock buddies and Lewis close behind. Every face in the class turned to look as Rod pulled up a chair, leaning against Jojo's desk. She could smell the garlic from his carb-loading lunch.

"So, what do you have against Barnsley Toole?" he started. "Is it him in particular? Or maybe all guys make you sick. Jojo's sort of a lezzie name, isn't it?"

Lewis guffawed, "Dude, she's a lezzie."

"It's short for Josephine," Jojo corrected him. Her heart thumped nervously at the class's eyes turning toward her.

"So, Josephine, would you puke on me too? 'Cause I

bet you couldn't handle this either." Rod stood to his full gargantuan height, displaying his bulk.

"You wish," Jojo muttered, her whole body shaking with anger. With one quick move, she could corner kick Rod's shin. Then again, all she needed was to be the barfing girl who also had an anger management problem.

"Yeah, right," Rod said. "Like I'd wish for that. Who do you think you are? You might be Barbar's kid but that don't mean shit if you're a puke-filled lesbian."

Jojo dug her nails into the underside of her cherry-wood desk. How long had this ignorant homophobe gone unchecked?

Before she could reply, Jojo's phone vibrated in her pocket. She slid it out, looking down at the screen under her desk. She silently prayed it wasn't a goofy message from Willa that Rod would see, or a picture of her dads on their sabbatical, arms around each other. If Rod knew the girl he was wrongly calling a lesbian had a set of adoptive gay fathers, he'd have ammunition to last the school year.

To Jojo's surprise, it was from Myla. *Don't let that asshole talk to you like that,* it read.

"Hey, Rod," Myla cooed sweetly. "I was wondering something."

Rod turned, looking Myla up and down as he bit his lip. She was a picture of cool composure, looking model-perfect in her red and gray Phillip Lim cadet jacket over a short violet Marc Jacobs pleat dress. "Don't worry, I still think you're hot even if your sis is nasty."

Myla sighed heavily, every eye in the classroom turning to her with interest. "No, I thought you should tell

Jojo about last year's game with Malibu. You know, the one where you got so nervous, you wet yourself at halftime."

Rod's red face grew almost purple as he turned to his buddies in shock. "Dudes, you promised you'd never tell anyone," he yelped, his voice almost a whimper. He tore from the class as it broke out in peals of laughter.

Jojo beamed. Someone had ammunition, and it wasn't Rod.

After class, Jojo waited for Myla in the hall, leaning casually against the cool cinder-block wall. Her hood was down and she felt free, and a little less like she had to hide.

Myla was the last student to file out, thanks to the crowd that gathered around her desk, wanting to know all about Rod's nervous bladder.

Jojo hugged Myla hard, hoping the gesture wouldn't annoy her. "That was amazing. Thank you, thank you, thank you."

Hitching her silver Balenciaga tote over her shoulder, Myla shrugged. "No big deal. He deserves it. Hey, want to go to tea?"

Jojo squinted at her, puzzled. "What about seventh and eighth?"

"You have to stop hiding in the library already. Those classes are canceled today—they announced it at lunch. They're doing a montage of Kady Parker's character thinking she's going nuts seeing her angel everywhere. They need a bunch of classrooms and the hall. Too much disruption, I guess."

Jojo raised her eyebrows. So far, *Class Angel* didn't

seem like *enough* of a disruption. She'd been hoping the movie's arrival would take some of the interest off her, but so far kids at BHH seemed more annoyed than awed that the movie was being filmed at their school. Grant Isaacson was the only real distraction. His trailer was next to the tennis courts, and girls who'd been excused from PE all year had actually shown up today, preening as they waited for turns with the auto-serve machine. But they'd never be so déclassé as to actually ask for his autograph. Willa, Jojo's best friend back home, had texted her asking for it, but even if she was locked in a room with Grant—with a stack of his headshots, and a million working pens—she would never risk additional scorn by doing something so *not* BHH.

Jojo grinned. "Sounds good. But is this, like, going to be okay with Billie and Talia and everyone?" It wasn't that she was scared of them, but she was just getting comfortable with Myla and didn't know how the whole pack-leader thing worked.

Myla scoffed. "They're going to stay here, and hang around to see if Grant Isaacson will, who knows, make them his official groupies or something."

"Really?" Jojo said, rolling her eyes. "How lame."

Lame was right. Myla was beyond annoyed with her girlfriends. They'd practically shrieked when Grant strolled by their table in the cafeteria today. The very last thing she wanted to do, besides ever see Lewis Buford's face again, was watch her friends burst into preteen giggles at some one-hit wonder who just got his Screen Actors Guild card.

If she hadn't been on the outs with Ash, Myla might

have put up with it, maybe even played along. But as it was, her friends seemed to care a lot more about how Grant's copper hair hung over his topaz eyes than about how Myla needed them. Sure, she'd never been one to talk about her feelings ad nauseam, but her best girl-friends had always been there to plan shopping trips, spa visits, and evenings out whenever she and Ash had fought in the past. Now they were actually broken up, and her friends' best effort had been an offer to join them when they invited Amelie Adams and Kady Parker to lunch.

"Yeah, completely lame," Myla said, gesturing Jojo to follow. "The car's waiting. Let's go."

Myla and Jojo sat on the outdoor terrace of the Bel-Air Hotel's restaurant, which overlooked Swan Lake. Jojo couldn't believe it contained actual, majestic-looking swans and not the dingy gray ones she'd seen at the Sacramento community golf course. The hotel's famed bird-of-paradise plant loomed overhead, casting jagged shadows on their white linen tablecloth. Around her, the clink of silverware chimed daintily as well-dressed ladies nibbled on finger sandwiches.

Jojo breathed in, loving the smell of fresh apricots that wafted from a nearby tree. The hotel's glam pink stucco buildings, set deep off Sunset Boulevard, had made Jojo feel underdressed. Now she felt just right, wearing Myla's cadet jacket over her soft cotton T-shirt. At the table next to them, a set of blue-haired ladies who looked like iden-tical twins in their pink Chanel suits squawked to one another about how "adorable" Myla and Jojo were.

Bel-Air tea was Myla's bad-day destination, a fact

she hadn't wanted to share with Jojo. Her new sister
had gone through enough today. Just the fact that Jojo
had no interest in Grant had been a monumental lift to
Myla's spirits. Myla laughed to herself. A week ago, the
last person she'd have imagined bringing to tea was this
intruder, who arrived and seemingly claimed all their
parents' attention instantly. But then again, a week ago,
Myla had still thought her breakup with Ash was just an
extended bout of his stubbornness to give up in a fight.
And a week ago, she'd have been here with her friends.
Myla knew they'd be back . . . eventually. In the meantime, a little sisterly bonding couldn't hurt.

"Thanks again for your help in class. I could never do
that," Jojo said. "I just clam up. It's like you studied for
that moment."

"No," Myla said, brushing off the compliment. "I was
raised by Barkley Everhart and Lailah Barton is all."

Jojo rolled her eyes. "I wish that was it. Come on. I'm
genetically tied to Barkley and Lailah. If you get that from
them, shouldn't I too? Maybe they made a mistake."

The reminder that Jojo was her parents' flesh-and-
blood true kid stung Myla, but the prickle passed quickly.
There was no doubt in Myla's mind that Jojo was Barbar's real kid. Jojo's eyes were the same one-in-a-million
violet as her mom's, and her grin was 100 percent pure
Barkley. Jojo's problem was that she didn't know *how* to
be their daughter.

"Nurture versus nature. You were raised by two men
who, no offense, think hip is just a bone in your pelvis.
Our parents taught me plenty about charity, but I grew
up in Hollywood. I learned how to do cutthroat when

the time is right. You didn't have that advantage." Myla looked into Jojo's eager violet eyes as they twinkled in the sun. With her easy smile, open face, and trusting gaze, Jojo seemed the perfect candidate for a Myla makeover. And if she was going to be part of the family, shouldn't she live up to the Everhart name? Myla leaned across the table, an idea forming. "I can change all that."

Jojo shrugged. "Thanks, but it's not like you can swoop in every time some jerkbag lays into me."

"Stop being dense. I'm not going to be your pit bull. I can do way better. Teach you everything you need to know to be part of America's most famous family."

Jojo laughed, several scone crumbs flying from her lips. She reddened, covering her mouth with her hand. From under her palm, she said, "It's not like I'm a simple twelve-step program away from ruling the school."

Myla let go of Jojo's wrist, sinking back into her chair like a queen evaluating a gift of jewels from one of her subjects. "Maybe not overnight, but I'm Myla Everhart. My program doesn't need twelve steps. Just follow my lead, and you won't feel a thing."

Myla folded her arms neatly over her chest, cocking her head in that powerful half-grin. The mere tilt of her chin seemed to pull the waiter back, almost magnetically, and he asked, "Can I get you anything else?" His eyes spoke differently. They said, *Please let me get you something else, Miss Everhart. I live to serve a girl like you.*

As Myla sent him away with a sweet "No, thank you," she turned back to Jojo, eyebrows raised. "So, you in?"

"In." Jojo nodded.

As if she had a choice.

AMERICA'S NEXT TOP MYLA

"Okay, so, you're getting ready for school the day after someone bitchy—let's say the female Rod Stegerson—trashes your Prada shoes for being last season. What do you wear?" Myla swung open both sets of double doors to her massive closet. "Show me."

Jojo felt her jaw drop in awe. She pushed a strand of her thick, almond-hued hair out of her violet eyes to get the full view. Myla's closet qualified as the Eighth Wonder of the World. Each type of clothing had about twelve feet of rack space in the double-decker closet, which stretched all the way up to the twelve-foot-high ceiling and across the longest wall of Myla's sprawling room. Fabrics of every texture, organized by color, loomed overhead like a rainbow. Myla even had one of those library ladders that slid across the top so she could reach things on the highest racks. At the center of all this was a twelve-foot-tall shrine to Myla's shoes, lit from above and below with small recessed bulbs. The lights cast each pair of shoes in a glow, giving every designer stiletto, sandal, wedge, and boot an aura of divine magnificence.

"Holy shit," Jojo croaked. She'd already been impressed

with Myla's four-poster bed with its pristine black-and-white duvet of vintage fashion magazine covers, the white dresser painted with brightly hued Pop Art–style daisies, the hulking wide-screen TV and velvety purple couch, identical to Jojo's burgundy one. But the closet was intimidating, like some significant artwork that you'd go see on a field trip and not know how to describe in your essay afterward.

"Do you have an answer? Or are you just going to stare?" Myla was sitting across from the closet in one of three low fuchsia armchairs clustered around a black cube table. She tapped the toe of her Christian Louboutin T-strap sandal against the wood floor, the shoe's fiery orange butterfly design appearing to flutter as she did. Her eyes were a jade mystery as she coolly regarded Jojo, with her familiar half-smile.

Jojo frowned. "So you're giving me word problems? If Jojo wears last season's Prada shoes, and female Rod makes fun of her, what does Jojo wear tomorrow to show that bitch who's boss?" Jojo still wasn't sold on the whole makeover project—mega-makeovers were for the movies, or at least reality show contestants. Jojo was just . . . Jojo. And no quantity of designer clothes or Myla maxims could change that. But if going along with the scheme was a means to hanging out with Myla, Jojo would take it. She stared down at her feet, thinking. Her favorite new shoes, a pair of silver Hollywould wedges that her mom had given her last week, seemed to wink back up at her.

"It's a trick question," Jojo finally said, feeling triumphant. "I wouldn't wear last season's shoes!"

Myla pursed her lips dispassionately. "It *is* a trick question. But you're wrong." She popped up from her chair with a swish of silk, pacing in front of her wardrobe like a general checking the barracks. She began to toss items of clothing onto her bed.

"You could wear this." She threw out a low-cut red Vivienne Westwood sweater. "You could wear this." A pair of black sequined leggings flew past Jojo's nose. "You could wear this, this, or this." She plucked out a green Juicy Couture minidress, a brown Burberry safari dress, and a black Fendi cashmere sweaterdress and tossed them on the bed like she was dealing cards.

"I don't get it," Jojo said, her violet eyes scanning the items. "You picked that stuff at random."

Myla shook her head. "Random is exactly right. The outfits are immaterial. The key is, those shoes are the *only* thing you absolutely *must* wear the next day. Show girl-Rod that—last season or not—if they look good, and you rock them like a pair of Pradas should be rocked, no one gives you shit about where they came from, or *when* they came from."

Jojo processed this information with greater concentration than she'd paid to the Pythagorean theorem in geometry class at JFK. "So I can do whatever I want? Then why do I need these lessons?" She flopped into one of the chairs, already exhausted. As far as she might have come from her Aéropostale sweatshirts and Forever21 jeans, she sincerely doubted she could ever achieve Myla's poise and flawless style.

Myla pulled Jojo up by the arms. "Because you don't get what it means to do whatever you want. In the back of your head, you're always wondering what people think of you and you get so caught up wondering that you paralyze yourself. Take your whole Barnsley incident. Let's role-play. I'm you, you're Barnsley."

Jojo rolled her eyes, even though she was intrigued. She didn't exactly care what people thought but she did overanalyze every little thing. It had taken Jojo sixteen years to figure that out about herself, and Myla had done in it a few weeks. "Do we have to?"

Myla ignored the question. She tottered on her heels until she was an inch away from Jojo. Pretending to be drunk, she cuddled up to Jojo. "Sure, Barnsley, I'll kiss you." She lolled her head onto Jojo's neck, and Jojo cracked up at the impersonation. Myla shot her a *don't laugh* look. Jojo squashed her lips.

Myla leaned into Jojo, moved her head back and forth like a deranged puppet, and then fake-hurled with a dramatic heaving noise.

Jojo jumped back, just like Barnsley had. The words she couldn't forget came easily. "That fucking bitch puked in my mouth!"

Myla-as-Jojo cocked her head to one side, fake-scanning her outfit for wayward puke. Then, she looked into Jojo-Barnsley's eyes, and said, loudly and slowly, like each word was a well-aimed arrow, "Barnsley Toole, you disgusting pig. Your mouth tastes like"—she pondered the bouquet, like she was at a wine tasting—"dead fish. Old blue cheese. And . . . is that Zima? Thank God I did everyone the service of putting you out of commission."

Jojo cracked up, falling onto the bed, as Myla prissily

dabbed the corners of her mouth with a Kleenex. Then Myla was giggling, flopping down beside Jojo.

"'And . . . is that Zima?'" Jojo repeated as they caught their breath. Jojo had heard Myla's infectious laugh before. But she'd never expected to see someone as poised as Myla roll around in a fit of giggles with her. It was just like hanging with Willa, her best friend in Sacramento, but Myla was more than that—they were *sisters*. Jojo suddenly didn't care that the video of her and Barnsley was featured on YouTube. So she'd hurled on a guy. At least she wasn't Barnsley Toole, who would wake up one day and realize how pathetic he actually was.

Jojo sat up on the bed, staring in awe and wonder at Myla, who was dabbing the corners of her eyes. "That was amazing. But do you really think *I* could pull that off?"

Myla refluffed her hair in the mirror, catching Jojo's eye in the reflection. "You wouldn't be here if I didn't. When you embarrass yourself, think of a way to make it more embarrassing for whoever is messing with you." She slung an arm over Jojo's shoulders, sort of nudging her up. "Remember, it's never you, it's them."

Jojo thought the mantra sounded a little absolute. But now wasn't the time for asking questions. If a magician was revealing how she did her tricks, you just enjoyed the show.

Two hours later, Jojo was ready for a nap. But Myla wasn't finished. "Let's review what you've learned, okay?" Myla sat on her bed, holding up a hand so Jojo would remain standing. "You're at a social function and you've been dancing. It's time for a touch-up. Show me what you do in the bathroom." She held up her iPhone's video camera and turned it on Jojo.

"Um, pee?" Jojo said, waving off Myla's frown. "I'm kidding!" She went to Myla's vanity, sitting in the swiveling plum leather chair in front of the round golden mirror. She fluffed her hair, which Myla had expertly straightened and then tamed into loose curls. She applied a fresh coat of Myla's favorite lip gloss, Philosophy Red Licorice, blotted her nose and cheeks with a piece of rice paper, and pressed the side of her index finger to each of her eyelashes, curling them up slightly. She cocked her head over her shoulder to check her backside in the mirror.

Myla nodded enthusiastically. "Good, exactly what I would have done. You don't want to come out with a completely remade face. Now, demonstrate your walk to, say, history class."

Jojo picked up the red Balenciaga hobo they'd been practicing with. It was much lighter than the backpack that made her lean to one side like a hunchback. The trick was to only take what she needed for each class, instead of carrying everything around all day. She slung the bag easily over her left shoulder, then grabbed Myla's textbook from the desk, carrying it neatly in the crook of her right arm.

Jojo usually walked without thinking about it. Now she put one foot in front of the other, heel to toe, her head up high and her eyes straight ahead. It was a *nothing to see here* walk, which Myla said showed people they should be more interested in her than she was in them. She didn't even look to Myla for approval as she passed at a clip, the bag gracefully swinging at her elbow. For good measure, she strode across the room twice more, only making direct eye contact with the iPhone's video lens at the very end of her strut. She wanted a memento of the cool look on her face.

"Very nice," Myla said. "Now you see why we stop at our lockers before each period. Carrying all your books may be efficient, but efficiency can be the enemy of grace and beauty."

Jojo shook her head, astonished. "How do you know all this stuff?" She wondered if Myla locked herself in the room to practice her walk and her blasé expressions. There was no way she'd keep track of all these rules and maneuvers.

Myla made a *who, me?* face. "Years of practice. But you're a very fast learner. Of course, you're the first one I ever gave lessons to."

Jojo felt herself beam goofily, and then quickly corrected her smile into a Myla-patented satisfied half-smirk. She dropped the bag onto the bed and neatly sat down in one of the chairs. She smoothed down the fluffy full skirt of the red Alexander McQueen cashmere flannel dress Myla had lent her, admiring her Chanel Lotus Rouge–polished toenails as they peeked out the top of Myla's Miu Miu open-toe black bow pumps—at least her pedicure had lasted.

Jojo looked at their reflection, sitting in their matching chairs, both with their legs neatly crossed at the ankle. Myla looked exotic, with her tanned gold skin, her gleaming pinup-girl hair, and her candy-heart lips. But it was her own reflection that made Jojo stare. She caught

Myla's eye in the mirror. "Can I tell you something? I didn't think this would work." Myla's face remained open, so Jojo pressed on. "But I can't believe it. I didn't think I could look like this . . . be like this."

Myla shook her head as if to say, "Silly Jojo!" She shrugged. "I knew you could. We're sisters."

Jojo let herself grin in full, looking once more at her polished and perfect self in the mirror. At the modelesque way she posed, hand on hip, one tan leg slightly bent at the knee. At her shoulders, thrown back as if to say, *I'm wearing this dress. It is not wearing me.* Even her shoulder-length hair had a *look at me* sheen. The violet eyes staring back at her belonged to a different person. A person just as fabulous, just as L.A., as Myla. Who knew some smoky eye makeup, a quarter-sized dollop of Fekkai glosssing cream, and a little attitude could make her into a whole new person? A person who—though she shared no DNA with her—clearly *was* Myla Everhart's sister.

DUDE, YOU'RE MY ONLY HOPE

Jake stared furtively around Meltdown Comics on Sunset, at the wall of Japanese capsule toys, new graphic novels shimmering under the lights, and the posters of buxom superheroines with faces that were simultaneously sneering and seductive. It was an hour before closing on Wednesday night, and even though Jake had vowed to shed all traces of geekdom, Miles had insisted. Besides, he wouldn't exactly run into any other BHH people here.

Eyeing his reflection in a collectibles case, Jake took a deep breath and rattled off one of Tommy Archer's speeches, the one in act two where Kady started to see him as more than a jock. "I know you're not as tough as you look, Lizzie. I've seen you at your softest, when you think no one's around. At the café, when you give a little kid extra whipped cream on his cocoa or you share half your sandwich with a homeless woman. I know you, Lizzie Barnett. I know you hide how kind you are under sarcastic comments." He narrowed his eyes in what he hoped was a penetrating stare, picturing Kady-as-Lizzie's face. But in the case's mirrored back wall, his own bug-eyed reflection stared back at him, like Wall-E with a Jewfro.

"Hey, bro! Look what I found! A variant cover of *Secret Invasion* number one! Sue Storm looks hot!" Miles waved the floppy comic in the air for Jake to see, breaking Jake's concentration.

Jake sighed and picked up a stuffed animal from a half-off bin. He tried to hold the yellow doll like a football. Tommy Archer was a quarterback, and Jake needed the practice.

Miles shuffled over, adjusting one of the Spock ears he wore to get the store's Trekkie discount. "Dude, I hate to be the one to say this, but you look like you're breastfeeding Pikachu."

Of course he did. In his mirror at home, practicing with a real football, Jake's little brother, Brendan, had caught on to what he was doing and wasted no time mocking him.

Jake tossed the yellow plush toy back into its bin. He missed and shook his head dejectedly. He'd taken the part the other day before realizing that Tommy Archer was this awesome, popular jock. Jake's only experience with popular, awesome jocks was being on the receiving end of their popular and awesome torture tactics. Not that anyone on *Class Angel* could ever find that out. Jake had spent a summer bulking up, in a bid to go from dud to stud. In some small part of his brain that wasn't anxiety-wracked, he was glad that his newly gained muscles, braceless teeth, and improved posture were fooling *someone*. Amelie, at tutoring, had given him constant reassurance that he would do just fine. It didn't really help, though. A guy like Tommy Archer wouldn't be so naive as to fall for a megastar like Amelie and think he had a chance. Tommy Archer wouldn't have spent half his savings account on trendy, overpriced Kitson clothes. And he wouldn't have believed Amelie's invitation to Lewis Buford's Hollywood party was a date. At least Jake's new acting worries had helped him put Amelie out of his head. Still, she was going to be disappointed when shooting started in two days.

"Why so serious?" Miles cackled in a vocal hybrid of the Joker and Peter Brady. "You're not yourself, dude. *Secret Invasion*, first issue, variant!" Miles, who had the treasure gingerly pinched between his thumb and forefinger, practically shouted. The guys at the counter shot him dirty looks. "I'll let you have it, if it'll make you feel better."

"No, it's okay, dude." Jake sighed. He felt totally weak. Even though he had declared them verboten in his effort to be a whole new guy, Jake had amassed a foot-tall stack of fresh comic books in just a half hour at the store, and now he ran his fingers back and forth over the stapled spines, feeling a mixture of relief and disgust, like a dieter who'd just scarfed a plate of Pink's chili cheese fries.

Miles dropped the comic atop Jake's stack. Miles had been searching for the variant cover all summer, even sending Jake updates while he was away at camp. "I'm freaking out. Me, playing a jock?" Jake confessed. "My motor skills are pretty much confined to turning comic book pages with tweezers, not tossing a football." Jake continued for several more minutes, a stream-of-consciousness parade of worries.

Miles listened intently and, when Jake was done, scratched behind his Spock ears thoughtfully. "This isn't so bad. You just need to do a character study. Remember last year, when I was chosen for the part of Giles in that reenactment of the *Buffy* musical?" Jake winced at the memory. Last year, it hadn't even occurred to him how dorky it was for his friend to appear in a bad fanboy reproduction of the show. "I just went to the Beverly Hills library and studied that old English dude who works in the rare-books section. Totally worked."

Jake chuckled. Mr. Dornan, who was ancient and nothing like Giles, had caught Miles sitting in his wingback chair, wearing the tweed blazer he'd left behind when he got up to help a library patron, sticking his nose into a box of Mr. Dornan's Earl Grey tea. Miles had been banned from the library for six months. Miles nodded proudly, probably reminiscing about his big role. That was the thing with Miles: As stereotypically nerdy as he might be, he was okay with it. And frankly, that made Jake a little jealous.

"So, what's your point? I have to stalk someone?"

Miles removed his glasses and cleaned them with the hem of his shirt, and Jake could tell a plan was forming.

"No, no, no. Jake, it's simple. You find someone to model your character off of. At BHH. Hmm, who could you use? Ash Gilmour! He's your neighbor, right?"

Jake shook his head. Ash would probably be totally patient and obliging if Jake dropped by and asked to study him. But in the company of his former best friend, who'd gone from Jake's equally geeky best bud to the crown prince of BHH, Jake would feel like a ragged beggar. "Tommy's an all-American heartthrob guy. Ash could get any girl he wants, but he's more like a rock star. He doesn't even play any sports, just surfs and stuff."

Miles nodded, making his way to a set of chairs upholstered in a tapestry of classic Superman comics. Jake followed, sitting down next to him. Having serious discussions in these very chairs was sort of a tradition for him and Miles, but their debates usually sounded more like the one going on at the counter, where the cashier and a customer were arguing over whether Hermione could take Sarah Connor in a fight.

"Okay, I got it," Miles said, snapping his fingers. "Lewis Buford. His dad was an athlete, and doesn't he play polo or something? Plus, he acts like he owns the school. And he's really popular. Like, he even makes *Us Weekly*."

Jake sighed. "No way. He's too Hollywood, and a total pretty boy. Tommy's supposed to be kind of normal and, like, not some guy who can get a different girl every night. Or maybe he could, but he wouldn't. And, he's modest. Lewis wears clothes with his own picture on them. He's the male Paris Hilton."

Miles sighed, leaning back in the chair and putting his feet up on the black table shaped like the Batman symbol. "Okay, you're not gonna like this, but he's perfect. *Rod Stegerson*. He letters in everything and went to state last year for basketball. And he's never had a girlfriend."

Jake almost threw up in his mouth at the thought of shadowing the meathead. "That guy is not Joe Normal. Or Tommy Archer. He's a psychopath. And the reason he hasn't had a girlfriend is that he terrifies people. He's like a bizarro version of Tommy. Rod is all darkness and fear, and Tommy is . . . good. Like the kind of guy who's even nice to guys like us, just because that's his style."

Jake had been thinking a lot about this—Tommy Archer was the guy he longed to be. It was what his summer makeover had been all about. But the thing was, the more Jake tried to be a cool guy, the farther he felt from the mark. It was like cool guys had mastered some secret philosophy, and Jake had bought the wrong textbook.

"So couldn't you just study Rod and do the opposite?" Miles asked.

"What, and get my head shoved in a toilet bowl and 'homo' written on my locker? No. I'm done for. We go to the most not-normal school in the world. That's why they said they cast me. Because I'm so socially retarded from a Beverly Hills perspective that I'm the closest thing we've got to a decent, popular jock. If we went to school in the burbs, I might be Captain Cool, like Tommy. But if he went to BHH, Tommy Archer as we know him would never survive."

Miles shrugged. "Well, can you visit a school in the burbs?"

Jake could feel his first smile in days take over his face. It was so obvious. He could almost see the solution spring from his head in a comic book thought bubble. "Miles," he said slowly, "I have a better idea."

Sitting across from Jojo at a cozy sidewalk table, Jake hoped Ingrid's French didn't seem too romantic. It was close to his house and school, and his parents came here on their dates, a thought that made him even more nervous. If his mom and dad showed up while he was out with Jojo, they'd introduce themselves and treat Jojo like she was the first girl Jake had ever gone on a date with. Which, okay, she kind of was. But this wasn't a date. This was business.

The restaurant was on Santa Monica Boulevard, tucked just far enough from the street to make you feel like you were in Paris, and not just under Century City's monolithic but architecturally insignificant office buildings. Through the brocade curtains, Jake could see several older couples dotting the tables inside the low-lit café.

"This place is nice," Jojo said, as Ingrid, a grandmotherly lady in a floral apron, set down a ham-and-cheese crepe in front of her, beaming at them. "Way better than cafeteria food."

Jake nodded. "Yeah, I haven't been here since my mom's birthday in April." He cut a corner off his turkey-and-spinach panini, relieved that Jojo was acting so casual. Jake had stopped by Jojo's locker during a break in filming, pretending to be checking it for more graffiti, and invited her to lunch off campus. Despite the cryptic invite, she'd accepted. She looked different, somehow, more confident. Jake attributed the change to the fact that she was wearing a thigh-length off-the-shoulder black sweater with white trim and black buttons down the sleeves, atop a pair of white leggings and insanely high red open-toe heels. Missing was the hoodie that she'd been hiding beneath earlier in the week. Her hair, which usually spilled over her shoulders in a carefree way, was tied back in a sleek bun. Seeing the "new" Jojo, Jake had feared she'd blow him off. But not only had

she accepted the invite, she'd told him his powder blue
Corolla was "nice and cozy." Jake almost felt like he was
getting away with something. Girls so glamorous weren't
supposed to be down-to-earth, were they?

"That's cool that your family has a usual place. I used
to go to Sadie's Pizza with my dads all the time. Did I
tell you I have two dads? And Barbar, of course." Jojo
felt like she was rambling, which was definitely against
Myla's rules. *Nerves,* she told herself. Maybe her makeover would push her into princess territory with the rest
of BHH. But Jake had known her when she was just Jojo,
hopeless new girl–slash-outsider. She didn't want him to
think she was desperate to fit in. She was just doing what
she had to do to survive.

"No, I don't think so. Where are they?" Jake leaned
forward when he asked her, like he really cared about
the answer, and Jojo wondered again why he'd asked her
here. Not that she minded having a lunch plan that didn't
involve quietly chewing a sandwich in the recesses of the
BHH library. Jake was welcome company, especially since
he looked so cute in his Tommy Archer clothes, a tight-
ish navy T-shirt with *Reavis Rams* emblazoned across the
chest.

"Sabbatical, in Greenland. Thank biological parents
for small miracles. I mean, I thought growing up in
Sacramento was boring. Me, tundra, and a town named
Nuuk wouldn't exactly qualify for living the dream."
And I wouldn't be having lunch outside with a cute guy,
she thought, visions of the burly, fur-hatted Viking guys
she and Willa had imagined muscling their way into her
head.

Jake smiled, half-pondering why it had never occurred to him to invite Jojo to lunch before. Even though he'd convinced himself that Amelie was grounded and easy to talk to, he was truly comfortable around Jojo, not just lying to himself because he had a crush. He almost felt bad, knowing he'd invited her here with a goal in mind. And now he had his opening. "So, Sacramento. Was it really that different from living here?"

"Let's put it this way. Every car in the BHH student parking lot probably cost more than my dads' house. Except yours. In Sacramento, your car has, like, identical octuplets. Squared. No offense to your car." Before she'd ever ridden in it, Jojo had felt comforted by the sight of the Corolla, taking it as proof that someone at BHH wasn't completely obsessed with status. When Jake had led her to it today, everything clicked—of course Jake was the owner of the only normal car at BHH.

"Yeah, about Sacramento. I wanted to ask you about that guy, the popular one who you said would never survive here?" Jake hoped he didn't sound like an idiot. When Miles had suggested he visit a school in the suburbs, Jake had remembered what Jojo had said about Sacramento's BMOC. If a role model for Tommy Archer existed, it had to be that guy.

Jojo bit her lip, and a slight flush crept up her face. "Justin Klatch?" She sounded shy mentioning his name. Jake wondered if she'd had a thing for him. "Yeah, what about him?"

"Well, I'm trying to figure out my *Class Angel* character by basing him on someone real. But BHH isn't exactly full of the kind of all-American, popular guys who everybody likes, you know? And Justin sounded like he . . . is that guy?" Jake trailed off, realizing how ridiculous that sounded. He wondered if George Clooney ever had to do this.

"Yeah, he definitely is," Jojo said, shyly toying with an orange slice at the edge of her plate. Before Jake had asked about Justin Klatch, she'd briefly wondered if this was a date. But now it seemed like he was just doing research for his role. She was surprised to feel a ping of disappointment at the realization.

"What does Justin drive?" Jake asked.

Jojo noticed that Jake's hazel eyes had little flecks of green in them, like sprinkles on a sugar cookie. Her face felt warm, as if Justin himself were the third guest at their table, listening to the conversation. "Well, he has this cool blue Toyota Scion. It's the nicest car at our high school, and that includes most of the teachers. But his dad sells cars, so he got a deal." Jojo hadn't liked Justin for his cool car, though she had on several occasions pictured Justin pulling up her driveway in it.

"He paid for it himself?" Jake looked surprised, probably because kids in Beverly Hills merely had to exist to have cars presented to them. Jojo remembered that just because Jake didn't exactly fit in didn't mean he wasn't part of this world. Sacramento was probably as foreign to him as Beverly Hills was to her.

"Yeah, he worked in the body shop there over the summer. Not that I knew because I rode past on my bike or anything." Jojo smiled sheepishly, picking nervously at the crepe's edge. Actually, revealing her former semi-stalking ways wasn't that embarrassing. She'd caught

Jake studying *Fairy Princess* websites on the day they met. Now they were even.

"You liked him!" Jake wished he could put the exclamation back in his head, where it belonged. He didn't want to embarrass Jojo when she was helping him. Still, if a girl like Jojo thought Justin was worth spying on, it meant he was Jake's Tommy Archer. This was perfect.

She shrugged, not seeming annoyed at all. "Maybe, but that's unimportant. You need to know *why* I liked him. Why every girl at JFK liked him."

"He was probably built, right? Isn't that why girls always like guys?" Jake could almost hear the *wrong answer* buzzer going off in his head. After all, he'd worked all summer to get built, and he was still girlfriendless. And clueless.

Jojo rolled her eyes. "Way more than that. It's a whole lifestyle, the way of the Klatch or something. Like, take Lewis Buford. If a girl dropped all her books in front of his locker, he'd probably say something like, 'Wow, if you wanted to show me your ass, you could have just asked me out' or something. Now, what do you think Justin would do?"

"Maybe stop to help her pick them up?" Jake said. It was what he would do, or would do for a girl like Jojo. Other BHH girls would swim through mud before letting Jake help them over it.

Jojo nodded. "Yeah, exactly. You do the right thing, but always keeping in mind that you're not *obligated* to. And that's what makes the person feel special: You don't have to be nice to them, but you're choosing to be." Jojo was surprised by how good it felt to actually be able to

offer advice on something. Just as Myla was the expert
on getting respect at BHH, she was starting to feel like
the expert on what it took to be popular in Anytown,
USA. And it was nice, too, to think about her old school,
her old life. It all seemed so far in the past now, like looking in the rearview mirror.

Jake was practically taking notes, so she went on.
"When you're doing your part, just think of scenes with
a girl like it's not that much different than being around
a guy. But in your head, you're thinking, 'She wants to
kiss me.' And you don't let on that you might want to kiss
her. You're just chill in every situation. And not some
guy who's only nice to see if you can hook up with someone." Jojo knew from experience. The anniversary of
Dropped Books Day, the one and only time she'd been
truly alone with Justin, was coming up. Justin's sweet
assistance as he corralled her spilled papers and books
had launched her crush on him. But she'd never had the
guts to really flirt with him. "And when he talks to you,
he smiles and never breaks eye contact, like you're a
puzzle he's trying to figure out. He has these great blue
eyes, and longish blond hair that sort of hangs over his
forehead. I don't think he uses any product."

Jake self-consciously ran a hand through his own hair,
coated in pomade in an attempt to tame it. "How would
he treat a geek like me?"

"That's the best part. Justin is, like, captain of the soccer team, captain of the baseball team, has a great car and
is totally ripped. But it would never cross his mind to
rip on a geek. The thing with Justin Klatch is, it's like
he doesn't see categories. That's not true for every cool

kid at JFK. There are plenty of cliques, too, just at JFK, they're formed based on common interests, not your parents' net worth. But Justin treats everyone like they're the same. Well, not the same, but equal."

"Is he some kind of saint? If I weren't Jewish, I'd say he's the new Jesus." The corner of Jake's mouth turned up in a grin.

"WWJKD?" Jojo caught Jake's eye across the table and they both cracked up.

Jake was beaming, and Jojo felt really good, like for once there was a use for her here. Jake glanced at his cell. "Hey, I have to get back." He left money for the check and stretched out a hand to help Jojo from her seat. When she was standing, Jake's hand moved to the middle of her back. He looked down into her eyes, a floppy curl freeing itself and falling in front of his eyes. "I really appreciate this, Jojo."

As his hand fell away, the sound of her name on Jake's lips echoed in her ears. She still felt a warm tingle where he had touched her, and suddenly she barely knew how to form words. Even though they'd just been talking about Justin Klatch for the past half hour, the memories of her former crush were fading fast.

JUST ONE OF THE GIRLS

"So what do you do for fun, Jake?" Kady asked, leaning back in her bean bag chair so that her short, raven-colored hair fanned out around her little doll face. As she stretched, her amethyst belly button ring peeked out from beneath her tight aqua tank top. Light from the curvy white lamp in the corner glinted off the jewel.

Amelie suppressed the urge to roll her eyes. Could Kady be more obvious?

"Uh, you know, the usual," Jake said from his spot on the blue couch, beneath the trailer's high, vent-style window. He picked up his sandwich, a chicken Caesar wrap from La Vincenza, and set it back down on the blond wood coffee table. He'd yet to take a bite, Amelie noticed, because he'd only had eyes for Kady since they began their lunch break a half hour ago. It was Thursday, the day of their big football game scene, and they'd only shot a few short takes, but it was enough for Amelie to see she was going to be odd co-star out. "Hang out, hit the beach, that kind of thing. What about you?" Jake hadn't been much of a beach guy two weeks ago, Amelie thought, when the two of them traded sci-fi and fantasy book recommendations during her math tutoring session.

"You know, the usual," Kady replied playfully. "A little clubbing, a little dancing. I'm up for anything, as long as I like who I'm with." Picturing Jake at a club with Kady, Amelie squirmed in the flimsy plastic chair, her knees bumping the folding dinette table. Earlier she'd heard the crew making bets on how long it would be before Kady and Jake were an item. Probably by week's end— Kady worked fast. And though he hadn't gotten Kady's hints to ask her out, Jake was flirting back. And pretty much ignoring Amelie. Last week, she'd thought they were becoming fast friends. Now she was more useless than a third wheel.

"I'm the same way," Jake said, leaning toward Kady. "It's all about who you're with." He brushed back a wayward curl with his hand, seeming like a totally different guy than the one who'd taken her to Lewis Buford's party last weekend. Thinking about that night made Amelie think of Hunter, and she wondered what he was doing now. Certainly not sitting in a corner, watching other people flirt and feeling sorry for himself.

As Kady launched into the positives of MyHouse, a new Hollywood club, Amelie charted the trajectory of her week. Hadn't she been ecstatic about shooting at BHH? Feeling like she could be part of semi-normal teenage life? Her sheltered existence was her own fault. She was at a high school and still sitting in a trailer.

She stood up. "I'm going to eat outside," she said, stretching her legs. She picked up her script and her turkey pesto croissant. Jake nodded blankly, but Kady beamed gratefully, a thank-you to Amelie for giving her alone time with Jake.

Amelie swung open the trailer door and hopped onto the metal steps. She was still wearing her costume, an ivory Milly shift dress and gold sequined Miu Miu sandals. Students turned to look at her for a swift second before going back to what they'd been doing. It was lunchtime at BHH, and since *Class Angel* was using a lot of the cafeteria, people were eating on the lawn. The plush green grass was a sea of cashmere blankets, a sizable number of them clustered around the door to Grant's trailer. Girls had kicked off their designer shoes and sunned their bare legs, looking up to see if they could manage a glimpse of their crush. Farther away, guys leaned back on the grass, casting sideways glances at the girls camped out for Grant. Laughter and chatter echoed against the looming front of the high school, before bouncing into the cloudless blue sky.

Where other kids her age fantasized about her life, to Amelie, *this* was the fantasy. Normalcy. And she'd always be standing on the steps, like she was now, watching instead of taking part.

Amelie was about to trek to her trailer when the two blond girls and the pageboyed brunette who'd been tailing Grant stopped outside her door, the brunette holding a cashmere throw.

One of the blondes spoke first, extending her slender arm to shake Amelie's hand. "Amelie Adams? I'm Fortune Weathers," she said, tossing a buttery lock of hair over her shoulder. "This is Billie Bollman and Talia Montgomery." She gestured to the other horsey blonde and the brunette, who gave tiny finger waves.

"Um, hi," Amelie said. She recognized them as friends of Myla Everhart, the daughter of Barbar, who even an outsider like Amelie could see ruled the school. She was glad to not be wearing *Class Angel*'s crazy-person halo. She already felt like enough of a conversationally challenged freak, not even able to eke out a decent hello.

"We've been wanting to properly introduce ourselves," Talia said, checking her off-the-shoulder Rebecca Beeson sweater for invisible lint.

"We've been so rude not to try to meet you sooner," Billie sang, dramatically punctuating her comment with a light slap of her forehead. "You must think we're awful."

Amelie suppressed a smile. They'd been so ardently tailing Grant, she was surprised they didn't leave strands of drool behind. "Not at all," she finally said. "It's nice to meet some real students."

"So," Fortune cut in, all business, "let's sit in the shade, because, hello, skin cancer!" She said this despite the fact that her tan was clearly 100 percent natural. She pointed to a patch of shade directly beneath Grant's trailer.

"Oh, are you . . . inviting me to sit with you?" Amelie said, feeling even lamer than she already did. What surprised her was how badly she wanted to sit with them. She was too smart to believe Myla Everhart's friends would be genuinely interested in her; befriending a sheltered child star didn't seem like their kind of thing. Still, it was better than sitting alone in her trailer.

"Of course we are," Billie said, waving at Amelie to follow them. Talia carried the blanket to the area beneath Grant's trailer window. She spread it out, straightening the edges in an OCD way, keeping her eyes on the window.

"I wanted to tell you, I L-O-V-E-D what they did with your hair for that scene in the cafeteria," Talia said, pulling one of Amelie's red curls. "The bun with the wispy pieces around your face? You should do that all the time. It softens your eyes. So romantic."

"Thanks," Amelie said, looking for something of Talia's to compliment. "I really like your necklace," she said awkwardly. As a star since practically birth, Amelie was great at working rooms of adults, from top-tier executives to agents and directors, but she'd never really had girlfriends her own age. Unless you counted girls like Kady, who'd probably never notice Amelie if they hadn't been thrown together on a movie.

Talia's hand shot up to her diamond-coated star pendant. "You can totally borrow it."

Billie rolled her eyes, fluffing her three-tier Rag & Bone striped miniskirt. "Talia, look at her." She gestured to Amelie's dress. "Does she look like she needs your accessories?"

There was a slight edge to Billie's voice. The three of them were all competing to be the best ass-kiss, with Grant as a living, breathing door prize.

"We're planning outfits for the big football game scene," Fortune said, looking to Amelie like she was sitting on a throne. "We thought it would be really cool to actually be in the shot."

A few of the girls on a blanket not far away twittered amongst themselves. Amelie distinctly heard the words, "Why didn't *we* think of that?"

The football game scene taking place that evening would involve the entire BHH student body. In it, Kady's character, Lizzie, and her friend Knox, played by Grant, attended the school's big homecoming game, just to play a nasty pyramid-toppling prank on the cheerleaders who'd framed Kady for stealing the school's trophy.

"I just don't know what to wear to a Midwestern high school football game," Fortune said. Amelie surveyed Fortune's perfectly curated bohemian prep schooler outfit—dark green fringy scarf emerging from a neatly pressed cream blazer over a navy tartan skirt and funky black motorcycle boots. It was like she'd already cast herself as a rich girl with a wild side.

"Yeah, maybe you could tell us what you're wearing," Billie said, looking like a punk-rock Alice in Wonderland, with her platform Mary Janes and artfully askew black bow headband.

"Well, I guarantee it will include that halo." Amelie sighed. "Have you seen that thing?"

"How could you not? It's awful," Talia said. Catching the mean-girl tinge to her voice, she backpedaled. "But, you would look cute in anything."

Amelie laughed. "You don't have to lie. It should come with a butter churn."

Billie giggled. "You're funny! Isn't she funny?" She looked at the other girls, as amazed as if her pet Chihuahua had started reciting Shakespeare.

Amelie felt a wave of affection for her new, not-really friends. It was liberating to have a conversation that wasn't about how to shoot act three, or her contract obligations for an in-store appearance. Okay, so maybe these girls wanted something. But if she were to be honest with herself, so did she.

"So, guys, I have a minor suggestion for tonight," she said. Why not help them out? Wasn't talking about what to wear to get a boy something regular girls did all the time?

"You want seats by Grant, right?"

The trio sang halfhearted protests. "Noooo," they insisted. "It's not that at all."

"Come on, I know he's hot," Amelie said, even though Grant—with his unwashed indie rock hair and penchant for secondhand-store tweed—was not even close to Hunter on the hotness scale.

"He's okay," Talia said, her eyes scanning his window above them again.

"Okay, fine, if you want to be in the movie, do this: Dress down. Something that an average girl would wear on a date. Like nice jeans, a cute V-neck sweater. You could do your hair in a ponytail, or just down. Lose the satin headbands. They're too Upper East Side. And it's supposed to be October in Ohio, so maybe a jacket, a light one?"

Talia clapped her hands, excitedly looking from Fortune to Billie. "Omigod, that sounds so perfect! Amelie, you're a lifesaver!"

They all clustered closer to her, folding her into an awkward kneeling group hug. As they split up, Billie kept a hand on Amelie's arm. "Amelie, do you think we're totally lame to be going after Grant this way?"

As Billie, followed by Talia and Fortune, turned their wide eyes on her, Amelie felt like the girl everyone knew could be counted on for good advice. She shook her head. "Not at all," she whispered conspiratorially, grinning at a group of guys who passed by, looking appreciatively at the four of them. "You never know what could happen, or if you'll get another chance." She was thinking of herself and Hunter, wondering if she could have done more.

"Someone's speaking from experience," Fortune said, linking arms with her. "Have you seen any cute guys here, or do you already have a thing for someone?"

Amelie could feel a blush rise in her cheeks as she thought of Hunter. "I've liked the same guy forever, but I don't think it's ever going to work out. I don't know if it's our timing, or if it's just me." She lowered her head shyly. Kady knew about her crush, but Amelie had never confessed her doubts aloud to anyone.

Talia scoffed, pulling her in the direction of the front doors. "Yeah, like it could be you. He'd have to be nuts. Or gay." Her mahogany eyes twinkled under the sun. "BHH has some semi-decent boys. Maybe it's destiny that you're here."

"Yeah, you never know. If you got a boyfriend here, maybe you could enroll. You would so be the most popular girl here," Fortune said. "You're, like, so smart and so nice."

"You should go here," Billie said, nodding, as if that settled the issue. She stood and took one last, longing look at Grant's window as she shouldered her Gucci tote. "Oh, and by the way, we're hitting the Bev Center Saturday. You should come."

Amelie pictured trying on clothes with girls her own age, instead of under the watchful, conservative eye of her momager, Helen. She was about to say yes, until she remembered she'd be shooting *Class Angel* both Saturday and Sunday. "I have to shoot this weekend, or I would love to," she said dismally.

"There'll be other shopping trips," Fortune said, her friendly smile a promise.

"Until then, come with me to my locker," Talia said in Amelie's ear. "I have this Benefit lipstick that's sort of a peach, and it's not right for me. But it would be really pretty with your complexion."

Talia pulled her into the retreating crowd of students, couples and BFFs in pairs, as they headed through the double doors. Amelie was unable to control the wide smile that took over her face as she stepped into the center of the crowd. So what if Talia, Billie, and Fortune weren't exactly her friends? And this wasn't exactly her school?

She'd only needed a taste of the normal life to know she wanted more.

KLATCH PERFORMANCE

"Do you think it's funny to give nonconformists like me and Knox . . ." Kady-as-Lizzie trailed off, staring heavenward. She huffed a frustrated breath and flopped backward onto a wooden bench that lined the BHH field house equipment room's wall. Grant, Amelie, and the production crew all straightened out of their filming positions. "What's wrong with me today?" she muttered to no one in particular, even though she was looking at Jake apologetically.

Jake shrugged. After just a few takes, he had figured out Kady's tell when she was about to mess up a line: Her gaze would flit skyward, like she half-expected her lines to be written on the ceiling. "No worries. It happens to everyone, right?" he said easily, feeling like he was in a dream. They'd done three takes of the scene already, but Jake didn't mind the starts and stops. Every pause gave him time to remember that this—him, as the lead in a movie and not completely screwing it up—was actually happening to *him*.

Kady was apologizing to Jake because so far, he was the only one in the cast to nail every take. Even Amelie

had stumbled over one of her lines. They were shooting the scene where Lizzie and Knox discovered that
Tommy—in addition to being an awesome basketball
player—also penned poignant essays under a pseudonym
for the Reavis paper. Amelie was in it, too, helping Lizzie
discover the storeroom where Tommy was writing one of
his pieces in private.

The equipment room was tiny and cramped, every
shelf stuffed with team uniforms, football shoulder pads,
and random sports paraphernalia. Reavis High's blue-
and-white gear replaced BHH's red-and-black uniforms.
Jake leaned against a basket of volleyballs, his feet resting
on a duffel bag of softball equipment. A notebook lay
open on his lap.

"Now, guys," Gary said. "Jake's perfect in this scene.
Tommy is a little surprised, but he trusts Kady and Grant
with his secret, and wants Kady to know he's more than
a jock, so he's also a little pleased. Amelie, you need to
look proud for bringing them here. Grant, you're seeing
this guy in a new light—he's a lot like Knox. And Kady,
you're impressed—you always believed you were in love
with this essay writer—but you don't want Tommy to
know that, so you're pretending you're angry with him.
Please, guys, let's nail this. Follow Jake's lead. He's got
it."

Jake stared down at the pages of scribbles, trying not
to grin like an idiot. He honestly had no idea what he
was doing to warrant all this praise. He'd just been trying to carry out Jojo's advice—treating Kady like she was
the only one in the room. As for his lines, he didn't feel
like he was doing anything special. He had a geek's gift

for memorizing, and several years of Torah recitations at Hebrew School aiding his enunciation. That was all. But as long as he had "it," for now he was, as in the words of many an L.A. bumper sticker, *driving it like he stole it*.

Gary clapped his hands twice. "This is it, I can feel it. We'll take it from Kady's line, 'Why do you do this?' Let's roll."

Kady, Grant, and Amelie clustered in the doorway. Jake took one deep breath and posed with his pen hovering over the pages of his composition notebook. He furrowed his brow. Like Jake, Justin Klatch would treat his essays with the importance of a state basketball title.

"And, action!" Gary stage-whispered.

"Why do you do this?" Kady said, taking a few steps into the room so that she was hovering above Jake. Kady crossed her arms over her chest defiantly, staring down at Jake with a mixture of surprise and anger. "For shits and giggles? Do you think it's funny to give nonconformists like me and Knox hope that there's someone at this school who doesn't think cheerleaders and ballers deserve special treatment?"

Amelie piped up, as Class Angel, but Jake kept staring at Kady's concerned face, partially because of Jojo's advice but also because he still felt like Amelie could see the remains of his utter infatuation all over his face. "Remains" was the right word, he thought. His crush on Amelie no longer hurt in the raw-wound way it had since the party. It was healing fast, but he had a feeling it would leave a scar. "I told you he was different. I may just be an apprentice angel, but I can read people."

"Shut up," Kady said through gritted teeth in Amelie's

direction. She leaned down so close to Jake, he breathed in the sugary aroma of her frosting-scented body lotion. "Are you going to answer me?"

Jake searched her blue eyes, noticing that diamonds of gray circled her pupils. "Isn't it possible that I just believe in sticking up for the little guy?" He puffed out his chest a little, liking Tommy Archer more and more. The guy was like a high school superhero. Jake could see why girls would go for him. He himself was a little in love with him too. "A jock like me wouldn't have much credibility, so I made up a student. I don't need credit. But I'm guessing you like the essays?"

Lizzie backed away, throwing up her hands.

Knox piped up. "Like them? Lizzie cuts them all out and saves them! She said, and I quote, 'If I ever meet X. L. Thursday, I'm going to kiss him on the mouth.'"

Lizzie spun on her heel, embarrassed. Looking at Class Angel, she muttered, "I hate you."

Angel gamely shrugged. "They told me that would be part of the job."

Lizzie dashed out, her Angel at her heels. Knox hung back.

"This is like meeting Captain America and Jack Kerouac rolled into one muscular dude," he said, holding out a fist toward Jake.

Jake panicked. The fist thing wasn't in the script. He extended a hand and awkwardly clasped Grant's fist, pumping it up and down in a handshake. Then he realized he was supposed to be *fist-bumping*. What kind of idiot didn't know that?

Jake's face was turning a dark shade of red when

Gary yelled cut. "That was hilarious, Jake, the handshake instead of the fist-bump. Good ad-libbing," he added, coming over to pat Jake on the back. "We're actually going to finish in time."

"Nice work, bro," Grant said, looking into a mirror on the door. He ran his hands over his hair to muss it more than it already was. "Can I give you a tip?"

Here it came. Grant Isaacson telling Jake not to be so transparently uncool. Tearing into him because he didn't know what a fist-bump was.

"Uh, sure," Jake croaked out, shifting uncomfortably under Grant's penetrating stare.

"You've had, what, four Diet Cokes today?" Grant's gold-colored eyes seemed to signal this was a bad thing.

Jake shrugged. "I'm not sure," he replied. "I don't actually keep count."

"Just be careful," Grant said, the gravity of his tone making clear he wasn't joking around. "Soda'll make you bloated and pasty. Keep it out of your system, and you'll be fine." Grant cracked a rare smile, displaying slightly crooked top teeth. "I'm really glad we found you, man."

"Me too," Jake said, meaning it. How else would he have known the power of the Klatch without this movie? Or be trading actor tricks with Grant Isaacson, who could get any girl he wanted? He stood up, handing the composition book to the prop master before heading into the gymnasium. He couldn't believe that three professional actors had gotten notes to follow *his* lead. He pictured himself as a guest on *Inside the Actors Studio*, telling James Lipton about his first role. "And, then, James, I thought, 'What Would Justin Klatch Do?'"

He headed toward the craft services table, where Kady was already assembling a plate of salad and cookies. Amelie was sitting in her chair about ten feet away, as a makeup artist removed glitter from her cheeks.

Kady grinned as he approached, her lips like a perfect red bow across her heart-shaped face. She set down her plate and hugged him. "That was spectacular, Jake," she said, her voice muffled as she spoke into his chest. She was shorter than Amelie, and Jake felt strong and manly against her tiny frame.

"Thanks," he said, looking down into her eyes. "You were amazing too."

Kady shrugged cutely as she pulled out of the hug, her hoodie falling down to expose one shoulder. "So, are you ready for tonight?"

Tonight was the big football game scene. Jake, as Tommy, was playing quarterback, and Lizzie, there to pull a prank on the cheerleaders, was supposed to get caught up in admiring Tommy on the field, against her better judgment. All of BHH was going to be in the bleachers, watching him make a perfect pass to win the game. After Saturday, with his ridiculous attempts to even hold a football, he'd spent several hours at ESPN Zone playing Quarterback Challenge with Miles as his coach. "Dude, what did you work out for all summer if you're not going to put it to good use now?" Miles had said. "Throwing a football is all physics and geometry. Inertia, arch, stuff geeks know way better than jocks." After a physics-driven football lesson, Jake had emerged from the restaurant with a perfect spiral.

"Sure," Jake said, grinning in a confident but not cocky

way. Even though the cameras were off, he was still using his WWJKD training. "I think it will be fun."

Kady play-shoved him. "Yeah, fun. Even Hunter Sparks was nervous about filming that scene, and he'd only be in front of a bunch of losers from Central Casting, not his whole high school." Her eyes danced over Jake's body. "Do you play football? I bet you do."

Jake looked away for one quick moment and saw Amelie looking his way too. *She* knew he was no athlete. She also knew he was not a ladies' man. And, yeah, Justin Klatch probably didn't lie, but *he* probably wouldn't have to say he'd never played football. Quarterback Challenge counted, right?

"I did," Jake said, swigging some water to wash down the lie. "When I was younger."

"Oh, really?" Kady slid along the table, coming closer again. She reached for his bicep and squeezed. Jake flexed at exactly the right moment. "Wow, yeah, you did. So, why not now?"

Jake flinched, he hoped not in a perceivable way. What now? He imagined the face of Justin Klatch, who looked like Matt Damon crossed with Thor. Justin was saying, "ACL."

"I had this game and sort of got cocky. I didn't run the play like Coach said, and I was tearing down the field when all these guys tackled me. I tore my ACL pretty bad and called it quits. I learned my lesson, though." He nodded solemnly, hoping that sounded convincing.

"Wow." Kady raised an eyebrow, sliding an inch closer. He could feel her warm breath on his neck. She looked up at him, her lips parted. "You wanna show me your scar?"

Holy. Justin. Klatch. Kady Parker was *flirting* with him. Big-time. Jake jogged—no, sprinted—his memory, trying to remember where an ACL even *was*. In his head, Justin rolled his eyes: "Leg, dude."

"Are you trying to get me to take off my pants?" Jake asked, before he even knew what he was saying. *Where did that come from?* His imaginary Justin nodded encouragingly.

"Maybe," Kady said, her night-colored eyes teasing. "And so what if I am?"

As Jake felt every muscle, bone, and ACL in his body tense up pleasurably, he congratulated himself. *Totally Klatched it*, he thought to himself.

BLEACHER BUMMERS

"Okay, we need to fill in these empty seats near Grant. Can we please have Talia Montgomery, Billie Bollman, and Fortune Weathers?" The casting director, a plump blond woman wearing oversize chunky blue beads, scanned the sidelines along BHH's bleachers. She looked like Meryl Streep's younger sister.

Myla covered her ears as her friends let out a piercing squeal. She hadn't heard them get that excited since she'd chartered a jet to take them all shopping in New York for her fifteenth birthday.

"Omigod, it's happening. I get his right side, next to his dimple," Fortune said bossily, adjusting the V-neck of her blue J.Crew sweater.

"Fine, I'll take his left. His hair looks better from that angle, anyway," Talia sniped back, her hair tamed into two low pigtails wrapped in navy ribbons.

"What about me?" Billie said sadly, unzipping her hoodie and straightening her shoulders, displaying the cleavage afforded by her navy tank top. It was clear to Myla that her friends had dressed down in an effort to appear "authentic." But they could have gone suburbia casual in C&C pieces from Fred Segal, instead of mall brands. Movie parts or not, nothing was worth defiling one's skin with cheapo clothes.

"You can sit next to me," Fortune said, generously patting Billie on the shoulder. "I'll lean back so you can see the dimple."

Myla rolled her eyes. She couldn't believe the whole school was being forced into servitude for a dumb teen movie, or that her friends were so excited about it. She knew they'd gone to Amelie Adams for "fashion" advice, and it annoyed her. Myla would have given them better wardrobe counseling, but her three besties were all extra grateful because Amelie had supposedly spoken to the casting director. Like that was such a big deal.

As her friends shoved their way past other students to get close to Grant, Myla scanned the bleachers, pulling her hands into her cashmere sweater as a chilly breeze swept across the field. The casting director had directed all the BHH B-listers to fill in the visitors' section across the field. Olivia Abdabo had been sent to change out of her self-designed blue sequined jumpsuit and was now glumly texting in the back row of the bleachers, wearing a shapeless Reavis High sweatshirt and ill-fitting Gap jeans. Higher up, poor Jojo had been given a Reavis High band uniform, and sat between two freshman boys, holding a trumpet. She was guaranteed to be on-camera in her foot-high plumed band cap. But Jojo held her shoulders back like she was daring someone to tease her. She looked like a Zen master crossed with British royalty. Myla felt a surge of pride. Jojo was definitely getting the hang of Everhart Life 101.

A few feet away, Ash and his buddies stood in a circle, playing Hacky Sack as they waited for instructions. Ash knocked the little ball out of the game, and it landed with a dull plop by Myla's feet. She bent to pick it up just as Ash arrived in front of her.

"Hey," she said, her voice catching in her throat. She hadn't spoken to him since they'd met at their spot in Griffith Park to declare a truce. His sandy hair shone under the stadium's lights. Instinctively, Myla reached to lift his hair from his face, then pulled her hand away.

"Hey," Ash said. His voice filtered through her every pore. They reached for the ball at the same time, their hands brushing over its bumpy surface. Myla pulled hers away, laughing nervously despite herself.

"You two." The casting director suddenly loomed over them, exhaling a plume of smoke from her American Spirit. "You look adorable together. Sit behind Grant and the blondes."

Ash blinked, a shy smile crossing his face. He helped Myla up from her crouched position. As their fingers touched again, a surge both familiar and fresh shot through Myla.

"Sure," Ash said to the casting director. He dropped Myla's hand and she followed him to a seat behind Fortune and Billie, who both looked shell-shocked by their proximity to Grant. Myla shot the girls a significant look, trying to convey the excitement she was keeping reined in. But her friends were too starstruck by Grant to even notice. Irked, Myla vowed to ignore them for the rest of the scene. Let them have Grant. Ash, in Myla's eyes, was much hotter. His hair, though shaggy as always, was

obviously clean, contrasting with Grant's "the more
buildup the better" style. Ash had classic features—
slightly sun-tinged skin, a strong chin, a perfect aquiline
nose, sculpted red lips, and deep, soulful eyes that even
when sleepy or stoned could reduce a girl to butter. Grant
had the dimple and high cheekbones, but was what Myla
would call sugly—surly and ugly—with his nocturnal
pallor, perma-pout, glinty amber eyes, and a nose that
looked like it had been broken on more than one occasion. In profile, he looked like a bad Picasso knockoff,
the features all slightly off but not arranged in a way that
qualified them as art. But she could guess at his allure. He
had that whole *I'll ravage your body right after I finish this
bottle of whiskey* look to him.

Myla settled next to Ash on the bleachers, feeling
warmth coming off him even though he wore just a light
black windbreaker over a vintage Led Zeppelin tee. There
was a foot of space between them.

"Honey," the casting director called to Myla, gesturing with a freshly lit cigarette. "Scoot closer, like you like
him." Myla nodded and slid six inches over, not closing
the gap entirely. She couldn't just lean into him like she
would have a month ago. The casting director gave her the
eye. "When we start rolling, a little closer. Not like two
kids who take their purity rings seriously." Myla glared at
her. The woman had no clue something far more important than her stupid movie was going on here.

"How have you been?" Ash asked, not looking at
Myla. Instead, he stared at the field, where Jacob
Porter-Goldsmith was throwing passes with surprising
skill. Like the rest of BHH, Ash had been semi-shocked

at the news Jake made the lead in the movie. Jake was probably the last person most of their classmates would expect to play a star athlete. *More power to him,* Ash thought.

"Good," Myla said, even though the last week had been far from one of her best. She felt awkward and not like herself. Their truce gave her no sense of purpose. "So, this is weird, right?" she said, testing the water.

"What's weird?" Now Ash made eye contact, his eyes grazing over her face.

Myla gestured to the field, blushing as she realized how else her words could have been interpreted. "Jacob Porter-Goldsmith, movie star." As if on cue, Jake tossed the ball to a receiver at the twenty-yard line. Myla stopped herself from saying, *Do you think he invented some geeky robot arm so he could throw like that?* Ash hated when she ripped on his neighbor. Even though they weren't friends anymore, Ash annoyingly stood up for Jacob PG. He even hated when Myla called him PG, a nickname that had gotten started when a bunch of BHHers saw Jake getting turned away from a PG-13 movie—when he was fourteen. Boys had an odd sense of loyalty.

Ash shrugged. "People change, I guess."

Myla's head spun. Was he talking about Jacob, or about them? Did he mean he'd changed, and he'd never love her again? Or did it mean she had to change to win him back?

The director paced in front of them, megaphone pressed to his mouth. "We're going to start now, people," he boomed. "Everyone, look like you're enjoying yourself and in awe of your quarterback." He gestured to Jake, who was swigging from a bottle of Gatorade on the sidelines. The crowd giggled, but only slightly. Jake's success was getting to them, Myla thought. "Couples, cuddle. No one's asking you to get married."

Ash did as he was told, his arm circling Myla's shoulder stiffly. The crowd was dead silent now, waiting for further orders. The deafening quiet, and Ash's tenseness, made Myla feel like she was trapped under plastic.

"Um, we're not laying Tommy Archer to rest," the director shouted. "Talk, chatter, chant, 'Go, Tommy!'"

Myla figured that was as good a command as any for her to talk to Ash. "So, my parents have really missed you coming by for dinner." It was true. Lailah had sadly cleared the place setting next to Myla's yesterday for the third time that week. Myla missed him too.

"Oh," Ash said, a slightly pained expression on his face. "It would be weird for me to keep mooching off you guys, with, you know, everything."

"It's not mooching," Myla giggled, loosening up a little at Ash's odd, constipated look. "I bet you've been living on Pop-Tarts and takeout. You're always welcome. Lucy will make your favorite."

"Beef Wellington?" Ash's mouth curved up in a small grin. Myla felt hopeful. Maybe the way to a man's heart *was* through his stomach. She'd always believed that your hair, clothing, and attitude meant much more than a home-cooked meal. But at this point, she wouldn't have been surprised to find she'd had it wrong all along.

A few hours later, they'd watched the cheerleaders pyramid up and stunt-fall down a billion times. Now they were acting as the backdrop as the production crew worked to get several takes of Jake's big Hail Mary pass. Myla was still nestled in Ash's grip, like they were here on a date. Neither of them had brought up the Lewis fiasco. It was too awkward a topic for the situation. And Ash had seemed proud of her when Myla told him about her truce with Jojo. She made a point not to bore him with details of Jojo's makeover.

In front of them, Billie, Talia, and Fortune were discussing Amelie Adams, who was standing in the shadows of the bleachers in a white asymmetrical minidress with a ridiculous frilly halo perched on her red curls. Amelie was scolding Kady Parker, who—for the scene—was supposed to have greased the grass where the cheerleaders formed their ill-fated pyramid.

Billie surveyed the white-blond ends of her long tresses, her cornflower blue eyes crossing atop her nose—a perfect copy of Ashley Tisdale's new one. By the same doctor. "Amelie looks so good with red hair. Maybe I should go red too." She exaggeratedly leaned across Fortune's lap. Fortune squirmed, folding her arms over her narrow rib cage. She was sensitive about having the widest hips of the group and tried to bring attention to her ample chest. Billie batted her thickly mascaraed eyelashes at Grant.

"I was going to do that when my hair grows out," Talia said, adjusting a strand of her awkward bob. "My hair's so much nicer when it's long," she added, her mouth just inches from Grant's ear.

"Yeah, I can't believe I've been a boring blond for so long," Fortune muttered, pouting up at Grant, who looked as uncomfortable as a window shopper being swarmed by a team of salesmen. "What color hair do you think looks best on a girl, Grant?" Myla rolled her eyes, whispering to Ash, "Red hair, right. Maybe I should dye mine."

Ash leaned toward her, seeming to look at each individual strand of her hair protectively, his eyes falling on the inch-long chunk of hair at the back of her neck. In a furor, Myla had violently snipped out a long strand of her hair that years earlier she'd dyed a punk-rock emerald green at Ash's suggestion. Myla felt a tiny, not unpleasant, chill weave its way from her neck down her spine.

"Don't go red," Ash said, his voice thick and mournful. "I love your hair." He knew he'd said the wrong thing the second the words were out of his mouth. Saying he loved anything about Myla *to* Myla right now was too fraught with significance, and he knew he needed to keep things casual. But he couldn't help it. The idea of Myla changing anything about her beauty was sacrilege.

Myla bit her lip to stop herself from saying something bitchy about how she wasn't at all serious. Instead, her lips tilted into their half-smile and—locking her jade eyes on Ash's—she said breathlessly, "I won't."

Her heart thumped in time with the BHH marching band's percussion section. She felt closer to Ash in this stupid fake-couple setup than she had in months. She wanted to wriggle her hands under his jacket and cling to his warm chest, lay her head down in the gap between his shoulder and his head. But this was still too confusing. How long would they have to pretend?

"Eyes on the field, everyone!" the director shouted through his megaphone. "This is Tommy's big moment.

Reavis has won the big game! The cheerleaders are out, so it's all on you guys to celebrate the big victory. Remember, after this, you can go home!"

The crowd began to chant, "Tommy! Tommy!" Myla and Ash chanted too. Every so often, Ash looked at Myla with a goofy "I can't believe we're doing this" grin.

On the field, Jake cocked his arm back like a statue of an Olympian god as three members of the opposing team—who looked more like freshly released inmates than high school students—hurtled toward him. He released the ball into a perfect Hail Mary pass and the spinning mass of pigskin soared down the field like it was missile-guided.

"Holy crap, Jake," Ash said approvingly. Without thinking, he squeezed Myla closer to him, watching in suspense as the ball sailed downfield. As Myla nestled against him, Ash could feel how easy it would be to slip back into their old ways. The Golden Couple. Their being together was like predestination, which he'd learned about in world religions class. Were they only capable of two extremes? Either being a full-blown couple, or out-and-out enemies? He must have been nuts to think they could find middle ground.

The ball landed easily in the receiver's hands, and the crowd went wild. Billie, Talia, and Fortune group-hugged a puzzled-looking Grant. Jojo and the band crowd stood up, waving their brass wildly. Even Lewis Buford, several rows back, stood and yelled, "Yeah, motherfucker!"

Ash and Myla were on their feet, cheering and hugging like the rest of the crowd. Ash looked down at Myla, his eyes gleaming. Their faces were less than a foot apart,

and Myla felt the tingling sensation she got whenever
Ash was about to kiss her. Civility truce be damned. She
loved Ash. She gave him her most meaningful stare and
her most telling half-smile. *Kiss me,* she willed her eyes
to say.

Then he leaned back, held up his palm awkwardly, and
said, "High five!"

What. The. Fuck. High five? Was he *twelve*? Myla
forced her jaw back into its locked and upright position
and limply slapped his palm.

Ash smiled as he stood, and as he pulled away from
her, Myla felt like he took all the oxygen in the air with
him. "Well, I gotta go. See you around?"

Her voice catching in her throat, Myla nodded. They'd
known each other better than anyone else for three years.
She'd taken care of Ash when he was sick. They'd slept in
the same bed. And now they were high-fiving?

TRAIN WRECK CONDUCTOR

Ash turned onto Moreno and reached for his phone, ready to call Mulberry Pizza for a large pepperoni-and-mushroom pie. After his weird encounter with Myla, he wanted nothing more than to sit in his room, play the new MGMT EP on repeat, and eat until he fell asleep.

Just as he was about to hit Mulberry's number on speed dial, his phone lit up in his hand, his dad's scowling face on the screen.

Ash picked up. "Hey, Dad," he croaked, knowing immediately what this was about and wishing he hadn't answered.

"Hey, Ash," Gordon said, in a too-chipper-to-be-talking-to-your-son voice. Ash could hear the sound of hot-tub jets bubbling in the background. "So, did you forget our plan?" Gordon was using his salesman voice, which Ash recognized from years of his dad's bargaining. As a kid, Ash and his father had bargained and bartered over all Ash's chores—"Son, I thought you were gonna clean your room so we could go to Toys 'R' Us," "Ash, didn't we say you couldn't have Jake over until you finished your spelling worksheet?"

"Um, no, I didn't forget," Ash swerved in his one-handed turn onto Santa Monica Boulevard, nearly clipping a limo making a left into the rear drive of the Beverly Hills Hilton.

"Daisy needs a tour guide, kid," Gordon said. The goofy way he said "kid" made Ash cringe. Why was he being given an annoying grown-up responsibility if he was still a kid? "She said she can't get a hold of you."

"I had to be in a football game scene for *Class Angel*. My phone was off," Ash said, hitting the brakes hard to avoid a cluster of ladies laden with shopping bags as they crossed Santa Monica at Rodeo Drive.

"For four days, Ash Gibson Gilmour?" Gordon said, his upbeat tone giving way to veiled irritation.

Ash pulled the phone away from his ear and flipped it the finger at the use of his full name, shrinking into the leather bucket seat. It was true, Daisy had called countless times over the last few days and he'd sent the calls to voice mail, figuring his dad would call himself if it was really important. When he'd agreed to his dad's plan at Spago the other day, he really hadn't thought it would mean Daisy would actually *call* him. And he was kind of annoyed with his dad's power. A couple little *you're the only guy for the job* remarks, and somehow Ash had agreed to take on what was really just dirty work.

"I was busy," Ash lied, turning onto Beverly Drive, through Beverly Gardens Park. He turned onto Carmelita, toward home, his ravenous appetite for Mulberry's oily slices gone.

"Daisy is waiting for you at the W in Westwood. Be there in fifteen minutes, sport," Gordon said. "I know you don't want to. But my house, my rules. And it would mean a lot, bud."

Before Ash could protest, his dad had hung up.

Fifteen minutes later, Ash stood at the chrome front desk of the W, which looked like a giant staircase laid on its side. He was all business as he asked the pretty desk clerk, whose blond afro matched her golden tank top, to call Daisy's room.

She dialed, shaking her head at Ash after thirty seconds had passed. "I'm sorry, there's no answer in Miss Morton's room."

"Okay, thanks," Ash said, smiling. He was off the hook. He'd send his dad a picture of himself waiting in the W lobby to prove he was there—and Daisy, his pill-popping, non-bathing prodigy—was not. Maybe he'd still get that pizza after all.

Ash walked through the lobby, toward a dimly lit seating area the W called the Living Room. The room's flattering mood lighting made the half-dozen wannabe screenwriters hunched over laptops look almost like *GQ* models instead of agoraphobic insomniacs. Ash plopped down onto a chair that was nothing more than a huge cushion with legs. He was about to take his photo when a familiar voice rang out.

"Is that Ash Gilmour? Finally arriving for little ol' me?"

Ash looked up. Daisy lay like an abused rag doll across a long white sofa. She clutched one of the couch's striped pillows to her chest, covered by a flimsy tank top emblazoned with black type that read, *How Much?* Her glittery yellow tutu rode up around her waist, exposing her plaid boy shorts. One leg stretched across the table, her other bent at an uncomfortable forty-five degree backwards angle on the couch. Both her feet were clad in R2D2 slippers.

"I'm ready to go," she said, leaping up from the couch, her limbs splayed like none of them belonged to the same person.

Daisy looked worse standing than she did lying down. Her short hair was matted in back, a snarl of purple and fire engine red locks clumped to her skull, and one eye drooped closed under a heavy layer of glittery eye shadow. She looked like an asymmetrical disco queen who needed a V8.

"Okay, let's go," Ash said, grabbing her wrist and pulling her toward the door.

Daisy let out a low whistle. "You're a rough one, eh? I like it." A little wobbly, she leaned into him. She didn't smell like booze, so Ash wondered if she was drugged up. She waved like a hyper child at the hostess and every person she passed, yelling, "I'll see you later. And you! And I hope you too!"

Ash rolled his eyes. Anyone else would be getting paid to put up with Daisy's crap. All the compensation he'd get was a "thanks, sport." If he was lucky.

After prying Daisy from the arms of the valet, who she insisted on hugging goodbye, they were safely in the car. "Safely" being a relative term, as Daisy pushed buttons, rolled her window up and down, and reached for the steering wheel as Ash drove.

Ash searched his head for something to do. He'd never played tour guide to a rock star before and felt like he needed to come up with something to keep his charge occupied. It dawned on him that Daisy was a girl, and might like some of the things Myla did. "Where to? Barneys? Bloomingdale's? Saks?" Ash named Myla's favorite haunts near Rodeo Drive.

Daisy made a gagging noise. "Do I like look a fucking priss to you?" She rooted around in her "purse," a vinyl kids' pencil case with Dora the Explorer on one side. "I have directions." She fished out a piece of W stationery, on which were surprisingly neat penned directions to an address in Hollywood.

"Well, okay," Ash said. "Where are we going?"

Daisy put a finger to her lip in a *shush* gesture. "Secret. You'll see when we get there."

With the directions in hand, Daisy became oddly serious, navigating and pointing out landmarks from the passenger seat.

"You're not even going to give me a hint?" Ash asked, not moving his eyes from the road as Daisy stared out the window. They were stuck on the busiest stretch of Hollywood Boulevard. An army of tourists waddled along the crosswalk, headed from Mann's Chinese Cinema to the El Capitan. Daisy screeched with delight as two impersonators of Captain Jack Sparrow, an overweight version of Elmo with matted fur, and a Supergirl who'd long stopped being super anything wandered in front of the Camaro.

"Maybe I should give up this music thing and do that," Daisy said, not answering Ash's question, as a nearly seven-foot-tall black man in red platform boots, hot pants, and fiery-colored angel wings sauntered past the car. "Get my photo taken with American sods on holiday."

"Sounds good," Ash said blankly, wondering why Daisy would choose to shop here. The Hollywood & Highland shopping center had nothing you couldn't find everywhere in L.A. Actually, it had nothing you couldn't find everywhere in America. Ash mentally went over the mall's stores, trying to figure out where Daisy wanted to go. Forever21, a Virgin Megastore, Sephora, Guess, Lucky, Victoria's Secret. He winced at the idea of Daisy buying underwear. But then Victoria's Secret probably didn't carry bourbon-flavored edible undies.

"Yeah, I'd be good at it. Dressing up," Daisy said, picking at some crust of indeterminate origin on her tank top.

They parked, and Ash followed Daisy past the stores. "Everything closes soon, you know," he told her. He glanced at the time on his iPhone. He hoped this wouldn't take all night.

"Yeah, but the bars just got busy," Daisy said, striding toward the pedestrian crossing on Highland. They crossed and she beelined for a hole-in-the-wall bar called the Powerhouse, sandwiched between a Chinese restaurant and a Western Union. Against his better judgment, a vague flare of intrigue flashed in Ash's brain. As grimy as the place looked, at least Daisy wasn't making him chaperone her to some designer store or poser nightclub.

"Follow me, love," she said, pulling him inside.

The Powerhouse was not a nice establishment, which probably explained why neither of them was carded. The bar was a dirty gray steel, every leather stool torn or held together with duct tape, as though the decorator had been going for something called Urinal Chic. Few lights worked, and with no windows to the outside, it resembled a poorly lit subway stop out of a bad horror movie. Scattered around were old men with missing teeth, a few homeless guys nursing drinks as they guarded all their worldly possessions, and several terrified-looking hipsters who'd probably gone in search of a real dive bar experience and gotten more than they bargained for. *Maybe a poser nightclub would have been a safer choice*, Ash thought.

Seeing Ash looking around warily, Daisy patted his arm. "Don't worry, it's all bark, no bite. They're just supposed to have really great live music, and small crowds 'cause it's kind of a dump. The *CityBeat* reporter got it right." She smiled, her glossed lips parting to show off her gleaming teeth. She turned toward the bar, standing on tiptoe and placing an order. She stretched past a few overdressed guys who looked like lost members of Franz Ferdinand, who both stared at her shapely legs peeking out of the tutu, and the bare skin of her back where her tiny T-shirt rode up. Neither guy made an effort to hide the fact they were checking Daisy out, as if her looking so right-out-of-bed gave them a right to ogle. Ash glared at the guys, feeling oddly protective of Daisy all of a sudden.

She hopped away from the bar, holding two bottles of Budweiser. "Sorry, they don't have anything fancy here," she said, handing one to Ash with an unstudied shrug. She was so unposed, so natural about everything, that he kind of got why guys stared. There was something about a girl who didn't announce to the world how hot she was. And yet when you looked at her, you wanted to keep looking.

Daisy gestured with her beer bottle to the stage as a pretty girl, with red curls and a short flowered babydoll dress, strode out. "This is who I came to see," she whispered to Ash, her eyes scanning the singer.

Ash relaxed as they got settled in a spot by the bar. If babysitting Daisy meant an evening of checking out some good live music, he could handle this. It was actually a pretty decent way to spend a school night, minus the bar's down-and-out décor.

The girl picked up a guitar and started to strum a slow and somber medley. "I wrote this when I was feeling a little broken," she said. As she began to sing, the guys in the room shifted their stares from Daisy to the redhead.

> "*You think I'm just a feather in your cap*
> *Just a pin upon your map*
> *That I'm just a number, in this urban jungle.*
> *But when . . . will . . . you . . . realize . . .*
> *I . . . will . . . cut . . . you . . . down . . . to . . . size*
> *You're a lowdown dirty shame*
> *Promised you'd be different . . .*
> *But you're a different kind of same*
> *Ain't no way you'll get me back*
> *Not this feather in your cap . . .*"

"Do you hear this bollocks?" Daisy said, grabbing Ash's forearm more tightly with each word. Ash knew the song was one of Daisy's, though her version was a faster rock number, and the girl was playing it in a bluesy way. It was a pretty good song. Not that he'd ever tell

Daisy that. Or Gordon. Still, it was really shitty of the girl to try to claim it as her own.

"You fucking bitchhole!" Daisy suddenly screamed, the anger morphing her face from stoned Raggedy Ann to American Gladiator.

Before Ash realized what was happening, Daisy ran and lunged at the girl, instantly grabbing a fistful of her hair. "Hey," the redhead squealed. She reeled backward and then lashed back, grabbing for Daisy's T-shirt. The mic stand toppled, wailing feedback. The mostly male crowd watched the girls grab for each other, seeming to do nothing more than yank at each other's hair and clothing. A deep voice in back bellowed, "Catfight!" as an excited murmur floated through the crowd, like the five-dollar cover charge had just become a great deal.

"Who do you think you are?" Daisy cried out. "You don't just play my fucking music, my fucking heartbreak, like it happened to you, you little, nothing phony!"

Ash could barely hear the girl's terrified whimper of a reply. He jogged to the stage to break them apart just as a giant paw of a hand came down on his shoulder.

A guy with a bald head and a jet-black goatee towered over Ash. His arms, bared in his sleeveless black muscle tee, were huge. "Get her back to whatever methadone clinic she came from," he bellowed coldly. "This is my place, and we don't tolerate low-class behavior here. These are good people."

Ash looked at the lascivious stares of the crowd watching Daisy chase the girl around the stage, one shoulder of her T-shirt ripped, exposing her red bra strap.

"I'm gonna sue you, you intellectual property–stealing whore!" shrieked Daisy. In response, the redhead spit at Daisy's slippers.

"Yeah, good people," he said, sarcastically.

"What did you say, sonny?" Huge Arms said.

"Nothing. But that's Daisy Morton, and that's her song that girl was singing. She's just protecting herself." He sort of got where she was coming from. A cover was one thing. Claiming someone's song as your own was another.

The owner grabbed Ash by the collar, yanked him to the stage, and, with his other giant arm, grabbed Daisy around the waist and pulled her down from the stage.

He stomped, still dragging Ash and carrying Daisy, to the door. "Stay the fuck out," he said, kicking the door open with his combat boot. He dropped Daisy onto the sidewalk and shoved Ash so hard he almost landed in the middle of Highland.

Daisy instantly sprang up, almost gleeful. Slinging an arm around Ash, she leaned her head on his shoulder and guided him across the street. "I bet you've never been treated like a common nobody before, eh, Mr. Bigshot?" She burst out laughing, her tiny frame quaking against his side. The vibrato of Daisy's giggle almost tickled, and soon Ash was cracking up, too. The tourists taking pictures along the Walk of Fame stopped and stared, whispering, "Is that Daisy Morton?"

Before the crowd could descend on Daisy for autographs and photos, she took Ash's hand and broke into a run, zipping through the throngs to his Camaro. They finally caught their breath as he started the car.

"I hope I didn't ruin your evening," Daisy said, smirking, her gray eyes still twinkling.

Ash shook his head. It wasn't the night he'd planned, but Daisy Morton was definitely more interesting than pizza.

CHECK, MATE

"'We are the champions, my friend. . . .'" Miles tried to mimic Freddie Mercury, as he swayed in the passenger seat of Jake's Corolla. "'We'll keep on fighting till the end. . . .'"

Jake lowered the volume on the Queen tape. The Corolla's stereo wasn't exactly modern, and he and Miles only had about three cassette tapes that they could play in the car without seeming like two guys in a musical time machine. Miles had unearthed Queen, Tom Petty, and Billy Idol from his dad's collection. Jake had hidden the shoe box his mom had given him of her old favorites: Duran Duran, Air Supply, and Flock of Seagulls.

"Dude, why are you turning that off? We are the champions, my friend!" Miles hadn't stopped grinning from ear to ear the whole ride to school. "I'm not trying to ride on your coattails, but I am totally riding on your coattails. This is the best thing that ever happened to us."

Jake drained his Starbucks cup as he made a sloppy left turn. He was exhausted after a long weekend of filming. This movie star–high school student dual role was taking its toll. His mom, Gigi, had treated the news of his *Class Angel* role with the same kind of horror she'd shown in fifth grade when Jake had come home with Twinkie, the classroom's pet rat, to take care of for the summer. She'd wanted him to quit immediately, and had only reluctantly come around when Jake had played the *Don't you want me to be happy?* card. But Jake could only stay Tommy Archer if he kept his grades up. So whenever he wasn't shooting, he was trying to cram in assignments for his classes, and it seemed like he was always shooting, or reciting and re-reciting his lines in hopes of not making a total ass of himself. He hadn't slept for more than four hours a night, and his body felt leaden. And Miles, in hyper-enthusiasm mode, wasn't making it any easier.

"Maybe," Jake finally answered, pulling into the BHH parking lot behind a pink Range Rover. "But I won't be a student here much longer if I don't finish my homework. I was up till three last night working on that Golden Gate Bridge case study for physics. My paper's a half-page short. And calc, I'm behind. English, I haven't started *Crime and Punishment*. Or that essay on health care as a right or a responsibility for civics."

Jake parked in his usual spot, his whole body weak just from thinking about his to-do list. Miles grabbed his backpack and Jake's, hefting one on each shoulder. "I got it, dude."

"Thanks, Miles," Jake muttered, not even remotely concerned about being teased for Miles carrying his bag. What, was Rod Stegerson gonna say they were gay lovers? Big deal.

"So, okay," Miles said, his voice in battle-plan pitch. "You've got physic, calc, English, civics. I can help. I'll talk to your teachers for you. Get you extra time. I'll tell them I'll get them on the AV squad priority list for equipment." BHH teachers frequently fought over the school's flat-screens, to show their classes high-definition documentaries.

Jake grimaced. "What priority list?"

"Exactly," Miles said, nodding assuredly, like a politician selling a fiscal plan the public didn't understand. "AV has keys even teachers don't get; they'll believe whatever I tell them. Think of me as your personal manager. What else do you need?"

Jake grinned. It was a goofy plan, pure Miles. No way would Jake make his best friend some servant/errand boy. But at least he could help with the homework situation. Priority list? Classic.

"Dude, just talk to the teachers, that would be awesome," Jake said. "I have to hurry if I'm going to make physics between scenes. First, let's stop by the production trailer for my check."

Miles's eyes widened. "Sweet. The inner sanctum."

Class Angel's production trailer was at the edge of the school's courtyard, a site long ago claimed by the coolest kids at BHH. Jake and Miles normally had no occasion to walk through it. The courtyard, a sunny, red-bricked area surrounded by benches, a low stone wall, and an array of rosebushes in the school colors, red and white, was like a micro-paradise where Jake wouldn't have been shocked to see Greek gods lounging as loincloth-clad women fed them grapes.

Today, it thrummed with people who were not BHH students. It was payday, and the hundreds of workers it took to film even a midlevel-budget movie had come out of the woodwork. Jake knew he'd be getting something for his part, but he wasn't exactly sure what.

The trailer was long and white, like the actors' trailers, but instead of being a metal box, it had a long row of windows along one side. He could see Kady Parker inside, talking to the line producer, as the woman handed her an envelope. Jake felt a nervous tingle rush through his body. He hadn't talked to Kady since before yesterday's scene, when he'd told her about his fake ACL injury. Miles knew about his *What Would Justin Klatch Do?* mantra, but not the lie, and now he prayed silently that Miles wouldn't blow his cover.

Jake clattered up the steps and into the trailer. Kady stood near the Arrowhead water cooler, chatting with a PA about the new David Fincher movie.

Jake cleared his throat. "I'm here to pick up my check, um, Lorraine."

Miles extended his hand. "Lorraine, it's a pleasure. Miles Abelson, Jake's manager."

Lorraine eyed Miles, who was straining under the weight of two filled-to-brimming backpacks, but didn't laugh. "Nice to meet you," She pulled an envelope from her stack. "Should I give this to you, or to your manager?" she said, looking back at Jake.

Jake was about to say she could hand it to him, since the Miles-as-assistant thing was just a joke. But Miles spoke first. "I'll take care of it," he said, all business, politely taking the check and nodding to Lorraine.

He turned and tore it open, and Jake could read it over Miles's shoulder.

Ten thousand dollars?

Ten. Thousand. Dollars!

"Holy crap," Miles said with hushed reverence as they moved to an empty corner of the trailer. "This is a lot of money. This is lease-an-Escalade money."

Jake chuckled. Yeah, right. If most of that money didn't go directly into his college savings account, his mom would have a fit. He didn't want to say that here, though. And he couldn't stay much longer. He had to get to physics in five minutes. There was a break in filming as the crew erected a pep rally set, so he was going to try to squeeze in a class. It would help his case when Miles went to speak to the teachers.

Jake was about to grab Miles to leave when a petite hand tapped him on the shoulder. Jake turned and saw Kady behind him, wearing a silky blue tank top that brought out her otherworldly eyes.

"Nice pass last night, Jake," she said, her hand still on Jake's arm. "Or should I call you Tom Brady?"

"He's good, right?" Miles said, introducing himself to Kady. Jake wanted to leave the trailer immediately, before Miles revealed something embarrassing, like the fact that Jake previously couldn't even get a spot as a water boy on BHH's team.

"I'll say," Kady said, her eyes never leaving Jake. "Were you and Miles just talking about leasing an Escalade?" She was regarding Jake like he was captain of the football team, Hollywood heartthrob, and all-around stud combined into one wild-haired-but-muscular Jewish package.

"Well, yeah," Jake said, the words barely controlled by his brain. "Fully loaded, right?" He grinned at Miles, Justin Klatch style.

Miles took the bait. "You got it."

Kady raised one eyebrow sexily at Jake, nodding goodbye to Miles. "Can't wait to see it." She headed to the exit. As she unlatched the metal door, she turned back, winking at Jake. "Maybe you could give me a ride sometime."

Miles let out a long, low breath as he watched her hop down the trailer steps in her rhinestone flip-flops and purple pleated miniskirt. "Jake, that was badass. She got any friends?"

"I'll let you know." Jake grinned, feeling more victorious than he ever had as a champion Mathlete. So, fine, he hadn't had much experience with "badass" anything up until now. But if he wasn't mistaken, right now he was the definition of the word.

And badasses didn't worry about being late for physics.

YOU SAY IT'S YOUR BIRTHDAY?

Ash rolled his Camaro into the driveway of his house on Bedford Drive, just as KROQ started to play Cracker's "Happy Birthday to Me."

Fucking mockery.

It *was* Ash's birthday, not that anyone would know it. He was completely pathetic. Fine, so his mom had remembered, calling him this morning. Her present had arrived last week—an open-ended ticket to Austin so he could come down whenever he wanted and get a new amp for his guitar. His sister had mailed him her usual gift, books, including a she-hoped-it-was-subtle-but-it-wasn't self-help book titled *Damn the Man: A Four-Step Conflict Resolution Guide for Fathers and Sons.*

Damn the man was right. Gordon hadn't called to wish him a good birthday, or uttered so much as a thank-you, even though Ash had been tossed on his ass out of a shitty dive bar. If he knew about it—Daisy's ejection from Powerhouse hadn't made any blogs—Gordon would probably revel in it. It would be a great story to tell at cocktail parties; he'd cap it with, "That's just life in the music business." Admittedly, it was kind of funny, and Ash had recounted it several times over the weekend to Tucker and Geoff.

Ash stepped onto the driveway, pulling his iPhone from his pocket as he did. Myla had sent a text. *Happy Birthday, Ash. I wish a lot of things for you. Love, M. P.S. Remember, you're always invited for dinner.*

That Myla had remembered—and bothered to do something about it—only added to the sting. Even his best friends had forgotten. Tucker and Geoff had invited him to Zuma today to hit the surf, but it wasn't a birthday thing, it was a *we do this every day* thing. In years past, they'd remembered—as had everyone else he hung with at BHH—because Myla had *made* them remember. For his sixteenth birthday last year, Myla had rented out four cabins at Big Bear, and paid for two days of skiing for Ash and all their friends. And she always made him a card, complete with glitter and stickers, which sounded cheesy, but wasn't. Myla had a crafty side she rarely showed. More than any gift or party, the fact that she risked her manicure to glue hundreds of sparkly hearts to construction paper always made his birthday a reminder of how much she loved him.

Ash heard the squeak of brakes in the Porter-Goldsmiths' driveway next door and he looked up to see Jake pulling up in his Corolla. He'd been meaning to congratulate Jake on his part in *Class Angel*, and say something to his childhood best friend about his awesome "game."

Jake emerged from his pastel blue Corolla looking a lot different than the scrawny, bruise-prone kid Ash had traded Pokémon cards with. He looked like someone Ash would hang out with now. Even his crazy mop of curls resembled a style Geoff had tried and failed to achieve.

Ash nodded across the driveway, stepping onto the swath of grass that separated their yards. "Hey, Jake," he said, feeling awkward. "Congrats on the movie."

Jake grinned widely, making Ash glad he'd paid the compliment. He'd never intended for his best-friend status with Jake to morph to them not talking at all, but the more they drifted, the less they spoke.

"Thanks, Ash," Jake said, grabbing his backpack from the passenger seat. He took a few steps toward his house, then raised his eyebrows. "Oh, and hey, it's your birthday, right?"

Ash squinted at him. "Yeah, it is. How'd you remember?"

Jake looked down at his Converse. Just when his old friend might start to think he was unlame, Jake had to do something as girly as remember Ash's birthday. "Just good with numbers, you know? But happy birthday." He shrugged nonchalantly and looked up to see Ash grinning in an appreciative way. Maybe remembering wasn't lame and girly. He noticed Ash was about to head into his dark and empty house. Most nights, Ash's car was the only one in the driveway, and the only light on in the house was in Ash's room, on the second floor across from Jake's. In theory, it sounded cool that Ash got a mansion to himself at sixteen, but Jake knew it had to be depressing. Especially on a birthday. "You know, you're welcome to come over for dinner here. My mom always has a lot of food. And don't worry, she never cooks anymore. Takeout. So everything's edible."

Ash laughed. Mrs. Porter-Goldsmith once had served them grilled cheese sandwiches made with microwaved matzo bread and cream cheese. "Um, thanks, but I think I'm supposed to do something later." First Myla had invited him over, now Jake. He must have looked like an orphan.

"Cool," Jake said. "But the offer stands, you know, whenever."

Ash lay on his bed, eating leftover chow fun noodles from Dragon's Fire, a Chinese restaurant on Santa Monica. He flipped idly through the *Damn the Man* book, laughing at how poorly the advice would go over with Gordon.

Clear the air, read the start of step one. *Set a date to do something manly as father and son. Get your aggressions out on the basketball court, at an automobile race, or even by taking a long run. Then find a quiet place to have a coffee, or even a stiff drink if that makes you both comfortable. Whoever does the inviting should then announce, "It's time for a talk." Agree to a no-interruptions opportunity to list your complaints with your father or son, and then be patient as he does the same.*

Ash rolled his eyes, flopping onto his stomach and putting his head under a pillow. Yeah, like Gordon would listen to a list of complaints.

From under the pillow, Ash heard his muffled ring—reset to a new Raconteurs song. Lifting the corner of the pillow, he reached for the phone, seeing his dad's face on the screen. At least he'd remembered his birthday.

"Hey, Dad," Ash said, hating that he felt incrementally better.

"Son," Gordon said, sounding jovial instead of stern. "Heard you had quite an adventure with Daisy last week." He chuckled. "Bet you've never had a night like that."

Um, you're welcome, Ash thought grimly, but didn't say anything. His dad was waiting for some acknowledgment of the Daisy adventure, and Ash was waiting for his dad's birthday wish. *We could stay like this all night,* he thought.

"So tonight, I need you to come up here," Gordon said. "We're having a party."

Ash instantly softened. A party? For him? The last time his dad had planned him a birthday party was a paintball outing in the seventh grade. It was right before the divorce.

"You didn't have to do that, Dad," Ash said.

"Of course I did. Investors want to meet Daisy, and I need to show she's not a liability. You're good with her. To an extent, anyway. Be here at eight?"

"Um, actually, I have plans." Ash gripped the phone tightly, pissed off that his dad would plan a party for Daisy while forgetting his birthday.

"What kind of plans?" Gordon asked skeptically. "It's Tuesday night."

And my birthday, Ash thought. *Not that you care.* He racked his brain for an actual engagement, not just hanging with Tucker and Geoff. Ash glanced out his window at Jake's navy curtains. "Actually, I'm supposed to go the Porter-Goldsmiths' for dinner," he said, hoping his Porter-Goldsmiths invite sounded like an unbreakable obligation.

"Yeah, of course. Must be a big night for you," Gordon said, sounding more amused than hurt. "Have a good time."

And with that, he hung up. Ash exhaled, laughing to himself as he imagined stodgy investors chatting up Daisy in one of her crazy tutus. It might have been fun to go, but if Ash's birthday was so easily forgettable, so was his dad's stupid party.

He rang the Porter-Goldsmiths' bell, feeling like a tool. He'd fetched a bottle of wine from the cellar and now he hastily untied the gift tag signed by Francis Ford Coppola from the bottle's neck. He tossed it in the bushes just as Jake's mom answered.

"Ash," Jake's mom, Gigi, said, her familiar halo of auburn hair tied in a loose ponytail. She looked a little surprised to see him, but pleased. "What a nice surprise. Come in." Memories flooded Ash as he stepped through the door. He and Jake had practically lived at one another's houses until they were ten. Mrs. Goldsmith had seen him in his Power Rangers underwear.

He handed her the bottle of wine, as she protested that he didn't have to do that.

As he walked into the Porter-Goldsmiths' eat-in kitchen, every face registered surprise at seeing him.

"Hey, Ash," Jake said, looking confused as he brought a plate of spaghetti to the table.

"Ash, 'sup?" Jake's little brother, Brendan, said, nodding approvingly as he sat down. Brendan had always tried to hang out with Ash and Jake when they were younger. He had to be thirteen now, and was almost Ash's height. He'd been a little chubby as a kid, but now he was all muscle, with shoulders that looked broad and square compared to his face, his cheeks still a round reminder of his baby fat.

Jonathan, Jake's dad, stood, clutching Ash's hand in his solid grip. "Good to see you, Ash. Sit, sit. I hear it's your birthday." The Porter-Goldsmiths' kitchen table was still the same dark, round six-seater he'd eaten at hundreds of times growing up. The kitchen was updated with granite counters and a stainless-steel fridge, but Gigi's collage of old Hollywood stars still hung above the stove.

After the initial surprise wore off, Ash worked to be a good dinner guest, even if he felt a little odd. Everything was familiar but different at his old best friend's house, like walking out of a movie and coming back a half hour later to realize you'd missed the whole middle.

"So, Ash, how are things? Still playing piano?" Gigi asked, looking at him over the rim of her wineglass.

The question made Ash feel like he'd been gone even longer. "I stopped a while ago," he said. "But I'm playing guitar now."

"Dude, that's awesome," Brendan said, high-fiving across the basket of garlic bread. "Think you'll ever get a band going?"

Ash shrugged, grinning. "I've been trying," he said, coiling some strands of spaghetti around his fork. "My bandmates have a hard time making decisions. You know how it goes."

"I wish," Brendan said. Turning to Jake, he said sarcastically, "He's got bandmates and you've got Abelson. No wonder he doesn't hang out with you anymore."

Ash cringed at the reminder that he'd been the one who ditched Jake. They'd already started to drift, and the one time he'd tried to include Jake with his new friend Tucker, when they were all about eleven, the whole experience had been a nightmare. Jake still thought girls were gross, and all Tucker wanted to do was try to get 7-Eleven clerks to sell them *Playboys*.

Jake took the remark in stride. "Bren, you couldn't even get into band playing the clarinet," he snickered, making eye contact with Ash. "I don't think you'll have bandmates anytime soon either."

"I only tried out for clarinet 'cause all the cute girls play the flute," Brendan shot back, looking at Ash defensively. Mr. Goldsmith made a loud *shhh* noise as he blew on a hot meatball.

"So, besides music," Mr. Goldsmith said, setting down the fork, meatball and all, "how is your family? Tessa?"

"Still at Berkeley," Ash said, remembering how Tessa used to love getting into debates with Jake's dad about non-teenage topics like politics and religion. "Studying philosophy."

"Oh, your father must love that," Gigi said, the words sounding harsher than she'd probably intended. Ash knew she thought his dad was a dick for leaving him alone in the house. He'd been lying out by the pool one day with his headphones on and heard Mrs. Goldsmith over the fence, telling one of her friends on the phone how she'd like to give Gordon Gilmour a piece of her mind, leaving a growing teenage boy to fend for himself. Ash remembered thinking he'd have loved to hear Gigi rail on his dad. Gordon could string together a creative swear combination, but Jake's mom could outgun him any day of the week.

"Yeah," Ash said, rolling his eyes so that Gigi knew they were on the same page. "He asked her what philosopher has ever made any money, and she told him Bob Dylan. That sort of ended that."

Jonathan laughed heartily. "Tessa was always a gifted debater. How is school going for *you*, though?"

Ash took a sip of the bitter iced tea Gigi had made. "I don't think anything I tell you about me and school will be half as good as what Jake can say."

Brendan laughed through a mouthful of meatball. "Yeah, nerd," he chided Jake.

Ash shot him a look. "No, I mean with the movie."

Gigi plastered a smile on her face that Ash could tell was fake. "Jacob knows what I think. I think he should make school the priority, not Hollywood." She sighed. "But since when does a mother know what's best for her child?"

Across the table Jake's hazel eyes bugged out in Ash's direction. Ash had clearly talked his way into a conversational minefield. "Jake's working with that Grant Isaacson dude. . . ." It was all he could think of.

"Little prick turned down my proposal to do his publicity," Gigi muttered into her wine.

"Ma, he doesn't even need you," Jake said. "Today, these three girls—which of Myla's friends again, Ash?"

"Billie Bollman, Talia Shepard, and Fortune Weathers. All totally crazy for that guy. And probably a little crazy," Ash chimed in, grinning at Jonathan, who was listening intently.

"Yeah, them," Jake said, sounding excited. "They left a plate of cookies from Sweet Lady Jane outside his trailer door. And he was completely terrified."

Ash leaned forward, getting into the story. "Well, of course he was. They'd had all of them iced with his face. And they were hiding behind the bushes with binoculars watching him as he picked them up."

"He didn't even eat them," Jake said. "He doesn't do sugar. It screws up your system." He looked meaningfully at Gigi, who'd finished eating and was sorting discriminately through a box of See's Candies on the counter. Apparently, Jake's mom was still in the diet mode she'd been in six years ago: Scarf candy at night in private, guilt herself through a day of bland food, repeat.

Dinner wound down with the whole family helping to clear the table. Ash loaded the silverware into the dishwasher and Jake's mom—maybe because of the two glasses of pinot noir she'd had with the meal—threw an affectionate arm around him. "You've always been such a sweetie." As everyone headed back to the table for dessert, Gigi held Jake back and whispered something to him.

Because even Gigi's *whisper* carried, Ash could hear her. "I can't believe he's alone on his birthday," she said. "I was thinking we could . . ." Ash couldn't hear the rest because Brendan started playing drums on the table with his silverware, looking out the corner of his eye to see if Ash was impressed with his percussion.

Jake came back to the table, Gigi just behind him, carrying a sheet cake from Whole Foods. A faint blue imprint of the words *Congrats to Our Star, Jake!* was still visible, but she'd spelled out *Ash! 17!* in M&M's. As she placed it on the table, she looked almost guilty, ran to the kitchen, and came back with candles.

"We were celebrating Jake's big role," she said, sticking the candles into the chocolate icing. "And reminding him that his family thinks he's a star, even if we disagree with his choices and even if the movie is a bomb."

Brendan chuckled. "Ha, loser," he said, looking at Ash. "I'm calling him DVD. As in 'direct to DVD.'"

Jonathan's jaw clenched, every hair of his beard looking tense. "C'mon, Bren. If Jake's movie is a hit, you'll be taking credit. Success has one hundred parents, but failure is an orphan."

Brendan pursed his lips petulantly, the softness of his chin becoming apparent. Jake's dad's "rabbi with a touch of Buddha" made for guilt trips worse than any normal parent could deliver. Ash chuckled along with Jake, and they shared a glance across the table.

"But Jake said he agreed your birthday was more important," Gigi continued, putting the candles in at odd angles.

Jake shook his head earnestly, his face turning red.

"Thanks, man," Ash said, as Jake shrugged.

Gigi lit the candles and everyone stood up, save for Ash, who Gigi instructed to stay seated. As they sang, Ash tried to focus entirely on the moment. They asked him questions, and cared about his interests, and made him feel like he was worth listening to. The Porter-Goldsmiths were being nicer to him than his own father.

Ash blew out the candles and Gigi cut the cake, serving pieces all around. Taking a quick bite of cake, Jake stood up from the table. "Sorry, Ma," he said. "I have to go meet Miles about this physics project. And I just told you, sugar screws you up."

"More for me then," Gigi said, kissing him goodbye. Jonathan patted his back. Ash had just witnessed Jake getting more parental affection in ten seconds than he'd had all year.

"More for you, too, Ash," Gigi said, setting a continent-size piece of cake in front of him as Jake slipped out the door. Once everyone had a piece, they resumed eating, but the chatter of conversation was gone, and the only noise came from the screech of forks across dessert plates. Ash looked up to see Gigi, Jonathan, and Brendan smiling at him generously across the table. He felt like some straggly dog the Porter-Goldsmiths had found and brought home and were now watching to make sure he ate something. The person who'd invited him had left; this was definitely what they called overstaying your welcome. He took three fast bites of cake, wanting to get out of there as soon as he could without being rude. He was feeling too much like a charity case without any family of his own.

Jonathan gave him his opening. "Ash, my boy, you must have some big things going on for your birthday tonight. I still remember when Jacob came home wanting to be a jockey after your dad took you all to Santa Anita."

Ash suppressed a smile. He'd been ten and his dad had taken him and his friends to learn how to bet on horses. As nuts as it was, Ash had thought Gordon was the coolest dad in the world. Once.

"Ha, yeah, I remember that. Jake even bought that pink jockey hat," Ash said. "He kept insisting it wasn't pink, it was magenta, and a royal color."

"Oh God, how did I not know this?" Brendan said, running from the kitchen, probably in search of Jake's hat.

"But I do have to go," Ash said, backing toward the door. He wanted to go to the one place that always felt like home. "Thank you guys for everything."

He'd decided to take Myla up on her invitation to stop by.

Right now.

LAST IMPRESSIONS

"Okay, so what about Olivia Abdabo? Miss I Think I'm Donatella Without the Bad Tan?" Jojo pointed one Lotus Rouge–painted fingernail—chip-free, thank you very much—at the pretty face with deep-set eyes staring up at them from the pages of the BHH yearbook.

Myla laughed. "That's not bad. A little on the long side. Total head case. Like, camping-out-in-front-of-the-Jonas-Brothers'-house head case. She made a whole purity outfit to show her devotion to teen abstinence and sat there overnight, until the cops came. For weeks after, she ate and drank nothing but white foods, just to show her dedication. A few weeks later, she lost her virginity to a senior in the Young Republicans Club."

Myla and Jojo were in Jojo's room, going through old yearbooks. They weren't reminiscing, though. They were in the middle of a lesson, titled "Knowledge Is Power." Myla never forgot a juicy slice of gossip. While the rest of BHH moved on to the next thing, Myla kept every foible, flaw, and weakness stored in the Eames file cabinet that was her brain.

Now she was teaching Jojo everything that could be taught about their classmates' lowest points over the last few years. Much as she liked gossiping with Myla in the privacy of their house, Jojo couldn't imagine herself using any of the information publicly. Myla could do whatever she wanted; she'd reigned at BHH for years. And she'd probably ruled her junior high, grammar school, and preschool before that. But when Jojo told Myla she didn't think she'd ever use all this dish, Myla had said, "People say they won't use algebra either. It's the concepts that are important. And the concept here is, Everyone has a weak spot." So Jojo contented herself in bonding with her sister. And she had to admit, gossip here was way more interesting than gossip back home.

Jojo flipped forward a few pages, and her eyes immediately landed on Jake Porter-Goldsmith. She giggled unintentionally. "That's Jake? Oh. My. God." He must have been about twenty-five pounds thinner last year. His face was narrow, his neck so long and thin it looked like he was trying to stretch himself out of the shot. "He was so dorky! But he's still cute."

Myla's head swiveled in Jojo's direction. "Did you say cute?"

Jojo didn't take her eyes off the picture. "Yeah, in a hopeless kind of way. He's much cuter now. Like he blossomed from geek to chic."

Myla stood up, yanking the yearbook from under Jojo's nose, closing the heavy hardcover with a snap. Eyeing Jojo with the glare of a pet owner whose puppy had just peed on the floor, she said, "No. No. And triple no. You cannot have a crush on Jacob Porter-Goldsmith."

Jojo felt a blush run up her neck at being called out for her crush. She'd been wanting to ask him how WWJKD was going, but hadn't bumped into him since their lunch date. But when she, like the rest of the school, saw him throw his amazing pass, it was clear the lessons had worked. He looked cuter than ever as a quarterback. "I think he likes to be called Jake now," she said, tossing a strand of her loosely curled hair over one shoulder.

"Jake, Jacob, I don't care if his new name is James Dean," Myla said, a little more gently. "He's an NFW boy."

"A what?" Jojo stood up, so she was at eye level with Myla.

"A No Fucking Way boy." Myla spelled it out. "Going out with him would cement you as BarfBarf for the rest of your life."

So what? was Jojo's first thought, and it came as as much of a surprise to her as seeing Jake as a reedy nerd. But she stopped herself from saying it aloud. After her dreadful first few weeks, she didn't have a ton of faith in her own choices—and besides, maybe her sister knew what she needed more than she did. Myla's advice had worked so far. Jojo turned and shuffled to her vanity, a hand-carved table stained silver with different-size drawers and a moon-shaped oval mirror, which Barkley had made for her. Sitting down and flipping her hairbrush in her hands, she looked back at Myla's reflection. "He's in a movie, though. You saw him make that pass," she pointed out.

Myla came up beside Jojo, putting a light hand on her shoulder. She perched on the edge of the vanity and offered Jojo a sympathetic look. "I know it sounds parental of me, but it's for your own good. What we're working on here is so much bigger than you realize. I'm not showing you how to survive BHH. I'm teaching you how to *thrive*. Do you understand why Jake's not part of that?"

Emotions swirled in Jojo's chest. She didn't get why Myla was talking to her like a child. Then again, she didn't understand why *she* was resisting what seemed like sincere, sisterly advice. But most of all, the idea of being *somebody* at BHH pulled at her. Not so much for the popularity, but to be closer to Myla. What good was it having a sister who ruled the school if you were always hiding out in the library? "Not really," she said, hoping she didn't sound as petulant as she felt.

"Once a geek, always a geek," Myla dictated, like she was telling Jojo two plus two was four. "He might be appealing now, but he's PG. And when the movie's done, he'll go right back to being PG. Mathlete, dork, hopeless. Maybe even worse than that, if the movie bombs. I'll help you find an acceptable boy. You'll forget Jake. I mean, Jacob."

Jojo was about to argue further when the doorbell chimed Beethoven's "Ode to Joy."

"Myla, Jojo, we have company," Lailah trilled up the stairs. They could hear her Manolos tapping across the wood floor as she asked Lucy to set another place for dinner.

"I hope they didn't invite DeNiro over again," Myla sighed. "He just chews and stares. Worst dinner guest ever. Follow my lead, I'll introduce you."

She and Jojo headed down the winding staircase, Myla first. Just as she reached the curve from which the dining room was visible, Myla almost missed the four final steps in her shock, excitement, and delight.

Because standing there was her just-turned-eighteen ex-boyfriend, Ash.

A few hours and one dinner later, Lailah leaned back in her high-backed chair as Lucy reached in to clear her empty dinner plate. "Oh, Ash, we're so happy to see you. And on your birthday." She cocked her perfectly shaped face to one side, a wave of dark hair tumbling in front of her violet eyes, as she studied Ash like he was a long-lost prodigal son returned home.

Ash grinned, feeling a little bad that he'd barely touched his polenta-crusted chicken and eaten only half of the beef Wellington prepared just for him. He was beyond stuffed after two meals. But while his stomach felt heavy, Ash felt lighter everywhere else. The Everharts' just felt like home. He sat at his usual spot, next to Myla's head-of-the-table dinner chair, with Jojo on the other side. He'd been worried that Jojo would be less than thrilled at his arrival, after he'd rejected her at Lewis' party. But he'd been pleasantly surprised when she said simply, "Hi, Ash," and given him a hello hug.

"And now, cake!" Barkley said, patting his "belly," if a ten-pack could be called that, over his blue button-down Armani shirt. Barkley loved cake the way other men his age loved classic cars or golf clubs. He *admired* cake, just reveling in its pleasures until he finally had to take that first bite. He looked around the table—at what Ash and

Myla used to privately joke was the miniature U.N., with all its international children—for cake reactions. Mahalo, going on nine, gave Ash a double-thumbs-up and Ash chuckled, amazed at how long his hair was getting. Bobby, who'd sprouted from a chubby kindergartener to skinny first grader this year, hadn't removed his knit Spider-Man skullcap all during dinner. Now he threw the hat in the air and cheered, "Cake!" The toddlers—Nelson, Indigo, and Ajani—all clapped to no particular beat at all, chanting "Birf-day! Birf-day!"

Lucy emerged again from the kitchen, carrying a three-layer German chocolate cake with nineteen long, skinny candles lit on top of it. Setting it down in front of Ash, she said, "Eighteen, with one for good luck."

The family sang its rendition of "Happy Birthday," most everyone a little off-key. Lailah, who'd just taken a role in the movie version of *Spring Awakening*, demonstrated her perfect pitch. As he blew out his candles, Ash thought his happiness at this moment was more than good luck.

It was about being right where he belonged.

Twenty minutes later, Myla was still unsure that the feet inside her cuffed Jeffrey Campbell booties were hers. Her whole body felt like a fizzy champagne vapor, little sparkly clouds that surrounded her physical being. *He'd actually shown up*. For someone used to getting her own way, Myla should have been more blasé about having Ash over. But she was surprised by how much she enjoyed getting something she wanted that she hadn't thought possible.

She tried now to climb the stairs calmly, Ash behind

her, Jojo behind him. Myla wanted Jojo around, at least for a while, to serve as witness to her and Ash finally getting back together.

They reached her room, and Ash sank easily into his usual spot on her purple velvet couch. All of them were silent—Myla from a rare case of nerves; Ash from nerves, maybe, or just cake, chicken, and beef overload; Jojo probably from feeling like a third wheel.

Myla looked for something to do, hoping to get Ash to stay awhile. She glanced at Jojo, making a desperate *say something!* face. Jojo gave her best Myla-patented mocking half-smile, then said, "So Ash, Myla was just telling me which boys at BHH are good enough to date."

Myla smiled, relieved. Maybe Jojo *was* learning something. The subject of dating was exactly where Myla wanted Ash to be. She plopped down next to Ash on the sofa, making sure to maintain perfect posture, to hide the bloat of the cake she'd wolfed down anxiously. "Yeah, help us find a boy for Jojo."

Ash, who'd had his eyes half-closed in post-feast repose, opened one. "A challenge or a gimme?" he asked, using Myla's terms for unattainable versus attainable boys.

Myla examined Jojo. She was too pretty for a gimme, but too sweet for a challenge.

"Who's a little bit of both?" Myla said. Jojo made a *what the hell?* face.

"Simple," Ash said, yawning. "Tucker. Guy keeps talking about you." He pointed at Jojo. "His crushes usually fade fast. Something you did lengthened his attention span."

Myla considered this, folding her arms in satisfaction. Tucker was the very definition of man meat: a pretty boy, not a ton going on upstairs, and thus not likely to play games. Granted, he might not be a long-haul boy, since he could be a little slutty, but Jojo just needed a decent-looking guy to get her mind off losers like PG. And who knew? Maybe sweet Jojo would be just the girl to tame Mr. Prowl himself. "I would have slapped you if you said Geoff, but Tucker is good. Perfect. Give her the stats. Sit down, Jojo."

Jojo was so full, she'd slouched down in the pink chair. Catching herself going into slob mode in front of Myla, she straightened into a dignified position. Fred and Bradley would be glad to know she'd finally started to control her posture. Who'd known that all it would take was one glamorous, judgmental stepsister?

"Stats? On Tucker?"

Jojo felt flattered. Tucker was cute, and she'd seen other girls watch him covetously. She didn't know what he had going on in the brains or sense-of-humor department, but Jojo felt proud that Myla thought she could land such a wanted guy at BHH. Maybe it wasn't noble of her, but now that Myla had said it aloud, she wanted desperately to *thrive*, not just survive. She looked around Myla's room. Pictures of Myla and her girlfriends poked from every nook and cranny. Her iPhone, tossed carelessly on the bed, beeped constantly with incoming texts. And Ash Gilmour, one of the cutest guys Jojo had ever met, was leaning back on the couch like he lived here. Jojo wanted it all. Not just the closet and dresser bursting with desirable things but the mementos of the ultimate life. And Myla obviously knew how to get it. Besides, if Jojo succeeded, she'd someday rise to a level of power high enough that she could date any guy she wanted . . . even Jake. "Yeah, like what does he like to do? What books does he read?"

Ash laughed robustly. "Skip the books. Tucker likes surfing, surfing, and more surfing. Toss in a little music appreciation. Keep it simple. Between that and the fact that you're a cute girl, you're done."

"O-kay," Jojo said. That wasn't the best start, but she was still on board for the plan. "So what do I do?"

Myla snapped her fingers like a choreographer. "You have homework. Go to your room and pick an outfit a surf-loving, music-loving, cute girl-crazy guy would like. Modern. So nothing Victorian, Gatsbian, or even sexy librarian."

"You got it," Jojo said, secretly thinking that "sexy librarian" sounded exactly like something Jake might appreciate.

It had been nearly a half hour, and Jojo hadn't returned. Myla appreciated her sister for sensing that she wanted to be alone with Ash. Jojo was too smart to not have already thrown together a miniskirt, tank top, hoodie and embellished flip-flops—Tucker bait.

Now they were talking like old times. Not quite old times, since as a couple, their conversations often led to them making out. But close enough. They were on Myla's couch, only a few inches of soft fabric separating them.

"So what's up with your friends?" Ash asked, his playful smile teasing her. "Did you hear about the stalker cookies?"

"Yeah." Myla sighed, rolling her eyes at him. Her friends' ardor for Grant Isaacson had showed no signs of waning, and they hadn't even consulted her about their cookie plan, which, frankly, made her look bad by association. Rumor was, they'd used secret camera phone shots they'd taken of Grant during the football game scene and had them iced onto cookies. *If* they'd even bothered to ask, she'd have told them they were veering into restraining-order territory. But they'd hatched the plan without her, probably after the game. They'd invited her to go to dinner with them that night, but almost seemed relieved when she declined. Much as she wanted nothing to do with their plan, she couldn't believe how distracted they'd been acting toward her. "But I had nothing to do with it," she quickly added.

"I kinda figured," Ash said, making eye contact, still laughing. "Not your style. You can tell them it's the lamest and creepiest thing I've heard in a while."

Myla giggled, feeling like she was with the old Ash. Before her trip, before the breakup, before Lewis Buford. "At least my friends wouldn't forget my birthday," she retorted, before realizing what she'd said. Her eyes got wide, and she brought her fingertips to cover her mouth. "I'm sorry, I didn't mean—"

Ash waved it off. "My friends? Come on. Could you see Tucker and Geoff out getting a hundred red velvet cupcakes with my name spelled out in little candy guitars?"

Myla blushed. The cupcakes were something she'd served at Ash's birthday bash last year at Big Bear. "I'd think they could manage at least a taquito or something."

Ash smirked. "Not those guys. Unluckily for me, they don't have a Myla Everhart bone in their bodies. Jake Porter-Goldsmith remembered, though. Weird, huh?"

What's with everyone's obsession with PG? Myla wondered. She didn't want to talk about Ash's birthday anymore, because she didn't want to think about the party she'd planned to throw. She'd had the idea to rent out Club 33, a top secret New Orleans–style honky-tonk hidden in Disneyland. Ash secretly loved the Pirates of the Caribbean ride, which was right below it. She'd wanted to close it down so the two of them could ride through the "seas" as if on their own private love boat.

Saddened by the things they'd already missed in just the short time they'd been broken up, Myla changed the subject. "So your dad asked you to an investor party for Daisy Morton? Are you sure it wasn't a surprise birthday party?" she asked, leaning closer to Ash on the plush cushions. At dinner, he'd told Lailah and Barkley that Gordon was busy with the fête. Much as her own parents got on her nerves, she felt grateful to not have a father as completely unavailable as Gordon. She also knew she was probably the only person in the world, besides his sister, with whom Ash would discuss his relationship with his dad.

Ash shook his head. "Definitely not," he monotoned. "The worst of it is, she's staying in Beverly Hills, and he appointed me her babysitter. I had to go to the shittiest bar in Hollywood so she could try to kick this poor girl's ass last night."

"So she's really as nuts as they say?" Myla said. She was hoping the answer was yes. Even though Daisy

Morton was a complete and utter mess, she was also hot in that completely ungroomed way that a lot of guys found sexy.

Ash shrugged. "I guess. But I hate that shit. I mean, my dad's label used to stand for something. Integrity. Quality. Actual musical skills. But even if you cleaned her up, she's still not that talented. People are just interested in seeing a train wreck. And I'm stuck with her against my will."

Myla leaned back a little into the couch, relieved. When they'd been dating, Myla sometimes had creeping insecurities. Every time Ash got hooked on some new female singer-songwriter, or a girl band, Myla worried he'd start to wish she played guitar, or wrote songs, or some other hippie, soulful stuff. "It can't last forever. She's probably a one-hit wonder," Myla reasoned. "But I think your dad has a long career as an asshole ahead of him." She straightened herself up into her *Gordon Gilmour, I'm so awesome* pose—shoulders back, chin jutting out, eyes squinting, and her hand tucked into an invisible blazer like a tiny Asian Napoleon. Then she spoke in an approximation of Gordon's booming voice. "Ash Gibson Gilmour, are you trying to tell me that you're sixteen and rich and good-looking and don't want to follow around a hygiene-hating head case like some entry-level nursing home employee? What's wrong with you? You should appreciate these things I let you do for me." Myla watched as Ash's frown tugged upward in a smile. "Are you smiling?" she continued in the Gordon voice. "The celebrity lunatic market is booming. And it's *serious business.* If you walk around *smiling* when you're getting Daisy's tutus dry-cleaned, you're going to cost me years of future profits."

Ash burst out laughing. Myla cracked up too, and they collided in the kind of exertive laughter that felt like a heavy make-out session, leaving them barely able to breathe. Just as they came up for air, Myla looked into Ash's eyes and couldn't take the temptation.

She leaned in and kissed him. It was like those old movies. Fireworks burst behind her eyelids; a symphony played in her ears. If they'd been standing up, Myla's leg would have involuntarily bent at the knee, the heel of her bootie pointing heavenward.

To Ash, great kisses were like great music. You felt a good song with your whole body, and you felt a great song with your whole body and something more. A great kiss brought to life parts of you that could never be detailed or diagramed in any textbook. The glow around your heart. That tickle in the back of your brain. The starburst just behind your eyes. He and Myla were kissing. Great kissing. Kissing like they needed each other, wanted each other, could never be torn apart. Until, unbidden, his mind flashed to Myla kissing Lewis. Myla curled next to Lewis, his hands all over her.

Ash pulled away, hearing in his mind the familiar ripping sound of a needle being pulled abruptly from a vinyl record. The Myla-Lewis scene sent waves of pain through his body, like he was getting kicked in the balls while his heart was being stomped on.

"What's wrong?" Myla said, her lush green eyes glittering and wet at the corners. She leaned in again, putting her hands on his chest.

Ash sprang back from the couch, standing above her. Nothing and everything was wrong. He wanted more than anything to kiss her again. But his vision stood between them like an invisible force field. Kisses like his and Myla's were supposed to be all theirs. But she'd kissed Lewis, and maybe that kiss had been just as great. "I can't do this," he said, looking at Myla but feeling half-blind, like he could only see the bad things. "Every time I see you, I see . . . that night."

Myla hastily wiped away a tear. She pressed her eyes closed, and when she opened them again, all signs of tears were gone. "The thing with Lewis, it meant nothing," she said, sounding businesslike, rational, even though there was a telltale quaver under the words.

"Doesn't matter," Ash said, grabbing his Paul Smith jacket off her bed. Of course she would tell him it meant nothing. What else would she say? That it was a great, amazing kiss and she'd never forget that night with Lewis?

Myla rose, striding silently over to Ash. He was right. How could he believe her? She'd scrubbed her mind, and her lips, dozens of times to forget the sliminess of Lewis's mouth on hers, and the way Ash had looked at her when he saw it happen. But for all Ash knew, the kiss with Lewis might have been her idea of everything a kiss should be—the symphony. She left a gap between them, staying close enough that he could feel her warm breath on his neck. She didn't know what she was going to say. She just knew she wanted to be between Ash and the door. "How can I make you believe me?" she uttered, more to herself than to him.

Ash shrugged, pulling his coat tight around his shoulders. Even behind the stubborn lock of hair that fell in front of them, Myla could see his eyes were glistening. She hated that she'd hurt him. Knowing she'd betrayed him hurt worse than if she'd been the one to catch him in the act. Which gave her an idea . . .

"Kiss someone else," she blurted out.

A small, sad chuckle broke free from Ash's lips. "Why, to make you feel better?'

Myla shook her head, regaining her strength. "No. Because it's the only way you could ever understand." Myla grabbed for his hand with urgency, locking her green eyes onto his. "I want you to. Kiss someone else, and see that the only kisses that matter are the ones between you and me."

Ash looked at her like she was Crazy Daisy. Wouldn't another kiss be another scar on their relationship? More irreparable damage?

"That's ridiculous, Myla," he said, ambling toward the door. "Look, I need to go. I'll see you . . . at school."

And then he left.

Myla folded herself into a corner of the couch, her knees pressed to her chest, and let the tears fall.

SPARKS WILL FLY

"Are you at all freaked out by those three girls who are following Grant around?" Kady said, tearing off a piece of her pretzel croissant and "mmm"-ing in ecstasy as she took a bite. It was Wednesday afternoon, and Amelie was sharing a table with Kady and Jake at the City Bakery in Brentwood. She'd finally gotten Jake to talk to her long enough to schedule a tutoring session. She'd agreed to meet him here, at the only Western outpost of the famous New York bakery, before realizing it was the spot where he and Kady would be filming a scene without her later that day.

So much for tutoring. Kady never shut up, and Jake had lazily checked Amelie's worksheet, but seemed distracted as he listened to Kady. The three of them were crammed around a small circular table only meant for two. Kady had pulled up a chair and smushed herself between Jake and Amelie.

The place was packed to the point where three teenage celebrities could skate by unnoticed. Not that Brentwood's rich denizens didn't see celebrities every day. A dozen or so trophy wives clustered around the salad bar, competing to see who could make the smallest salad. A honey-tressed woman, baring her slim but defined upper arms in a sleeveless tank, placed three roasted brussels sprouts on her otherwise empty plate. Her narrow-waisted brunette friend added just one to a plate that contained four small tufts of arugula.

"I never thought we'd find groupies at a Beverly Hills high school. We were doing his big speech about how he, well, Knox, used to be in love with me," Kady continued, tearing off another piece of pretzel croissant and hastily chewing it. "Oh my God, this is so good. Anyway, Grant's fan club were all staring at me so hard, like they wanted to switch bodies with me. I got this freaky chill. They're like cute versions of Macbeth's witches."

Jake laughed, catching Kady's eye over a forkful of his tofu salad. "I've been trying to tell people that for years," he said, emptying his second bottle of Smart Water.

Amelie giggled, feeling a little guilty as she did. "They're harmless, though," she protested. Amelie had had lunch with Billie, Talia, and Fortune again yesterday, and she'd had a blast, flipping through fashion magazines and letting the girls try out a braided updo from the Phillip Lim show on her red hair. Maybe they weren't officially her friends, but gossiping about them made her uneasy. Someday, when she went to BHH, they'd be more than just lunch buddies, and friendship meant not saying nasty things behind one another's backs.

Kady rolled her eyes. "I know. It's just so weird. They're not even really fighting over Grant. They're like the three lovesick Musketeers—all for one and one for all. Imagine asking them out. He'd have to buy three dinners, hold three doors, look deeply into six eyes. I don't even want to know what happens during a make-out session. I'm a woman of the world, but that's too worldly for even me."

Amelie noticed a blush creep up Jake's face and he instantly reached for his empty water bottle.

"Oh, I'm out of water," he said, shaking the bottle. "I'll go get another one."

"You can have some of my Diet Coke. I forgot I had one from craft services when I ordered," Amelie offered, pulling the fresh bottle from her tote bag.

Jake smiled politely. "I'm trying to stay away from soda. Grant says it makes you pasty," he explained. "I'll be right back."

Kady watched as Jake ambled to the cooler in the corner. She wrapped her red Free People cardigan tightly around her tiny frame and turned to Amelie conspiratorially. "I don't fully get Grant mania. What's the appeal? He's so broody, and way more full of himself than he lets on." Her gaze trailed over to the cashier, where Jake was paying. "Jake, on the other hand, is so cute and sweet. And hot. Where are *his* groupies?"

Amelie mulled this assessment with a swig of tea. Kady was right, of course. With his new leading-man status, Amelie expected Jake to be surrounded by eager females. But then again, Jake was no Hollywood himbo. "He's smart, so maybe they're intimidated," Amelie reasoned.

Kady flipped up her hood, so that just a fringe of her silky black hair wisped around her tiny doll face. "I'm going to tell you something, and you can't make that face where you look like you've digested a bad tuna roll." She paused, her sapphire eyes scanning Amelie's face. "I like Jake."

Oh, big news, Amelie thought with a touch of annoyance. Instead, she smiled and teasingly said, "Yeah, I know. You've been flirting with him since pretty much the first time you saw him."

Kady took a deep breath, rolling one of her croissant's oversize salt grains around on the placemat. "I know. But I think maybe I actually *really* like him."

Every muscle tensed beneath Amelie's breezy gown. She'd known Kady had a crush, but the thought of her and Jake actually in a relationship made her shiver like she was stranded atop a diamond run at Big Bear ski lodge. Kady was a force of nature or, well, of nightlife, and Jake was several ego trips short of ruling the club scene. The last thing she wanted was for Kady to change him into the kind of guy who talked about "the scene" all the time.

Instead, Amelie just said, "Jake? Is he really your type?"

Kady, who never got embarrassed—not even when she'd tripped over a camera wire and split her pants the other day—actually blushed. "I can't stop thinking about him. He's not a scraggly, unshaven hipster, true, but there's something. But I don't know if he likes me."

"You're asking me for advice on that?" Amelie laughed, breaking off a piece of her molten chocolate cookie. "I don't really have much luck in the guy department. I mean, he seems to be paying a lot of attention to you." *And ignoring me, even though I'm three chapters behind on geometry,* Amelie thought. She knew she should be more helpful. Kady *had* helped her be alone with Hunter that night at Area. She had no say about who Jake should date. He was just her tutor. And, okay, the guy who made her laugh even when she was feeling sorry for herself. But she didn't own him or anything.

Jake returned with his fresh Smart Water, plopping down in his seat. Kady had nudged her chair a little bit closer while he'd been gone. "When are we supposed to shoot this scene?" he asked, looking at Kady.

"We have time," she said, gazing at Jake like he was the only person in the room. "Have you ever tried one of these?" She waved her pretzel croissant under Jake's nose temptingly. Jake's eyes surveyed her pixie-like face. Amelie felt as invisible as Ryan Seacrest on the red carpet with Brangelina.

"Uh, I don't know if I should eat so much salt," Jake said, evidently taking all of Grant's food rules to heart. Amelie rolled her eyes. Grant's health obsessions were ridiculous, especially from a guy who hadn't set foot outdoors since he'd left the birth canal. "Maybe a little piece. It's kind of carby."

Kady tore a piece from the pastry and brought it to Jake's lips. Feeling like a ridiculously unnecessary chaperone, Amelie stared down at the open geometry textbook until her eyes blurred. Jake "mmm"-ed in delight. Amelie couldn't have felt more embarrassed than if he and Kady had been making out. Mercifully, her cell phone vibrated across the table, the number coming up restricted.

"Hello?" she said tentatively.

"Amelie? It's Hunter."

Amelie took a deep breath. Hunter sounded tinny

and far away. Still, it was unmistakably his toe-curling baritone coming through the receiver. She watched from the corner of her eye as Kady fed Jake another bite of pretzel. *You have Hunter on the phone. Pay attention!* She focused on making her voice sound less irritated.

"Hi, Hunter," she said. Kady and Jake looked up at his name. Jake's face flickered with something, maybe worry that Hunter would swoop in and take his part. Or maybe it was just surprise that Amelie was there and had a life of her own. *Good,* she thought. She had concerns beyond *Class Angel* and tutoring, too.

"Can you . . . meet me for coffee? The 101 Coffee Shop? I just . . . I need to talk."

"Meet you now?" Amelie's eyes blurred, but she saw Kady give an enthusiastic nod. Whether she was enthused for Amelie's romantic prospects or her own was unclear. *Let Kady have the tutor,* Amelie thought. *Hunter Sparks* was calling her. It was what she'd been waiting for.

The 101 Coffee Shop teemed with teenage hipsters in skinny jeans, beat-up Vans, and ironic tees. Right now, they were all staring at Amelie, who stuck out like something larger and more glittery than a sore thumb in her sugary white dress. Her new white metallic Chloé bag seemed to scream, *I cost more than a used Hyundai!* under the low lights. A girl with rumpled black hair wore an American Apparel tee screen-printed with Amelie as Fairy Princess, Miley Cyrus as Hannah Montana, and Demi Lovato, all standing beneath the words *Girl Power?* She whispered something to her guy friends, and the table laughed caustically.

The 101 looked like a family room from the 1970s, and it was poorly lit. A long cordovan banquette ran along one wall that was a mosaic of flat brown, white, and beige rocks. Along the other wall were booths in the same brown hue, each table beneath a dangling spherical light fixture. Amelie finally spotted Hunter, sitting alone at the booth farthest from the door. He gave her a little wave.

She slid into the booth, feeling his eyes on her. Even sitting down, Hunter's five feet eleven inches of gorgeous was apparent. He leaned forward, his chiseled jaw resting atop one of his muscular forearms.

"Hey, Amelie," he said, reaching over to touch her arm. "I'm glad you could make it. I ordered us both cappuccinos, hope that's okay."

Amelie nodded. "Yeah, that's fine," she said, pleased that he'd ordered for her. It meant he'd been thinking about her before she arrived. Hunter stared forlornly at his reflection in the stainless-steel napkin dispenser. Amelie wondered if they were on a date. If so, why was Hunter acting like it was the end of the world?

"Is everything okay?" she asked gently. Maybe he'd been regretting that they hadn't seen each other since the night of Lewis Buford's party. Or maybe he felt shy about what he'd said that night, when he'd admitted he couldn't resist her.

Hunter heaved a sigh. "No," he said, glancing up with a polite nod as the waitress set down a cappuccino in front of each of them. "I've never been fired before, Amelie."

Oh. So he wasn't thinking about them; he was still caught up in getting the boot from *Class Angel.* "I don't think I'd call it fired, Hunter," she said, giving him her best soothing smile. She wished she knew whether to listen wholeheartedly or try to flirt him out of his doldrums. "I don't think you were bad. I think producers just get ideas in their heads sometimes and think they need to change things." It was true. Sometimes studios made last-minute changes just to exert their power. But after watching the dailies, Amelie knew that Hunter really *had* been phoning it in. She didn't have the heart to tell him, though.

Hunter smiled weakly. "That's what I'd been thinking. They just changed it for no reason," he said, brushing an invisible piece of lint from his cashmere V-neck. "It's like they fixed something that wasn't even broken."

Amelie paused, not knowing what to say. Hunter was handsome and already a star, but the reality was, Jake was *better*. Like Tommy Archer, Jake was a guy who didn't know how great he was. With Jake at its core, the whole movie now had true sweetness and that *je ne sais quoi* teen angst factor. She had a feeling that Jake was just being Jake, not Mr. Superstar Method actor. But even if the producers had just gotten lucky, Jake had given *Class Angel* the true authenticity they'd been hoping for.

"I wouldn't worry about it, Hunter," Amelie said, thrown by how grown-up she sounded. "I mean, you've got a lot coming up, right?" Just last week, Hunter had landed a part as Iron Man's illegitimate son in the next installment of the franchise. And she'd just read about his casting in an indie role as a gas station clerk being stalked by a famous actress. She'd practically been ready to stalk him at the time. But now . . . things felt different.

"Yeah, I guess," he said, dolefully catching the eye of a trio of Hollywood High School girls who were staring at him. "But I feel like I don't know what I'm doing. Is the new guy a lot better than me? Jacob What's-His-Name?"

Amelie stirred her coffee surreptitiously. She was somewhat relieved that Hunter hadn't connected the name with Jake. They had met, after all, at Lewis's party—when Amelie had let Hunter believe that it was Jake who'd left her brokenhearted.

"He's . . . got a different style than you," she said carefully. "He's new at this. It's kind of hard to compare." Of course, it was easy to compare them. She'd been doing it from the moment she'd sat down, mentally tallying the pros and cons of Hunter and Jake as Tommy Archer.

"But different, good? What's his method? Is he a real high school jock? How often does he work out?"

Amelie glanced at the time on her Sidekick, a bit put off. Was Hunter always this insecure? Had he always fished for compliments this way? "I don't know, Hunter," she said. "Jake's just a regular guy." She shrugged, maybe a little impatiently, half wanting to shake Hunter and ask, *You dragged me out here for* this? Where was the confident, semi-cocky object of her lust? The guy who could make her heart thump like parade music just by saying her name?

"Oh," Hunter said, perking up a bit at the words *regular guy*. He flashed his megawatt grin, his coffee-colored eyes finally meeting Amelie's full-on. "That's kind of gimmicky. I was kinda glad not to have to shoot at BHH. It's hard enough just going out at night without being recognized. I bet it's a nightmare."

"It's not that bad, actually," she said, her mind cutting away to a vision of herself toting books down the hallway with her group of girlfriends. "It's nice to be around normal people. And most people there have parents or family in the business, so they're used to being around filming."

Hunter shook his head affectionately. "You're too nice," he said, cocking his head as his gaze scrolled over her face and her bare shoulder. "Come on, you can tell me. It sucks, doesn't it?" he asked, reaching across the table to fold her hand beneath his.

Hunter's hand was warm and dry, and hers was cold, as always. But when he touched her, she felt oddly detached. Maybe being away from him for a while had given her calm. Or maybe it was that since she'd started dreaming of going to high school, she'd sort of put her Hunter fantasies on the back burner. Whatever it was, it felt both satisfying and a little disappointing to not feel her heart flip at Hunter's touch.

"I'm serious," she said insistently. "At first I was nervous. But I've been thinking about trying to enroll."

Hunter squinted at her across the table before breaking into a wide smile. He laughed, letting go of her hand and running his fingers through his dark, shiny hair. "You're good. I forgot how funny you are, Amelie," he said. "We should hang out more often."

Amelie bit the inside of her lip, clenching her fist around the white satin bow draped at her waist. Hunter didn't get it. Or, he didn't get *her*. A piece of her heart, the spot she'd reserved for him for years, cracked at the realization that her crush was based on nothing but a fantasy. All this time, she'd thought that if she could just have Hunter to herself for a while, instead of sharing him with costars and directors, they'd really understand each other. She'd built him up so much that she'd imagined him being like her, a guy with an extraordinary life who just wanted a taste of the ordinary. "Yeah, we should," Amelie said dismissively, wishing he'd leave so she could stew in the anger of years of disillusionment.

Hunter swigged the last sip from his coffee cup. "I'm so glad you met up with me. I feel a hundred times better," he said, his eyes lingering on her exposed shoulder. "I'm about to hit a pre-party at Social, some *Us Weekly*/ Ray-Ban thing. Want to come?"

Amelie shook her head politely. "I have to get back to the set," she lied, without an iota of regret. "But thanks."

"Okay, maybe next time," Hunter said, standing up and leaning over to kiss her on the cheek. He threw down some money for the check and was off.

Amelie brushed the side of her face with her fingertips, realizing that the last time Hunter had kissed her cheek like that, she'd nearly fainted with joy. Last time, too, he'd invited her to meet him at Lewis Buford's party, and she'd felt like a rocket-guided missile, determined to get to the event no matter the consequences. This time, she didn't yearn to go with Hunter.

Amelie felt all her nerves come to life as her mind drew the face of the guy she wanted.

Jake?

THE BIG PAYBACK

U*nreal. Fictional. Fake. Phony. Make-believe. Imag-ined. Pretend.*

Unreal.

Jake cycled through every synonym he knew for *this can't be happening* and kept landing on *unreal*.

Because that was what this was. Kady Parker, she of the glossy black hair, pixielike face, and mesmerizing blue eyes, was sitting so close to him, he could smell the delicate top notes of her raspberry-scented perfume.

Kady bit lightly on the tip of her finger, the crumbs of their shared pretzel croissant dusted across the place mat between them. The bakery's crowd was changing. Instead of bored Hollywood wives picking at their salads, the place had filled with businessmen on late lunches. Some of them made no effort to hide the fact that they were checking Kady out. Jake himself felt pervy; he couldn't tear his gaze away from her lips. But it was almost like she was pointing at them.

"So, um, what should we do while we wait?" Jake said, extracting his script from his new Kenneth Cole messenger bag. "Should we go over our scene?"

"I wouldn't mind another croissant," Kady said, her voice a breathless whisper. She reached out a hand and pulled him up from his seat. The momentum of the movement forced their bodies to knock together, and Jake felt every one of his muscles clench as Kady's body collided with his. She stepped back, but only by an inch, and giggled. "We can share. Outside."

Jake didn't need anyone to tell him Kady was beautiful. But he couldn't help but puff his chest, imagining BHH guys like Rod and Lewis Buford if they could see him with Kady right now. Her eyes twinkled up at him as they waited in front of the glass bakery case. She paid for her order, clasped Jake's hand, and dragged him out of the restaurant.

They were sitting at a table at the center of the Brentwood Country Mart's courtyard, just outside the City Bakery. The crew was positioning mics for their outdoor shot as customers filed around them, used to seeing movie shoots as part of their daily routine. A group of cute UCLA girls in workout gear filed past, swinging bags from the Mart's James Perse store, gossiping. Their chatter trailed off as they saw Kady Parker sitting with Jake. They paused, their eyes flickering over him as if he'd become more interesting with Kady's seal of approval.

"Have another bite," Kady said, offering up yet another piece of pastry. Jake really couldn't eat any more, but it was impossible to refuse Kady's pleading, fluttering eyelashes. Or that fact that she was feeding him, letting her fingers linger a little longer by his lips each time she did so.

It was starting to sink in. Kady liked him. Not just

liked him, but *liked him* liked him. The notion felt foreign to his body. He was used to unrequited crushes. Just an hour ago, when Amelie had departed to meet Hunter, he'd even felt the twinge of a reopened wound. He'd been successfully putting her out of his head for the whole shoot, even if it meant ignoring her a little. But her mentioning Hunter had brought Jake back to the humiliation of Lewis Buford's party. Amelie was more sweet and innocent than some of her Hollywood peers, and yet he'd still been taken advantage of. Right now, though, Kady was coming on to him. And Jake couldn't come up with a reason for her to play him. She was beautiful, cool, and in demand. And she certainly didn't need him to add excitement to her life.

Kady sipped her Pellegrino with a straw, a smirk turning up the corners of her lips. "Look over there," she said, faintly gesturing with her chin. Jake turned.

"Don't look right at them," she said. "Stay casual. . . ."

Jake pretended to be stretching and craned his neck back. Several guys with cameras were attempting to hide behind the neatly shorn hedges that ran along the courtyard's edge. Paparazzi? Whoa. He thanked whatever deity had made this possible. He was about to have his first run-in with the paparazzi as he flirted with a gorgeous girl. Justin Klatch would be proud.

"Let's give them a proper photo op," Kady said, pushing the croissant aside as she leaned forward. Her eyes looked a darker shade of blue in the sun. Then she closed them, and the cherry lips that he'd been staring at for what felt like centuries were on his.

He kissed her back, twirling a strand of her dark hair

in what he hoped was a Justin Klatch–sanctioned way. Her lips were cool from the frosty water, but her breath was warm. He was kissing a girl who made movies. Kissing a girl who had no fewer than six hundred thousand hits on Google. Kissing a girl who hadn't been dared, and who wasn't one of his mom's friends' daughters willing to kiss anyone at her bat mitzvah just to get it out of the way.

His eyes closed as he added a little extra pressure to the kiss. At the height of Jake's Amelie obsession, Miles had torn a tip from *Details* about the proper amount of kissing force: *You should always give her a fraction more pressure than she's giving you.* Thankfully, Jake was good at fractions. And he seemed to be doing something right, as Kady's fingers languidly feathered against the back of his neck. Jake could hear cameras whirring, and sense eyes on him as a hushed collective whisper flitted around the courtyard.

Yeah, world, you're looking at Jake Porter-Goldsmith kissing Kady Parker, he thought to himself.

Talk about getting the star treatment.

WAX ON, WAX OFF

"This looks like crap on me," Myla said. "I don't know if I should wear orange. Ever. I think it would work on you, though." She tossed a Tang-colored Alexander Wang tank dress over the dressing room wall as though it was nothing more than toilet paper she was handing Jojo in a public bathroom.

They were at Barneys New York on Wilshire, and Jojo had amassed a pile of things to buy, all of them Myla-approved. Shopping with her sister was even better than shopping with her mom, or with Willa. Myla made funny comments about the other shoppers, like Willa did, but her taste was impeccable, so it was like being with a friend and an authority figure all in one. Jojo pulled the orange tank dress over her head. Flowy and looking like tropical fruit, it seemed like something Tucker would like, Jojo realized. Ever since Ash had suggested Tucker for her, Jojo had made a point to notice him at school. With his surfer tan, and a lean Michael Phelps–ish body visible through his tight T-shirts, there was nothing to complain about. He had a good laugh, too, one that gave her a little tingle.

A sense of humor was important to her in a potential boyfriend.

"I'm going to go pay," Myla said, her voice wafting over the wall. "Meet you out there."

"Okay," Jojo chirped happily. Being tormented for her BarfBarf incident was the best thing that had ever happened to her, because it had prompted Myla to spend time with her. Even if her stepsister did seem a little harsh at times, Jojo felt closer than she'd thought possible to Myla.

Her phone trilled out the Ting Tings song from last week's *Gossip Girl*, and she dug beneath her to-buy pile to find it. Willa's sassy tongue-out face popped up on the screen. "Hey," Jojo answered. "What's up?" Willa was her best friend from Sacramento, and Jojo had more than ten years of homemade friendship bracelets, photographs, and passed notes to prove it.

"Hey, Miss Thang," Willa said, speaking loudly enough to be heard over the high-pitched voices on her little brother Damian's cartoon. Willa was the de facto babysitter for him any time her mom had to work late. "You didn't answer my e-mail about the invitational."

Jojo had totally forgotten that Willa had e-mailed her about JFK's annual soccer invitational. "Oh God! I'm so sorry, it's been crazy around here." Though she'd spent her first few weeks in L.A. frequently trading IMs and texts with Willa, all Jojo's time with Myla had put her way behind on her correspondence. She flopped down on the changing bench.

"But you're coming, right?" Willa sounded hopeful, like she half-expected Jojo to say no. "Justin even asked about you."

Jojo was surprised—not so much that Justin had mentioned her, but that his name caused no tickle to run through her body. Instead, she thought, *What Would Justin Klatch Do?* and a vision of Jake's smiling face popped into her head.

"Well, who cares about him?" Jojo said, realizing that she meant it, even if it was flattering that her new, tabloid-worthy adoption story had gotten her former dream guy's attention. Maybe absence did make the heart grow fonder after all. "I'd be coming to see you."

Willa chuckled. "Yeah, right, like you won't be salivating when he takes his shirt off after the game." *Maybe he'll be salivating when he sees me in this dress,* Jojo thought, twirling one of the narrow straps around her index finger.

"Maybe a little." Jojo wondered if her crush on Justin would return as soon as she saw him again. Even Myla would probably be impressed by Justin's toned physique. Jake's body was equally sculpted, though, and he was an NFW boy, so maybe not.

"So you're coming?"

"Yeah, definitely. It feels like so long since I've been there. Like Sacramento will be future Sacramento, all silvery with flying cars when I get there," Jojo said, not really meaning it. Beverly Hills was a shiny, glittery wonderland compared to her old hometown, and she knew that Sacramento would probably seem duller than ever now that she'd had a taste of the good life.

"Nah, still the same old dump," Willa said cheerfully. "But it'll be so much fun. Coach said you can sit on the bench by the team, which is perfect, 'cause we are so dumping the water cooler on his head when we win. And if you come down early, we'll teach you the dance we made up for the boys' game. We're using that song you picked, 'Kick It' by Peaches. You'll have to slap my ass, though."

Jojo wrinkled her nose involuntarily. A few months ago, Jojo had been the ringleader, planning all the goofy stuff they'd do during the invitational. She'd even run a fake summit about it at Sadie's Pizza. Now she was almost nostalgic, thinking about how simple her life had been. But as she held a sexy Robert Cavalli chiffon halter dress up to her creamy shoulders, she was also grateful for the new, more complicated version.

"Of course I want to slap your ass. Who could resist it in those shorty soccer shorts?"

Willa laughed, sounding relieved. "You better watch it, or I'll be dumping water over your head, not Coach's. Bet Justin will like it," she singsonged temptingly.

Jojo heard the distinctive cadence of Myla's walk. She promised to e-mail Willa and hung up, just as Myla's brand-new Louboutin platform pumps became visible under the dressing room door.

"Stop lollygagging," Myla said. "Oh my God, lolly-gag, how grandma of me. But really, stop. We have waxing appointments at BeeHive."

She opened the door to her dressing room. "Waxing? Why?"

Myla rolled her eyes. "I told you earlier, beach party this Saturday. You can't go looking like Sasquatch."

Jojo winced, not just at the idea of having her hairs yanked out. "But I'm supposed to go to Sacramento this weekend. There's a soccer invitational."

Myla shook her head. "Sacramento will—sadly—still

be there next weekend. Tucker is throwing the party. It's not up for discussion."

Jojo saw her waxen face in the mirror beyond Myla's shoulder. Her sister could be a little like a drill sergeant sometimes. Not to mention snobby. Sacramento wasn't *that* bad. But Jojo reminded herself that Myla was just on edge about the whole Ash thing. After he'd left the other night, Myla had told her everything, about the kiss and how Ash had practically run off. She'd tried to sound breezy, saying Ash was being stupid, and that he'd come around. But Jojo could tell that Myla had been crying.

"But can't Tucker wait?" Jojo protested. "I promised I'd be there. Shouldn't I go to show them how freshly fabulous I am?"

Myla folded her arms. "You'll be even more fabulous if you don't go and they all wonder about you. I won't take no for an answer." Myla's voice was firm but playful, and Jojo felt a little flattered that her sister wanted her to come so badly.

"Besides, I need you there," Myla cajoled. It was true: Talia, Billie, and Fortune were currently on her shit list. Without Jojo, she'd be going to the party totally alone. Right now, Jojo was her de facto right-hand man. Make that right-hand, newly fabulous Myla-in-training. And if that made her other friends jealous, well, *sweet*.

It was the final push Jojo needed to make a decision. Between Ash and her inattentive girlfriends, Myla actually needed Jojo for a change. What kind of sister would she be to ditch her in her time of need? "Okay, gimme a sec to call and cancel. I'll meet you in shoes."

Jojo dialed Willa's number. She knew her friend would be disappointed, but hopefully she'd understand.

Willa answered on the first ring. "Nice of you to hang up on me," she said, more teasing than angry.

Jojo sighed. "I just remembered something about this weekend. I have to go with my parents and my family to a fund-raiser. I can't come to Sacramento," she said, her stomach bubbling with the lie. She could have told Willa the truth, about Myla having boyfriend and friend problems, but after bitching to Willa about Myla for her first week here, she knew Willa didn't have the highest opinion of her stepsister. Besides, saying she needed to support Myla at a big BHH beach party didn't sound like such a dire situation.

"Oh no! You can't get out of it?" Willa asked, sounding downcast.

"I really can't, Will," Jojo replied, wishing Willa didn't have to make her feel guilty about it. "Don't worry, there'll be other invitationals." As she said it, Jojo realized that Sacramento *could* wait for her. But a party in Malibu, that Myla actually *wanted* her to attend? That wouldn't happen every day. Who knew—next week, she could be back on the shit list with the rest of Myla's clique.

"Yeah, next year," Willa mumbled. Jojo bristled with irritation. She'd been away from Sacramento for less than a month. Were they really that desperate without her?

"Look, I have to go," Jojo said, not wanting to keep Myla waiting. "We'll make plans for some other time."

Jojo hung up as Willa mumbled her passive-aggressive agreement. She had a wax appointment to get to, and she knew that after that, Willa's needy guilt-tripping would no longer be the most painful part of her day.

ICING ON THE KAKE

Amelie sat outside BHH, on a bench near the front doors, waiting for her mom to pick her up after a long day of shooting. It was almost ten o'clock, and the grounds were dark and silent. A cool October wind blew beneath Amelie's hair, the crisp air sending a shiver down her spine. A lone light shone down overhead, casting a soft glow on the pavement.

Amelie was tired. Shooting had been long, and mostly painful. They were well into their second week of filming. The end of it, really. It was Thursday, and things were getting hurried so they could wrap next Friday. But that wasn't causing the strain. Amelie had dealt with tight shoots, and the rippling tension that came with them, many times before. *Fairy Princess* was always hectic, whether they were waiting on product-placement notes from a last-minute sponsor or altering one of the unicorn's horns because standards and practices deemed the first one "too phallic." But on *Fairy Princess*, she never had to watch two of her costars sneak kisses between takes.

Almost overnight, Jake and Kady had gone from flirty

costars to "Kake," a tabloid-sanctioned new Hollywood couple. Their on-set PDA would have been annoying for any costar. But since her crush on Jake had dawned on Amelie as if the sun itself had smacked her across the face, every smile he shot in Kady's direction was agony.

"Hey, Amelie." Jake's voice shook Amelie out of her daze, and she turned to see him approaching. He was alone, thankfully.

"Hi, Jake." She smiled at Jake's now-familiar face. How had she not noticed how cute he was before, back when he was just her tutor? The green flecks in his hazel eyes were apparent even in the low light, and his smile moved easily over his face. Several errant curls poked cutely out from under his *Class Angel* baseball cap. "I thought you'd have left by now."

Jake shrugged, sitting down next to her. "Waiting on Kady," he said, like they'd been going out forever.

"Oh, that's nice," Amelie lied. "Are you giving her a ride home?" She remembered riding in Jake's Corolla on the way to Lewis's party. If only she hadn't been so obsessed with Hunter at the time, maybe *she* would be the one heading home with Jake tonight. Not that she'd have kept him waiting, like some chauffeur.

"I think she called us a car," Jake said, smirking as if he couldn't believe his luck. He peered down at his cell phone, clutched in his hand. "But my assistant, I mean friend, Miles, is supposed to be tracking down an Escalade for me. I can't wait."

"That's cool," Amelie said, even though she found it impossible to picture Jake plowing down the freeway in one of those obnoxious trucks. His Corolla wasn't exactly cool, but there had to be a car more suited to Jake. Something attractive but unassuming. Like him.

"We're going to some place called the Kress. Have you ever been?" Jake asked earnestly. He was probably the only person on earth who hadn't seen her first and only nightclub experience detailed on TMZ.

Amelie shook her head. "No. That's a club, right?" She felt like the kid still stuck on a tricycle as her friends zipped away on two-wheelers.

Jake chuckled nervously, zipping his hoodie against the quickening wind. "You'd know better than me," he said. "Up till now, the coolest place I've been is the masquerade at Comic Con. But don't tell Kady that."

Amelie nodded, liking knowing something Kady didn't. Then again, maybe she shouldn't be happy he was telling her secrets he thought were too dorky to share with his girlfriend. *He doesn't care about impressing me,* Amelie thought sadly.

Jake blushed. "I can't believe I just told you that," he said, shaking his head. "This is almost as bad as when you thought I was stalking you." The color in his face grew deeper as he recollected the tutoring session where he'd blurted out all of Amelie's favorite things.

"I won't tell," she said, giving Jake the best smile she could manage.

Jake studied her for a second, his hazel eyes locking on her aquamarine ones. "Is everything okay?" He patted her arm a little awkwardly. The gesture sent her heart springing from her chest, and she fought the urge to nestle her head on Jake's shoulder.

If she'd been some other version of herself, she might

tell him the truth: That she hated that he'd hooked up with Kady. That she thought Kady was all wrong for him, and that *she* was all right. That she regretted not seeing him, from the start, for who he really was—the funny, smart, kind guy she never knew she needed—because she was so caught up in her childlike Hunter fantasies.

She knew she'd never say those things, though. Because she never told anyone what she was really feeling. With Jake, though, she felt comfortable enough to reveal the other thing that was on her mind.

"It's all this," she said, spreading her arms wide as if she could hold up BHH. "Shooting here has shown me . . . I don't know. What I'm missing out on, I guess." During what was supposed to have been her lunch break today, Talia, Billie, and Fortune had invited her to go off-campus for mani-pedis. It had been an especially tempting offer, since she'd wanted to get away from Kake all day, and, purse on shoulder, she'd been ready to go. But then Gary had needed another take of the scene where Class Angel sat in on a high school English class, just to see how real people lived. Yet another terrible example of art imitating life.

Jake pulled off his baseball cap, massaging his flattened curls back into place. He looked across the lawn, watching headlights dance over the shadows as cars passed on Moreno.

"You think I'm crazy, don't you?" she said, embarrassed.

Turning to look at her, his eyes dark serious, Jake shook his head. "No, I get it," he said. A smile crossed his face. "I guess I've spent so much time dreaming of the day I'll get out of this place that I never thought about what I'd do if I *didn't* have it. Don't get me wrong, being in the movie has been fun and all, but I don't think I'd want to look back and not have had the experience of going to high school. It's one of those things you need, but for reasons beyond what they tell you in the brochure."

"Do you really mean that?" Amelie asked. Hunter had literally laughed at her when she'd said she wanted to go to a real school. And here Jake was, reading her mind.

Jake nodded. "Yeah," he said, sounding like he'd surprised even himself with his answer. "Really. As much as BHH has beaten me up over the years, and I mean beaten up literally . . ." He laughed, the sound emanating from deep inside him. As it filled the air between them, Amelie found herself laughing too, her eyes closed and her body soaking up the warm feeling of being really, truly understood.

"Hey, guys. I hope you weren't talking about me." Kady threw herself down on the bench, halfway on Jake's lap. She grinned hello at Amelie, then leaned back into Jake and cooed, "Sorry I kept you waiting." She planted a huge kiss on his mouth. Amelie's heart dove, lodging itself firmly in the pit of her stomach.

Just as Kady ran her Russian Navy nails through Jake's curls, Amelie saw her mom's Jaguar pull up in front of the school.

Amelie jumped from the bench. "Have fun tonight, guys," she said, speed-walking down the main path to her mom's idling car before Kake even had the chance to say goodbye.

As they started to drive, Amelie could see that her mom was tired. Helen's short, always-perfect red bob was mussed in some places, flyaway hairs gleaming every time they passed beneath one of the light posts lining the 405 freeway. With every lane change, she sipped from her venti espresso. The fact she was having caffeine after 4 p.m. was a dead giveaway.

"Did you have a good day, Am?" she asked, touching beneath her eyes, as if the dark circles might sprout into something grotesque.

Amelie nodded, looking out the window at cars whizzing by. For a week now, she'd been itching to hear what her mom would think of sending her to BHH. She hadn't had an opening, though. Some nights, it was hard to get Helen to go from momager to just Mom.

"I have to say, I'm having the worst time getting the Kidz Network people to schedule your Christmas special so you can still do the voice-over for that Pixar short. It's like they're jealous of you working with other companies."

Amelie leaned back in her leather seat, watching as the Getty Center came up ahead of them. She realized there would never be a perfect moment for her to say, "Hey, Mom, I want to go to high school." But after her conversation with Jake, she felt invigorated. She had to just do it.

"Maybe I don't have to do both," Amelie offered, testing the water. "I mean, Pixar is due for a bomb. And maybe there's something else I could be doing."

Helen's eyes flicked sideways, one perfectly arched eyebrow raised with interest. "Did you hear about something on set today? Are they still talking about a sequel? Because I don't know if you should do another teen movie right away."

"Not exactly," she said, a little hurt that her mom's mind always jumped to business. "Shooting at BHH made me realize something."

"Oh, really? And what's that?" Helen caught Amelie's eye in the rearview mirror.

"That I think that I should go to high school. To BHH."

Helen was silent for a moment, her eyes focused on the road. Her face was unreadable as she said, "And why do you want to go to high school?"

Because I could have friends, and live a normal life. And maybe even have a boyfriend, if Jake and Kady ever break up, Amelie thought. "I just think it's important," she answered, trying to paraphrase Jake's words. "I don't want to look back one day and not have had that experience."

Helen shook her head, her fingers kneading the skin beneath her eye. "So what you're telling me is that, all over the world, other girls want to be like you, but you want to be like *them*?"

Amelie knew the question was rhetorical, and there was no point in answering, but she nodded anyway. "Yeah," she said, a note of pleading in her voice. "Even for a little while, just to see how it goes."

Helen reached for her coffee and gulped down a long sip, as if the cup contained a rebellious-daughter elixir. "Honey, I wish it was so simple," she said, patting Amelie's knee. "But you live in a different world, and you're doing great in that world. You should be proud of what you have. Do you understand?"

Amelie felt so crestfallen that she was almost drinking her tears as she held them back. She rolled down her window. The air, now turned cold, coursed over her face in angry waves, like the whole world had officially turned against her.

Ahead of them, a driver flicked the still-orange tip of a cigarette out his window. As the butt hit the asphalt, hundreds of glowing embers exploded against the black and then died out.

To Amelie, it looked like the detritus of her now-extinguished hope.

WHY DON'T YOU WINE ABOUT IT?

"I'm here to pick up Daisy Morton," Ash said to the bored-looking receptionist at the front desk of the Beverly Hills Police Department. With its white pillars, columns, and floors so shiny your shoes squeaked, it looked like the White House's West Coast cousin.

Gordon had called in the middle of Ash and Tucker's band practice—really an excuse to eat and talk about girls—and told him he needed him, Daisy had been arrested and to pick her up at the BHPD. Ash thought jail was the perfect place for his charge, but said nothing to Gordon, who was already mad that Daisy had used her phone call on him, knowing Ash wouldn't answer.

The woman pressed a button and directed Ash inside. In a small, glass-windowed room Daisy was pacing back and forth like a caged beast, soaked head to toe in something red. Holy shit—was that dried blood? Had she finally snapped and killed someone?

A grim-faced officer with a head too long for his squat body stepped into the corridor. "You responsible for this one?" He gestured to Daisy, who was giving him the finger though the glass.

"I guess," Ash said.

"Bail's been posted already, by Gordon Gilmour." The officer held out a clipboard. "Sign here and here, and I'll let you take her home."

"What did she do?" Ash asked, afraid to hear the answer. "Is that . . . blood?"

"Charles Shaw, from Trader Joe's," the cop said, suppressing a laugh. Seeing Ash's puzzled face, he clarified. "It's two-dollar wine, son. People call it Two-Buck Chuck. She was in line, had no ID, and when they wouldn't let her buy it without proof of age, she started smashing bottles into a case of frozen shrimp. No injuries, fortunately, but the store is pressing charges."

Ash sighed, glad her crime wasn't serious but still dreading alone time with Crazy Daisy. The cop nodded, saying, "I'm gonna get a few more guys. I'm not going in there alone."

Great, Ash thought, watching as Daisy pressed her face against the glass like a blowfish.

Four cops emerged from a back room and somberly entered the holding cell.

"Well, if it isn't the fuckety fucks of Fuckville," Daisy screeched. "You need four of you big, strapping babies for little ol' me? You touch me in one wrong place, and I'll go all Catholic Church sex scandal on your out-of-shape asses."

Ash couldn't help chuckling at the horrified faces of four of Beverly Hills' finest. They gingerly took each of Daisy's arms, two to a side, and she dragged her feet along the tile floor, the cops practically lifting her off the ground.

Seeing Ash, she sprang back onto her feet, shook off the cops, and bounced over to him, like a girl chasing a butterfly. Her rainbow tutu fluttered with each skipping step. "Hi, you," she said, planting a wet kiss on his cheek. "Let's get the fuck out of this shithole. Toodles, wussyboys!"

They left the police station behind them, and Ash drove. But Daisy refused to get out of the car when he pulled up to the W. "No, the photogs know I'm staying here and they got enough for one night. See? I'm on TMZ already."

She reached over, taking Ash's iPhone from his pocket and pulling up the site. *Crazy Daisy Two-Buck Chucked*, read the headline. Accompanying it was camera phone video of her wailing like a banshee as she smashed individual bottles into a freezer drawer.

Ash glanced sideways at his passenger. She looked as bad as ever. Mascara dripped down from her eyes in points, her hair a multicolored snarl, like something two Muppets would leave behind after a battle to the death. Her T-shirt—which featured a gnome in the grass and read *Sod Off!*—was so wine-soaked he could feel the fumes making their way up his nostrils. Where could he take her? He didn't want to go back to Tucker's— Tucker's dad, the famous singer Dell Pearl, had outfitted the garage so it was *too* professional, with its state-of-the-art recording equipment and pristine lounge area. It was kind of embarrassing, actually, and for some reason he couldn't tolerate the idea of Daisy seeing how sleek, how *not* rock 'n' roll their practice space was. Besides, he wasn't confident she wouldn't destroy anything there.

Unfortunately, he also couldn't imagine another hotel letting Daisy check in. "Fine, we'll go to my house." He resignedly pulled a U-turn and headed toward his neighborhood.

Daisy closed her eyes, leaning deeply into the bucket seat. "Sounds perfect."

Looking at her almost peaceful face, Ash wondered if he was like the lead in a horror movie—just naive enough to invite the killer inside.

Daisy was . . . cooperating. So far, she'd agreed to take a shower and change into some of Tessa's old clothing. She'd even unhooked a menu for a new deli from the front door and deposited it neatly on the kitchen counter. She was upstairs showering now, as Ash waited fearfully downstairs. Would Daisy come out high and in full psycho mode again? He debated checking on her, but decided the longer she stayed in Tessa's room, the better. While he waited he called the new deli and ordered several sandwiches and mac and cheese.

Ash sank into one of the burgundy chaise lounges in the front room. He hadn't even walked into the room— dubbed "Fancy Land" by him and Tessa when they were kids—in months. As he glanced at the row of their class photos on the mantel of the double-size gas fireplace, he missed his sister. He reclined on the chaise, his eyes running over the keys of the baby grand piano where he used to take lessons. He'd never been that great at keyed instruments, and his dad had let him drop piano and double up on guitar when he was ten. He heard soft footfalls upstairs, and then a padding of feet down the steps.

Daisy softly entered with a barely audible "Hi." But she wasn't Daisy anymore. Or at least not Crazy Daisy. Her hair, still slightly wet, curled at her neck, but all the red and purple streaks were gone, leaving shiny walnut-colored locks behind. Her face was free of makeup, and her skin was like porcelain, a healthy glow visible now that she wasn't wearing caked-on powder. She was still thin, but wrapped in one of Tessa's old cream cardigans, she just looked petite, not painfully malnourished. Her light gray eyes caught the light, dancing happily over the piano.

Ash couldn't stop staring, unsure what to say. She didn't just look normal. She looked . . . beautiful.

The doorbell rang, startling Ash almost as much as Daisy's complete 180. "I ordered food," he said almost to himself.

"I can get it," Daisy offered.

"No," Ash said, leaping up and crossing in front of her. "I have to sign." The delivery guy, a pudgy kid in a torn UCLA sweatshirt, handed over several bags, and accepted Ash's signature and tip with an appreciative grunt, his eyes never leaving Daisy.

Ash brought the bags to the kitchen, splitting the sandwiches onto two plates. He put them down on the kitchen table. The first occasion he'd had in months to use more than one table setting, and it involved Daisy Morton? That would go first on the list of things he'd never thought could happen but had.

He gestured for Daisy to sit and she thanked him, sitting down. Ash tentatively bit into a roast beef sandwich, trying not to stare. But he couldn't help it. Fortunately, she broke the silence first.

"So, thanks for coming to get me, and for, you know, everything." She gestured to the food and then to herself, as if Ash was responsible for her makeover.

Ash smirked. "Well, I'm not going to leave a girl at the Beverly Hills jail," he said, finding himself unable to look away from her. "Even if it is fancier than the W."

Daisy cocked her head to one side, her shiny hair tumbling in front of her silvery eyes. "Just admit it, Ash Gilmour. You're a nice guy."

Ash took a bite of his sandwich and chewed, sort of teasing her as he mulled it over. "Not to everyone, I'm not," he finally said. It was true. He'd had no intention of being nice to Daisy until that night at the Powerhouse. Watching all those guys act like they had the right to ogle her had really upset him.

"Well, since you've been so nice to me, don't you think you deserve to know why I look so different?" Daisy took a healthy gulp of milk, eyeing him over the glass.

"A little, yeah," Ash said, scanning her silky hair. "Where are the red and purple streaks?"

"My mum would kill me if I dyed my hair with permanent stuff," she said. "I either use the wash-out stuff for all-over color or pin in dyed extensions."

"Okay . . ." Ash said slowly. "But, why do you care what your mom thinks? I mean, would you be going around destroying cheap wine bottles if you were her little angel?"

Daisy laughed. "I really thought you could see right through me. Guess I'm better than I thought. You can't say anything, not even to your dad. . . ."

"Not much chance of him listening to me, so don't worry."

"It's an act," she continued, watching as the knowledge spread over Ash's face. "I'm not crazy. Okay, no more crazy than any other girl."

Ash spun a piece of macaroni around on his plate. Could it really be *possible*? Did Daisy have a split personality or something? Her crazy side had seemed so *real*. "But why?"

"It's a long story, and of course it involves a boy," she said.

"Really?" Ash had heard she'd met her boyfriend through a prison pen-pal program. "That guy in jail?"

Daisy shook her head. "No, that's another stunt. This guy, you've probably heard of him, Robbie Tartan, he's a rock star in London."

Ash nodded. Robbie Tartan and the Screeches were a punk band with a few okay songs, but they'd never made it stateside.

Daisy shrugged. "We used to date, when I was sixteen. But I wasn't a pop star then. I did mostly singer-songwriter stuff, on the piano. I had classical training as a kid, so my music was kind of . . . mature. Not Billboard chart stuff, not stuff that gets you in the gossip columns. In England, the tabloids are even worse than they are here. There's no 'Stars . . . They're Just Like Us!' column. They want you to talk to pigeons and shoplift at Boots to take your picture. And Robbie, he liked attention, and he didn't get it with me. We would go to events and they'd pass right over us. So he dumped me."

Ash could see where this was going. "So Crazy Daisy was born out of a need for revenge?"

"More like out of insecurity." Daisy grimaced. "I wanted to show him that I could be bigger and better than anyone he'd ever date. And I wanted to show myself that I wasn't just some loser nobody. So far, so good. When I got the call from your dad, to record an American album with More, Robbie called me wanting to hang out again. I told him to bugger off."

She smiled wanly, her dark red lips shining.

"That's good at least," Ash said. "But I'm sorry that a guy would treat you that way."

"It's okay. I mean, I'd be lying if I said there's not a side of me that sort of enjoys letting my crazies out. And getting *rewarded* for it," she said. "I tell myself that as long as I know I'm pulling a Crazy Daisy move, that I'm still okay. I'm not too far gone. The only bad part is, the music I play now, it's not how I'd do it if I were just regular old Daisy. There wouldn't be a dance club remix of 'Feather in Your Cap.' It's a ballad, actually sort of the way that redhead was playing it at Powerhouse. It's about Robbie."

Ash was intrigued. He'd always liked "Feather in Your Cap," out of all Daisy's songs. The lyrics were beautiful, and he knew she'd written them herself. "Can I hear it?" he asked, gesturing to the piano.

Daisy nodded. "Sure." She took a seat at the baby grand, and began to play a slow, angelic melody. Her voice seemed to come from somewhere outside herself as she sang.

"*. . . I was just a notch upon your bedpost,*
Some guys' night talk, a drunken boast.
Just a scribble in your datebook,
Someone you let off the hook.

You think I'm just a feather in your cap
Just a pin upon your map
That I'm just a number, in this urban jungle.
But when . . . will . . . you . . . realize . . .
I . . . will . . . cut . . . you . . . down . . . to . . . size . . ."

She ended the song with a flourish, the sigh of each key caressing Ash's eardrums. Lyrically, the song bore no resemblance to his and Myla's epic romance, but the sad weight of the music reminded him of how lonely he was without her.

Daisy drew out the last few notes on the piano, the last key like a cool breeze floating through the room. She looked at him hopefully over the top of the dark wood instrument. "Did you like it?"

Ash finally exhaled, and it felt like the first time he'd breathed in months. "I loved it. I was just thinking . . . I can relate."

"Tell me," Daisy said, rising from the piano bench and crossing the room to take a seat next to him on the couch.

He didn't know what came over him, but he started to tell Daisy the whole story. About Myla being gone this summer, their fight, the Lewis thing, all of it. She listened intently, her eyes filled with the sympathy of someone who had had their heart broken into a million pieces too.

"You never know," Daisy said, when he was done. "It might work out for the best."

"Yeah," Ash said, feeling slightly embarrassed. Daisy was a great listener, just when he'd needed a great listener.

Tucker and Geoff had never been in serious relationships, so he never thought they'd understand his Myla stuff. But it wasn't like Ash really *knew* Daisy, or like they were even friends. For all he knew, she was just being nice because he was Gordon's son. He wanted to change the subject. "So, if you're not really nuts, does that mean Amy Winehouse is an act too?"

Daisy giggled, shaking her head so that waves of her light hair spun around her face like sunbeams. "No way. Girl needs some major repairs. She's absolutely *mental*. And that's coming from someone who just attacked a case of frozen shrimp with cheap merlot."

Ash threw his head back and laughed like a madman. Daisy was right. It *did* feel good to let his crazies out.

TUCKER IN

Jojo sat in the back of the Everharts' hybrid SUV on Saturday, flipping through old photos on her new iPhone. There was one of her and Willa, each with an arm inside a triple-extra-large JFK soccer hoodie that had arrived by accident from the uniform company. One of Willa, Samantha, and Debs, all huddled under a canopy during a game they'd played in the rain last year. Willa's beaming face seemed to say, "Wish you were here."

"What are you doing?" Myla asked, craning her neck from the row of leather seats opposite Jojo.

"Nothing," Jojo said, flipping the screen back to its wallpaper, a shot of her and Myla taken a few days ago in Myla's room. They both wore sheer Dolce & Gabbana bow blouses, Myla's in royal blue, Jojo's a deep green. Both girls' hair had the same sleek sheen, and their identical matte-red half-smiles were straight out of *Teen Vogue*.

"Your swimsuit is coming untied," Myla said, sliding along the seat and yanking the halter straps of Jojo's Trina Turk orange leaf-print bikini tight against her neck. Jojo winced as a strand of her hair got caught in the knot. Myla freed it, not as delicately as Jojo would've liked. Satisfied, Myla smoothed her own Milly daisy-print cover-up over her Betsey Johnson Black Magic bikini, which was basically waterproof lingerie.

Charlie, their driver, turned off the PCH onto Malibu Road, high up above the Pacific Ocean. The water was an inky blue dappled in sunlight, and all along the bluffs on the opposite side were homes teetering on precipices above the sea. Some were enormous, castlelike estates that reminded Jojo of the Everhart mansion in Beverly Hills. Others were modern, three-story squares, whole sides made of windows that overlooked the ocean. Behind them stood mountains. To live here would mean walking out your front door to the Pacific, with your back door leading you right into the hills.

As they drove further, the SUV came closer to land, until they were driving down a small road lined with beachfront homes, each one gated. Some had tiered buildings like Chinese pagodas painted in reds and oranges. Others looked like Spanish missions unfolding along the rocks. Finally, they pulled into a narrow wraparound drive, on the back end of what Jojo could only describe as an impossible house. It swooped and curved, with rounded walls made entirely of glass that reflected yellow and blue, with the rays of the sun and the rippling of the water. Orange blossom bushes and star jasmine encircled a rooftop balcony. Jojo could already see most of her BHH classmates gathered there, on a patio with a pool and a mile-long thatched roof bar.

She felt her nerves activate, and her stomach began

to whine from anxiety. She widened her eyes at perfectly poised Myla, as if to say, *Should I really be here?*

By way of answer, Myla said plainly, "It's Tucker's dad's place."

Hitching her Dior beach bag on one shoulder, Myla hopped out and impatiently gestured for Jojo to follow. Jojo stepped out tentatively, wishing she'd worn her beat-up Havaianas instead of Myla's four-inch Gucci heels.

Myla led the way, slipping in through the open glass doors. Every face at the party turned and waved. Jojo took in Tucker, Ash, their friends Geoff, Mark, and Julius, Billie, Talia, Fortune, Mai, Tosha, and a whole array of BHH's best and most beautiful.

Her body tensed. It was the first time she was seeing these people in a social setting since Lewis's party, and she was wearing a bikini and a skimpy cover-up. *Maybe this is how those dreams where you're naked in front of your whole class feel,* Jojo thought. Finally, Tucker cried, "Jojo and Myla are here!"

The guys, already feeling the effects of whatever was in the hollowed-out coconuts they sipped from, let out a "woo-hoo!"

Jojo smiled, relieved. Okay, so maybe a bikini and heels made that entire gender forget past party blunders. The girls weren't so easily impressed, though, offering Jojo a mostly bland chorus of hellos with a few stronger welcomes from hangers-on who'd never quite gotten in Myla's elite circle. Billie waved spastically at Myla, giving Jojo only a tight-lipped smile. Talia none-too-subtly scanned Jojo's outfit, comparing it to her own white halter one-piece and dark shades. Fortune Weathers hid her distaste for Jojo about as well as her two-tone green string bikini disguised her hips. She sighed audibly, allowing herself an irritated split-second smirk before sucking in her stomach again.

For a few seconds, Jojo imagined the soccer invitational, where her teammates would have wrapped her in a tight group hug. But, hey, a week ago she'd been losing her lunch on these people, and they were still saying hello to her. Besides, she realized, maybe Myla's friends were a little *jealous*. The idea that Myla would prefer Jojo's company to theirs thrilled Jojo as much as it probably scared them.

Tucker came up beside her, and Myla not-so-subtly shoved Jojo in his direction. He put a hand gently on her back and said, "I'll get you a drink." Book learning might not have been Tucker's thing, but apparently he was well versed in the art of smooth, flirty hosting.

He led her outside, where the pool was crammed with bodies bobbing along to a new Creases song featured in *Class Angel*. In the distance, the Malibu waves crashed along a vast expanse of uninterrupted, and privately owned, white sand. Tucker steered Jojo past Olivia Abdabo, holding court with a trio of girls on Myla's A-minus list. Olivia smiled at Jojo, and when Jojo realized that Olivia was looking at her, she responded with a friendly wave.

Tucker's guitar-callused fingers fluttered over her lower back as they stopped before the endless bar. Girls in tropical-print bikinis were mixing fresh fruit and rum, pouring the contents into carved-out coconuts.

"Daiquiri? Colada? Margarita?" Tucker asked. His pale blue eyes picked up the turquoise of the water, and he ran a hand almost nervously over his half-inch of naturally platinum hair. Ash had told Jojo that his buddy got just one haircut a year: a buzz cut in September that would grow to shoulder-length by the time school started again. *At least he's low-maintenance,* Jojo thought.

"Whatever has the least alcohol," she said, feeling a little dorky. She wished she'd asked Myla for tips on the best way to handle the situation. After her experience at Lewis's house, she wanted to stay far away from anything remotely close to the Long Island iced teas that had brought on BarfBarf. Still, she didn't want to seem lame.

"That's cool." Tucker grinned, sweetly pushing a strand of hair away from Jojo's face. "She'll have a frozen margarita, go easy on the tequila. And make mine the same," he told the bartender, a curvy brunette. He didn't look twice at her toned bare stomach, his eyes on Jojo the whole time.

Jojo felt a warm sensation flow through her body. So what if Tucker wasn't an A student? He was sweet. And he wanted to be with her.

Tucker handed her a coconut adorned with pineapple, mango, and papaya slices, and took her other hand. "Come on, I'll make sure you have a good time."

As he steered her through a crowd of her dancing, laughing peers—each of whom gave friendly nods and greetings—she felt pretty sure he would.

Jojo smoothed more SPF 32 into her chest. She ran her bare toes over the warm sand as she took a deep breath of fresh, salty air. The crack of every wave sounded like a burst of applause: Jojo felt wrapped in a blanket of social triumph. Okay, so maybe it was just the way warm ribbons of sunshine fell across her body that made her feel so good. She was returning from social pariah-dom with surprising speed. Not that she'd suddenly become co-ruler of the school with Myla. But she was definitely holding her own.

The party had moved from the house to the beach. The girls lounged on cushy orange sun chairs, lined up in order of ascension: Myla, then Jojo, Talia, Billie, and Fortune and a half-dozen others. Jojo was reaping the rewards from the Three Little Stalkers' behavior: Usually Talia got to sit next to Myla. But Myla had patted the chair next to hers and told Jojo to sit. Now Myla's friends were giving Jojo the cold shoulder, trying to pretend they weren't interested in everything Myla said to her. Out in the waves, the boys were acting the parts of laid-back alpha males, trying to outsurf one another. Music still poured from Tucker's deck to the beach, and the bikini-clad waitresses made their way back and forth bearing fresh fruity drinks. Down the beach, noise from another shindig wafted out to the shore. The BHH girls kept checking in that direction for revelers to stray from the other party and emerge on the sand. Rumor had it a Young Hollywood party was being held at the Polaroid House, which had been built expressly to entertain celebrities and had its own gifting room where swag was handed out. Some of the *Class Angel* stars were supposedly there.

"I swear that's Grant," Billie said, as she not-quite-stealthily put her rhinestoned binoculars up to her face. She bit her lip in concentration as she focused the lenses.

"Give me those," Fortune scolded, yanking the binoculars from Billie's hand. Peering through the lenses, she shook her head. "That's not him. It's just Robert Pattinson."

Jojo and Myla exchanged a look of disdain. The idea of Grant Isaacson shirtless had pulled every girl to the beach. They'd all posed, somewhat pathetically, displaying their assets in hopes of catching Grant's eye.

"Oh, I see someone coming," Fortune squealed, before sighing in disappointment. "Oh, it's Kady Parker. And Jake."

Jojo turned and saw Kady and Jake approaching, Jake's arm around her. He looked cute in his long trunks and a pair of aviators. A tinge of regret coasted over her body. She'd helped Jake get to the costar-dating point, after all. And now he didn't even notice her.

Myla poked Jojo in the arm. "Check out your man," she commanded. As Jojo watched Tucker through her Versace lens, she saw why Myla had picked him for her. He'd never cure cancer, but damn if the boy couldn't surf. He was better than every guy out there, even Ash.

Tucker wore just his Hawaiian board shorts, even though the water was freezing—after September, you had to be crazy to go in without a wet suit—his sculpted chest and abs bare and tan. He looked like a bronze god as he rode his board.

"I wish Grant surfed," Olivia said, practically shouting from her chair at the end of the line, as she rubbed

Clinique sunblock onto her cheeks. "Tucker is so good, Jojo," she noted, as if Jojo were responsible.

Jojo raised her eyebrows beneath her shades. After two hours, she was getting complimented on Tucker's skills? They'd been pretty much strangers as of this morning, but with approval from Myla, they were now a bona fide couple already. *Does it even matter what I want?* Jojo suddenly wondered, thinking of Jake walking hand in hand with Kady.

Tucker rode his wave in to the shore, hefting his board under one arm and striding across the sand. He made a beeline for Jojo, ignoring the scantily clad females surrounding her. His lips cocked in a satisfied grin.

"You were watching me," he said mischievously.

Jojo felt her face grow hot. She thought she was *supposed* to watch him. And he *was* awfully nice to look at. *Myla wouldn't be embarrassed in this situation*, she reminded herself.

"You were watching me too," she said, her voice composed.

"How could I not?" He knelt in the sand near her chair, his cold forearm brushing Jojo's thigh. She felt the slightest of tingles activate in a wave over her body. He leaned forward, and put his lips softly against her face, just next to her lips. Another tingle. She turned her head ever so slightly, and their lips met—hers warm and dry, his cool and salty—and he kissed her. It was a solid kiss—passionate, with gradually increasing force, almost like he'd practiced. Jojo couldn't deny that he had skills. And maybe once they got to know each other better, there'd be more behind their kisses than a mutual physical attraction.

As he broke away, Tucker squeezed Jojo's arm. "I'll see you later, okay?"

"If you're lucky," Jojo teased him with the half-smile again. Over Tucker's shoulder, Jojo glanced at Myla. Her sister nodded approvingly, even though she never took her eyes off Ash out in the surf.

Jojo reached out and clasped Myla's arm. "You should talk to him," she whispered, so none of the other girls could hear.

Myla grinned appreciatively, shadows falling on her face beneath her wide-brimmed sunhat. "You're right."

Myla hated the idea of trailing Ash as he left the water and headed up to the house, but Jojo was right. She stayed twenty paces behind him, having excused herself to visit the powder room.

She clipped through the glass doors, to find the big party room empty, save for Ash, checking his texts.

"You're getting better at your cutbacks," Myla said, quietly sinking into the custom couch that was big enough to seat ten comfortably.

Ash looked up from the phone and grinned. "Thanks, but not really. I sort of reversed direction on that one wave by total accident. But I'll take the compliment." Little specks of sand dotted his face just above his eyebrow. Out of habit, Myla reached up and brushed them away.

"Sorry," she said, drawing her hand away and rubbing a grain of sand between two fingers. "It just looked itchy."

"It just looked itchy"? Who tries to have an intimate moment with their ex and uses the word itchy? *Myla*

thought. She was nervous. She wanted to ask Ash if he'd kissed anyone yet, but she was almost scared to know the answer. It would probably hurt, and she'd probably be jealous. But as crazy as her suggestion that he kiss someone else sounded, the only thing crazier was their not being together. And if the only way Ash would know her kiss with Lewis meant nothing was for him to have a meaningless kiss of his own, then so be it. The pain would be worth it. Right?

"It's okay, My," Ash said, his gentle eyes seeming to ask why she'd followed him in here.

"So," Myla started, taking off her giant hat so he could see her eyes. "Have you . . . you know . . . yet?"

Ash pushed a wet strand of hair, falling adorably in front of his eyes, out of his face. "What's 'you know'?" He grinned, half-amused. Myla cursed herself for being so uncharacteristically fidgety.

"Kissed anyone," she said, looking at her hands. She couldn't look him in the eye.

Ash sighed, sinking backward into the cushions. "Seriously, this is ridiculous," he said. "Who am I going to kiss, anyway? I'm not gonna make out with some BHH girl that I have to see every day."

Myla winced at the idea of Ash kissing Fortune, or Billie, and suddenly she understood how hard this was for him. But she needed him to understand that all kisses weren't created equal. She wished he'd stop being so stubborn and get this over with. "Then pick a different girl," she said, as an idea formed in her head. "Kiss Crazy Daisy. It's perfect. You might even get that nut job out of your life if she gets mad and your dad finds out."

Ash said nothing, just hefted himself off the couch and sauntered back toward the door.

He looked back at her, chuckling lightly but with affection. "You know, you're a little bit of a nut job too, My. It's why I fell for you in the first place."

He opened the door, the *whoosh* of the waves flowing inside. He headed back in the direction of the beach, pulling up his wet suit as he went.

Myla felt her neck for the gold chain she used to wear Ash's ring on. It wasn't there, she remembered, as her fingers kneaded against her collarbone.

But maybe she'd be wearing it again soon.

MACHIAVELLI WITH A MACCHIATO

"Oh my God," Kady squealed, running at Jake and jumping into his arms. "You look so hot!"

Amelie rolled her eyes as Kady wrapped her thighs around Jake's waist, her green leggings wrinkling his Hugo Boss suit. Jake glanced at Amelie, smiling in a semi-embarrassed yet proud way, as if to say, *Sorry for our public displays of affection. But not really.* Then he turned away, kissing Kady deeply as she twirled one of his curls around her finger. To Amelie, the towering Jake and petite Kady resembled a giraffe with a garden gnome attached.

She pressed her lips closed and paged through her copy of *Elle*, the ink thoroughly smudged from multiple trips through the magazine. It wasn't even that great an issue. But it gave her somewhere else to look. The weekend had passed, and Kake was still going strong.

"Hey, so why weren't you at the Polaroid House thing this weekend?" Jake asked, sliding on the new pair of aviators Kady had given him at the party Saturday. Amelie didn't get why Jake was so eager to adapt to every trend Kady told him was cool. The glasses made him look like the dime-a-dozen wannabe actors who worked as personal trainers and office assistants at every cheap-rent locale from North Hollywood to Atwater Village. At least he was talking to her, though.

"I was busy," Amelie said, careful to smile only at Jake and not at Kady. "Had an in-store at Barnes & Noble in San Diego for the new Fairy Princess book."

"Oh, that sucks," Jake said. She couldn't tell if he was looking at her through his reflective lenses. "Wish you'd been there."

Kady looked at Amelie like she was a puppy who had just peed the carpet. Almost cute, even when she disappointed you. "Amelie's *always* working, Jake," Kady said. "She's a machine. All work and no play. Maybe we should find you a boyfriend, Am," she said playfully. With that, she snaked her arms tighter around Jake's chest and rested her tiny face on his arm.

Amelie wanted to roll up her magazine and swat Kady away like a fly. Why the need to make Amelie sound like the lamest person on earth? "Well, that was just on Saturday," she said. "Sunday, I hung out with some friends." She was lying, since the only friends she'd spent time with Sunday were Ben and Jerry.

Kady raised an eyebrow. "Oh, really? Who?" Her dark eyes twinkled mischievously as if she saw right through Amelie. Amelie ripped the page she'd been staring at. An article about why workplace romances fail. *Because you chose the wrong costar* was not among the reasons. "Just some people," she said breezily. Suddenly she felt irrationally angry at Hunter for making her leave Jake and Kady alone together in the first place.

"Nobody you know." With that, she jumped out of her canvas chair and walked away. She didn't have any more scenes today anyway. Kady and Jake had to film their last scene together—the two of them finally a couple at a big school dance, after Class Angel cleared Lizzie's name, helped her get into art school, and won her the Big Man on Campus. After their PG-rated kiss, the movie would cut to Amelie in her heavenly wonderland, beaming with pride at receiving a promotion from apprentice angel to associate.

Why had she let Jake slip through her fingers? She stomped toward her trailer as much as a pair of Ugg boots allowed a person to stomp. She was supposed to be waiting for Gary to return from a meeting with the producers. But they could call her.

She stopped at the craft service table for a macchiato, Kady and Jake still making out in the corner of her eye. A few feet away, Grant sat on the edge of the auditorium stage, his legion of followers now reduced to the three most devoted: Billie, Talia, and Fortune.

The three girls waved, but Amelie pretended not to notice. Much as she would have liked to get the girls' perspective on her situation, they were clearly occupied with Grant. Besides, hanging out with them seemed almost pointless now that she knew she wouldn't be attending BHH. She was headed for a destiny as an abject, loveless loser, surrounded by cats who listened to tales of her glory days as Fairy Princess. Why rub it in by spending time with girls who would never really be her friends?

"Grant, we were thinking. It's unfair Lizzie ends up with someone," Fortune said, twirling a strand of hair in a way that looked painful. "And you don't. What if they rewrote the last scene so that you get asked to dance by a girl? Or even, like, three?"

Talia and Billie nodded vigorously behind Fortune. "It would be soooo perfect," Talia said, leaning onto the stage in a way that afforded Grant a view of her La Perla bra.

"I took ballroom dance with Fred Astaire's grand-nephew," Billie bragged.

Grant looked past the trio, at Amelie, his eyes practically flashing, *Help!* Amelie smirked as if to say, *What can I do?*

Grant put on his most charming smile. "Ladies, ladies," he said, shrugging apologetically. "It's probably too late for a rewrite."

As she made her way to the auditorium doors, a thought occurred to Amelie. In this business, it was never too late for a rewrite.

Amelie knocked on the door to the production trailer, where Gary was having his meeting. She was glad to be wearing jeans, a beige V-neck, and her Uggs rather than an angel costume that made her look like a couture-clad dessert.

A young studio executive swung open the trailer door, his smile displaying a set of oft-whitened teeth. He wore the guy equivalent of Amelie's outfit: blue Pumas, worn-in True Religion jeans, and a vintage Philadelphia Phillies tee. Amelie recognized him immediately as Sanjay Bhatt, a VP for Transnational's teen entertainment division.

"Amelie, hello," he said easily, welcoming her in. He gestured for her to sit in a chair across from Gary and Devin Phillips, *Class Angel*'s executive producer.

Gary squinted at her oddly. "What's going on, Amelie?" He was dressed up, for Gary. No hat, a button-down shirt that was ironed and tucked, and khakis.

"Sorry for interrupting, but I had this idea over the weekend and wanted to run it by you," Amelie said, pushing a wayward curl from her eyes as the men regarded her with interest. "It's about the ending. Another direction on this movie might really set Transnational apart."

Sanjay looked enthused. He leaned forward, his chin on the steeple of his hands. "I'm intrigued," he said, casting a glance at Gary and Devin. "Go on."

Amelie cleared her throat, projecting a businesslike voice that echoed her mother's. "It seemed to me it would be interesting, and surprising, if—in the last scene—Class Angel reveals herself to Tommy. She explains to him that she's been pulling the strings, that she's in love with him and that she can stay on earth as a normal girl if he'd just kiss her. Tommy would be entranced and they'd kiss. Then in flashback we see that all along Angel was really pushing Lizzie toward Knox. And by giving Angel a reason to stay on earth, we have franchise potential: Angel, recently turned human, tries to navigate high school." She shrugged nonchalantly, as if it was a random thought and not the event on which her happiness hinged. If she could just kiss Jake, just once, she knew he'd feel what she felt. She needed this kiss to show him being with Kady was all wrong. Jake was a cuddle-on-the-couch-watching-movies kind of guy, not a find-a-dark-corner-in-a-nightclub kind of guy. And he definitely wasn't a couple-nickname kind of boyfriend. Kake was ridiculous. Jake needed to see that, and not waste time on Kady the way Amelie had on Hunter.

"It would involve just a quick rewrite of the final few pages, maybe an endcap of Lizzie getting together with Knox, so the audience sees how perfect they are for each other. Right now, it just seems a little . . . pat," Amelie invented, knowing that executives hated to hear the word *pat* about their films, even when it was true.

Sanjay's eyebrows raised, and Devin and Gary exchanged a look.

Devin smoothed the lapels of his bespoke suit. He was the best dressed of the three, which in this town meant he was the least confident about how he did his job. "And what prompted this idea?"

Amelie instantly thought of a story she'd scanned in the *Hollywood Reporter* that morning. "*Frothed Up*, the teen comedy set in the magical coffee shop? It only made seven million and opened fifth this weekend, even though the producers thought Selena Gomez and Nick Jonas would put it at least second with twenty million," she quoted almost verbatim from the article. "Audiences said they could see the ending coming ten seconds into the trailer. I mean, of course Selena and Nick wind up together. We've fought predictability with *Class Angel*, casting Jake as Tommy Archer and bringing on Grant. Think of the buzz we'd get if we take the audience somewhere they're not expecting."

Devin sighed, holding his graying head in his hands. "What are we doing here?" he finally muttered.

Amelie's heart thudded in her chest. She suddenly realized what she was doing: She was a sixteen-year-old best known for playing a girl who rode pink, winged ponies, and now she was telling a group of male bigwigs how to do their jobs? She was playing dangerously close to the edge with her first teen role. What if she not only lost Jake but also gambled away her career?

Gary stared at her, almost like he knew why she was bringing this up. He offered her a sympathetic, fatherly smile.

Devin finally spoke again, not looking at her. "Sanj, I don't know what to do with these kids."

Amelie felt like she'd just been caught shoplifting. After years of being voted Most Professional and Most Likely to Succeed, she was about to be fired for the first time. She'd be blacklisted and turn up twenty years from now as a celebrity judge on some reality show about glamorous toddlers. Maybe she'd get to go to high school in the meantime. But if her mother heard about this, it would definitely be military school.

"Is this a good idea?" Devin said. He was looking at Sanjay. Amelie knew Devin's type. When he'd started in the business, he'd probably been an "idea man" like Sanjay, but now that he was in his forties, he'd convinced himself he needed the insights of a young up-and-comer.

Sanjay rubbed the back of his neck coolly. He was enjoying this dramatic pause. His eyes traveled from Gary to Devin to Amelie, drawing out the suspense, like one of them was about to be awarded a top secret prize on a high-stakes game show.

"Personally, I think it's a fantastic idea," he finally

said. "It could up our buzz with the twelve-to-eighteen demo. It's so unexpected and so meta. We should just try it. If it doesn't work, we cut it, and it's still a great bonus feature for the DVD. Great idea, Amelie."

Devin nodded, like this had been obvious to him the whole time. "Exactly," he said. "I'll have the writers do a few more pages, and we'll messenger them over in a couple days. Okay, Gary?"

Gary raised both eyebrows, a look indecipherable to Amelie. He could easily break this idea by citing budget overruns, scheduling problems, or even saying that Jake and Kady's grand finale kiss was perfect and shouldn't be messed with. Amelie caught his eye and knew she looked desperate. "Of course, it won't take long to shoot," he said.

Amelie grinned. It would take just long enough.

SHOCKER ROOM

Jake stared at himself in the mirror above the locker room sinks. Of course the first break in filming he'd had in a while came just in time for him to go to gym class. It was a cliché for a geek to hate gym, but technically he didn't hate gym—he hated the *people* in gym. Rod Stegerson in particular.

But, in Justin Klatch fashion, Jake had decided to change right out in the open. Justin wouldn't be worried about noogies or swirlies or whatever torture method Rod had picked up in the latest edition of *Psychopath Weekly*.

Jake headed toward the lockers, sitting on a bench that stretched across the dank locker room. He pried his feet out of the vintage Sambas Kady had talked him into buying and was shoving on his cross-training Nikes when a shadow fell over the bench. Jake looked up to see Rod Stegerson, surrounded by his football goons, arms folded over their BHH gym shirts. Why had he come to gym? It was totally unnecessary. Miles had cleared all Jake's absences with his teachers. And yet, Jake, who'd won the Perfect Attendance award for two years running, still harbored enough vestiges of geekdom that he insisted on making whatever classes he could. He'd really have to work on breaking this habit when he got his next movie.

"Hey, Rod," Jake said as casually as he could. Maybe he could convince Rod to not give him a black eye or anything else that would mess up what was left to shoot of *Class Angel*.

"Jake, my man." Rod slapped Jake's shoulder with his heavy palm.

"What's up?" Jake said skeptically. Had Rod learned some new tactic? Act friendly but carry a big stick of pain?

"So, we've always been bros, right?"

Yeah, sure, Jake thought, *if by* bros *you mean I felt a real bond every time every time you sent my head into my locker door.* "Yeah, we're cool," he said, standing up to grab his shirt out of his locker. If he moved quickly enough, he could keep Rod's abuse to the verbal variety, at least until they got out on the gym floor. "We're"—he paused as he contemplated the word—"bros."

"Cool. Bros," Rod said monosyllabically, his jock army nodding emphatically behind him. "And I thought it was time to show you some respect. You landed Kady Parker, bro. It's only fair I congratulate you."

Jake looked over Rod's shoulder, catching his own surprised face in the mirror.

"So, how'd you do it, dude?" Rod's main sidekick, Dave Brandt, asked, cocking his square head. His neck was the width of Miles's torso.

"Kady?" Jake said, willing his voice not to squeak.

Should he tell them that he had no idea, that he'd seemingly become Kady Parker's boyfriend through sheer dumb luck? That he'd spent nights pondering that same question?

What would Justin Klatch do?

He was a nice guy, but this was a locker room. And even Jake knew locker rooms were where guys made themselves sound like bigger studs than they were, even if he'd never had the opportunity. Imaginary Justin smiled cockily in Jake's head.

"She was all over me from day one," Jake began, liking the way it sounded. "Like, *bam*! I tried to keep it professional, but she kept getting me alone."

Rod bobbed his head knowingly, like this sort of thing to him happened all the time. "And then you just had to go with it, right?"

Jake grinned. If anyone had told him he'd be talking girls with Rod Stegerson a month ago, he'd have asked what alternate universe they were living in. But alternate universes were for dorks.

Jake pictured Kady's pixielike face in his mind. Okay, so she hadn't exactly backed him in a corner and had her way with him, but she'd come close. "Well, I *am* a guy."

Rod clapped him again on the back. "No way, dude, you're the *man*!"

Rod's friends erupted in a chorus of "hell, yeahs," just as Jake's phone beeped, signaling an incoming message.

Miles. He'd taken the day off school to hunt down the perfect Escalade. Wait till these jocks saw Jake pull up to school in a gleaming black badass-mobile. Jake clicked to the photo messages and pulled up four different pictures of fully loaded trucks in black, gunmetal, white, and navy. *There's gotta be a winner here,* read Miles's message.

Rod peered down at the phone. "Is that your ride?"

"One of them," Jake said, surveying the vehicles. "Which do you think?"

Rod shook his head solemnly. "If you're gonna go Caddy, do it right. Get the ESV. It's bigger, and the way you pull chicks, you'll want something that can fit all of them."

This sounded about right. He quickly pounded out a message to Miles. "Dude, show me the ESV."

"Sweet," hollered Dave, high-fiving Jake. Jake high-fived back, then collected similar hand slaps from Rod and the rest of the guys. It occurred to him that this was the first time Rod had laid a hand on him in a nonviolent way.

It paid to be the man.

FIERY REDHEADS

Myla wove around the cafeteria's blond wood tables, past the organic-dessert vending machine. *Class Angel* was starting to wrap its work at the school, and the cafeteria was finally reopened. Myla was relieved to have it back. She loved the maintenance of the social order here: nerds in the corners, Myla in the middle, everyone else fanned out around her. Besides, cafeteria time meant catching up on gossip, something she and her girlfriends hadn't done in weeks. While they'd been busy picnicking outside Grant's trailer with Amelie, or whatever the hell they'd been doing, Myla had made off-campus lunch plans, but now it was time to reclaim her territory.

Talia, Fortune, and Billie had texted her during history to say they had a surprise for her. She was hoping that one of them had heard gossip about Ash kissing another girl. As bad as it sounded, even in her head, Myla couldn't help but hope that Ash was taking her suggestion seriously. She just needed some proof that he was willing to do anything to move forward. She certainly was.

Myla grabbed a fro-yo parfait and a chicken avocado wrap from the Healthy Options window, then carried her tray to the center table, a five-seater that was the most exclusive in the whole room. For most of high school, she Talia, Billie, and Fortune had sat there every day, with one empty chair reserved for Ash's drop-bys. Today Jojo had gone off campus for lunch with Tucker, so it would be just the four of them, just like old times.

She moved past a table overflowing with band kids and saw Billie, Talia, and Fortune at their table, with a redhead who had to be Amelie Adams. Maybe she hadn't been here in a few weeks, but who would have the audacity to sit there without her express permission? BHH's administration might have gone lax on some policies with the movie's arrival, but Myla hadn't.

As she got closer, Myla gaped in surprise. Her friends were all wearing filmy white dresses of indeterminate designer origin. And Amelie Adams was sitting in *her* seat.

She counted to ten, staring at the swirl of pomegranate curving up her parfait cup. *This is not real. This is not real. This is not real.* When she looked again, Amelie would be gone. And her friends would not be dressed like members of a whorish cult.

But when she looked, the whore-or was still there.

Myla swished to the table, her baby blue Fendi stiletto sandals pounding out a dangerous rhythm. She ignored Amelie, looking from friend to friend. "What's up with the outfits?" she asked point-blank, mustering her best sour face.

"It's for Amelie," Talia said, tugging a fallen strap back up her tanned shoulder. "Like a tribute thing. It was this or angel wings." She giggled, and so did Fortune and

Billie. Amelie laughed nervously, as if humbled—maybe even a little embarrassed—by the gesture.

Myla rolled her eyes. "Oh, how sweet of you," she said sarcastically. She was still standing above the table, not really wanting to sit down until Amelie was gone, and noticed that people were starting to stare. A gaggle of cheerleaders whispered to each other, and a table packed with jocks looked over, their curiosity piqued by the strange scene: Myla Everhart giving up her lunch chair to Amelie Adams, interloper. Even the band nerds collectively shifted their gaze in her direction, not wanting to miss history being made. One of them was probably composing an original orchestral piece inspired by the event.

Myla wasn't about to get in a catfight with her former besties. That kind of low-rent behavior was fine for the Lohans and Hiltons of the world, but she was real Hollywood royalty. Subterfuge and mind games worked so much better. She slid into the empty seat. Even out of the corner of her eye, she could see that Amelie had one of those preternaturally perfect faces that looked gorgeous from any angle. Her Caribbean blue eyes were clear and innocent, like she hadn't just taken over another girl's lunch table, not to mention her social status and her friends.

Myla smiled sweetly at Amelie. "So, Amelie, which of the girls do you think has the best shot with Grant?" she asked. Really, she was asking, *You know why they're hanging with you, right?* From Amelie's taken aback expression, Myla knew she'd understood her meaning perfectly.

Talia shot an apologetic smile at Amelie, as if to say, *Sorry Myla's being such a bitch.*

Billie glared at Myla. "Why would you ask something like that?" she snapped. "Don't listen to her, Am. She's just PMS-y."

Amelie said nothing. She simply returned Myla's sweet smile, as calm and unflappable as an angel.

Myla tucked into her parfait, barely tasting the fresh-cut strawberries. She begrudgingly awarded a point to the princess.

Jojo was trying her best to see what other girls saw in Tucker. They were sitting shoulder to shoulder in one of Jacopo's red booths, sharing a pizza called the Don. The pie was cut into squares, the crust thin and crispy, the sauce an ideal blend of tangy and sweet, and the cheese warm and bubbly, just like at Sadie's, back home. It was perfect.

Tucker, on the other hand, was not. At least not for Jojo. Every time Jojo managed to turn the conversation to something new, Tucker brought it right back to his favorite subject: surfing. He knew more about Kelly Slater and Laird Hamilton than their own mothers did.

"So, who do you have for English?" she asked, watching as Tucker served himself another four squares of pizza. The second their order had arrived, he'd claimed all four triangle-shaped corner pieces for himself. Jojo and Willa had a pact to always share those pieces, two and two. Her best friend would be horrified to hear a guy had hogged them all. On a date.

"Uh," Tucker said through a mouthful of cheese. "Hot chick? Youngish? Miss Butterworth?"

"You mean Mrs. Ballman?" Jojo looked at Tucker

skeptically. Could he really be so oblivious that he didn't
even learn teachers' names? Or worse, did he confuse all
of their names with mass-produced food brands? Mrs.
Ballman, a thirtyish Megan Fox look-alike, was a favorite
among the male students. Tucker tossed his arm lazily
across the back of the booth, his fingertips tracing her
shoulder blade. Smiling through gritted teeth, Jojo did
her best to stay still. His grabby hands only served to
remind her that they were hanging out again tonight.
Last night's date had consisted of "movie night," except
she'd only seen ten minutes of *Lords of Dogtown* as she
fought to keep Tucker's hand from traveling up her shirt.
Tucker was growing more irritating by the second, and
she didn't think they'd be the new super couple much
longer.

"Yeah," Tucker said, grinning appreciatively. "Who do
you have?"

"Mr. Dietz," she said, wishing she could be in her
honors English class right now. Mostly to get away from
Tucker. "Have you guys read *Catcher in the Rye* yet?"
Every guy Jojo had ever known had loved, or at least
claimed to love, *Catcher in the Rye*. From Justin Klatch,
whom she'd seen reading a dog-eared copy on her summer stalking missions, to—she bet—Jake. She didn't
care if Tucker liked the book or not. She just thought she
would scream if she had to listen to him describe again
the yearlong process behind the hand-carved surfboard
he'd ordered from an Australian surf company.

"Uh, I'm not really into baseball," Tucker said, slurp-
ing his Diet Coke noisily. "It's so slow and boring."

Look who's talking, Jojo thought meanly. Out of ideas,

she reached for the last slice of pizza, greedily biting into it. Giving her taste buds a little joy was the least she could do, since every other part of her was suffering.

"Dude, you took the last slice," Tucker said flirtily, pulling her to him for a kiss. "You owe me next time." Jojo clamped her lips tightly as she kissed him back. She really did need to speak to Myla about breakup protocol.

She was starting to craft a lie about needing to meet Myla before lunch ended when her cell buzzed with an incoming text. Willa's face popped up on the screen. Jojo scooted away from Tucker so she could check the message in private.

Family function, yeah right. Thanks for missing the invitational. Beneath the text was a forwarded TMZ article, accompanied by a photo of Jojo on the beach at Malibu, laughing with Myla and the rest of the girls. *Barbar's Daughters Spotted at Malibu Bash*, read the headline. Jojo tasted the acidic tomato sauce rise back up her throat, picturing Willa as she realized Jojo had lied to her.

She clicked away from the text message, not looking Tucker in the eye. "'Sup?" he asked, in his annoyingly casual way.

"I just want to go back now," Jojo said flatly. Back to school, or to her old way of life, she wasn't sure.

Fifteen minutes later, Jojo marched into the cafeteria with Tucker, holding hands. Jojo kept her grip limp.

Myla was sitting at her usual table, with Talia, Billie, and Fortune, who'd all dressed like slutty angels. Jojo rolled her eyes when she saw why: Amelie Adams was sitting in Myla's seat.

Jojo led Tucker to the table. Every table turned to watch as they made their way past.

After the only awkward lunch period of her teenage life, Myla was relieved to see Jojo and Tucker walk through the cafeteria's double doors. Her friends really seemed to *like* Amelie. Maybe at first they'd just viewed her as an instrument to get closer to Grant, but their affection actually seemed genuine. None of them had even asked Myla what was going on with Ash. She really wanted to spill about telling him to kiss Crazy Daisy, to see if they thought she'd gone completely nuts. But apparently, none of her friends cared what was happening in her life anymore.

"Myla, did you hear me?" Talia, oblivious to Jojo's approach, cut into her thoughts. Myla swirled the melted remains of her parfait, looking into her friend's brown eyes. "Amelie invited us to a *Class Angel* charity event tonight. Some of the cast are going to work at the Angel Food soup kitchen for publicity. Get it?" Talia smiled admiringly at Amelie.

Myla flipped her long ebony hair over one shoulder. "I go there all the time with my parents," she scoffed. "Only they don't do it for publicity." She shot Amelie a cutting look.

Amelie didn't blush, though. She flashed a megawatt grin that made Myla want to slap her. "You sure you don't want to come? Everyone who helps is going to get to visit the VIP tent at the *Class Angel* wrap party this weekend."

Myla stared at Amelie in disbelief. How dare she imply Myla would need *help* getting VIP access? Especially to a lame school-sanctioned wrap party for a teen movie. The only reason Myla even planned on going to the wrap party was to talk to Ash.

Myla turned to Jojo and Tucker instead. "Hey, what are you guys doing tonight?" she asked, ignoring Jojo's *don't go there* look. She needed to get away from her friends, and from Amelie, but didn't want to give the impression that she was the one being pushed out.

"We were gonna hang at my place, but then I thought it might be fun to head out to Venice," Tucker said. "Get some eats on Abbott Kinney."

"That sounds cool," Myla said, standing up and throwing an arm around Jojo. She turned to face her friends. It was time to draw a line in the sand. "Sorry, guys, I don't really want to go with you. I think I'd rather hang out with my sister."

Jojo couldn't believe it. Myla hadn't seen her friends in weeks, and now she was blowing them off to hang out with *her*? Maybe she could deal with Tucker for one more night.

OOPS-A-DAISY

Ash flipped through the channels on his LG flat-screen, annoyed that every station he tuned to seemed to feature kissing.

Turner Classic Movies. *Casablanca*. "Kiss me. Kiss me as if it were the last time."

TNT. *She's All That*. That lame song, "Kiss Me," that Myla had played over and over for three weeks when the movie come out.

MTV. *Barnsley's Babes*. "Your lips, my lips, some tequila. Let's do this thing."

Ugh. Ash dropped the remote and shifted his recliner to its 180-degree position. Myla seriously was not backing down on her whole kiss-someone-else plan. And now it felt like she'd paid the cable company to remind him. Which he wouldn't put past her.

He rolled onto his stomach. Did other guys go through stuff like this? Or had choosing Myla meant he got the best and worst of both worlds—amazing girlfriend, terrifying ex?

He closed his eyes, hoping to wake up with selective amnesia, something to make him remember only the good Myla stuff. His phone broke out in its new ring-tone, "Don't Let It Get You Down," by Spoon.

"'Lo?" He was too spent to roll off his stomach.

"Ash? Are you in a tunnel or something?" Daisy's English accent bubbled over the line.

He surprised himself by not only rolling over but sitting straight up.

"Daisy? What's going on?" He instantly felt worried. Last time he saw her, he had to pick her up from jail. Even if he knew now she wasn't really crazy, he still didn't feel good about her getting into the kinds of situations she got herself in.

"I'm just bored is all," she murmured. He could hear television chatter in the background. "There's crap on the telly, and I feel like I've been trapped in this room since my tenth birthday. I was thinking about going out . . . if you'd join me."

Ash grinned. "Do you mean bail you out? Because we have this three-strikes rule in California. Maybe it doesn't apply to English rock stars, though."

Daisy's laugh rang over the line. "No, I promise. I'll go incognito, blend in. *L.A. Weekly* wrote up this place Largo. Maybe you could meet me there?"

He'd always wanted to go to the old Largo in Silver Lake before it had moved to its new spot on La Cienega. Myla had always refused, saying that the place was full of old hipsters with superiority complexes.

"Yeah, that would be cool," Ash finally said. "Half hour?"

"I'll see you there, by the main stage, not the little room," Daisy said. "I bought tickets already, so get yours at the door. But remember, I'm incognito. So this time, don't look for the girl who's flashing her knickers."

The second he set foot inside, Ash knew he was going to like Largo. With its pewlike rows of seats, and hushed, reverent crowd, it felt almost like a church, minus all the talk about your mortal soul. Everything was bathed in a burgundy light, except the stage, where blue lights shone as bright as a full moon on a rare smogless night. A couple who looked like twin emo lumberjacks in faded black-and-white checked shirts strummed guitars onstage. The song wafted through the club hauntingly.

Scanning the rows in front of the stage, Ash couldn't see Daisy. Myla was right about the crowd being older hipsters; the youngest people here had to be in their late twenties, but most were closer to forty, the men in slim blazers and the women in dark sweaterdresses over tights and slouchy boots.

The duo on stage slipped out of their mournful dirge into a cover of Albert Hammond's "It Never Rains in Southern California." The spotlights moved over the crowd, and Ash laid eyes on Daisy, alone in the back row, her toffee-colored hair up in a messy bun. She wore a filmy dress with tiny roses printed on it, a tiny gold locket draped around her neck. She *was* incognito, but that didn't mean she blended in. Her skin glowed beneath the flickering yellow bulb near the exit, and her eyes were silver in the dimness. She reminded Ash of Zooey Deschanel, but even more beautiful.

"Hey," Ash said, slipping into the seat next to her. "Thanks for inviting me."

"It's the least I could do." Daisy tilted her head so that a soft curl fell from her bun. "Though the police station does add a certain level of excitement to our relationship."

Ash grinned, signaling a waitress to bring him a beer. "Do you want anything?"

Daisy shrugged. "I guess a club soda."

"A Stella and a club soda," he said, as the waitress nodded and flitted off. He turned back to Daisy. "Not drinking tonight?"

Daisy pulled nervously on her earlobe. "I don't really drink all that much. Unless I have to work to be . . . you know."

Ash nodded. "I get it." The guitarists announced a set break, and the club's sound system took over. The Rolling Stones' "Beast of Burden" sauntered through the club. A couple near the stage wandered out to the tiny dance floor, clinging to each other in a tight embrace.

"I love this song," Daisy said. "You wanna dance?"

Ash stood, offering his hand to Daisy. "Why not?"

They made their way to the front, Ash spinning Daisy out onto the floor. Her dress twirled under the blue lights, and she looked like an indie rock angel. She spun herself back, curling herself neatly under his arms, careful to leave a foot of space between them.

"You can come closer," Ash said. "I do bite, but never in public."

Daisy inched closer and leaned her head on Ash's shoulders in an exaggerated manner. "So, do you want me to see if I can get us kicked out of here?"

"Maybe not tonight," he said. Her wrist felt light

against his neck. "You're kind of cool when you're not in handcuffs." He blushed as soon as he said it, and was glad she couldn't see his red face under the lights.

"Kind of cool? I'm *beyond* cool," Daisy said, raising one freshly plucked eyebrow at him.

"Okay, maybe you're right," he said, almost able to feel her lips as she spoke. Mick Jagger yawled on behind them, and Daisy started to sing along in a doleful voice. "'I don't need no beast of burden . . . I need no fussing, I need no nursing . . . Never, never, never, never, never, never, never be.'" She giggled. "I hope I haven't made you feel like my beast of burden." She looked right into his eyes, a look so direct and earnest it surprised him with its intensity. He tried not to think of Myla telling him to kiss Daisy. Daisy had enough problems without being dragged into one of Myla's crazy schemes.

When he was silent, she whispered sincerely, "I don't want to be a bother." At that moment, he couldn't picture ever thinking of her as a bother. He stared into her feather-gray eyes, wishing he could look away. But he couldn't.

He leaned in and kissed her. The music disappeared, replaced in Ash's head with Myla's words, *"Kiss someone else, and you'll see it means nothing."*

Daisy's lips were soft and inviting on his. She twirled a strand of his hair around her finger, sending a shiver up the sides of his neck to the nooks behind his ears. It was like music. Great music.

Maybe it wasn't exactly like kissing Myla.

But it definitely didn't feel like nothing.

WORKING ALL THE ANGELS

"Amelie, new pages are ready," one of the student production assistants called through Amelie's thin trailer door.

He could have been saying, *Amelie, puppies! For you!* The effect was roughly the same.

Amelie fluttered to the door, knocking over a pile of J Brand jeans the company had sent her. Grinning like a madwoman, she flung open the door but reminded herself to act professional. The PA was a scholarly-looking BHH senior who always wore a suit jacket and who'd become Gary's favorite of the student hires. She wanted to snatch the pages from his hands and hurry back to her bedroom to read exactly how her first kiss with Jake would go.

"Hi, Amelie," he said, watching Amelie's eyes cut to the manila envelope under his arm. *Patience,* she told herself. "Um, sorry, my name's Rush. Baxter?" He said it like a question.

"Oh, I remember," she lied. "It's crazy we're shooting another ending, huh?" Luckily, Devin and Sanjay didn't want her to tell anyone she'd come up with the new scene. The last thing they needed was word getting out that one of Transnational's stars had gotten an ending change. Kady, and most important, Jake, wouldn't suspect a thing.

"Yeah, totally," he said, waving the envelope back and forth. Amelie grabbed it as casually as she could, resisting the urge to rip it open this second. She hadn't been this excited to read anything since the last Harry Potter book.

"Gary wants to know if you could be ready for hair and makeup in an hour. We're going to shoot this today. Jake has a lot of scenes with Grant tomorrow," Rush explained. He looked bashful yet proud. A few weeks on a movie set and the guy was trusted with the kind of information the assistant director usually doled out. Shooting a movie at BHH had led to big changes for everyone.

Amelie wanted to squeal and hug Rush. She'd be kissing Jake in a few hours and afterward, she knew everything would be different. Maybe he'd dump Kady on the spot, and they'd have their first date tonight. Amelie wouldn't drag Jake to hot spots and nightclubs. That stuff was for the Kadys and the Hunters of the world. Not that Amelie hated Hunter or anything. She could just see clearly now. Before, she'd been trying to change herself to fit into Hunter's world, while all the while she and Jake had already been living in the same one.

"Thanks, Rush," she said. "I can do an hour. I just better read these." She shook the envelope meaningfully and Rush hurried off.

She flopped onto the IKEA couch and fished out

the pages. There was a note from Sanjay scrawled on a Post-it stuck to the cover. "Amazing idea, Amelie. This might draw the *Cruel Intentions* crowd to a teen romantic comedy!" She rolled her eyes. The studio execs only saw a business gain, not a victory for true teenage love.

The dialogue wasn't great. It had that weird, stilted quality of a dream. But the exchange she wanted was there: Class Angel told Tommy who she was, and that she could become human with just one kiss. Tommy would take off Amelie's halo—a true bonus in Amelie's mind—and lean down to deliver her eternal life-altering smooch.

Maybe someday she'd tell Jake what she'd done to land him. She could picture her tell-all interview with *People* about how she'd gone behind the scenes to get a first kiss with Jake. And how years later, they were still living their own happily-ever-after.

Amelie was out of hair and makeup, pacing near the empty stairwell where they'd shoot. She furtively used a tissue to blot away excess lip gloss. She wanted this kiss to be perfect. And she wanted to get it right on the first take, before Kady returned to the set.

For the scene, Amelie would get to dress completely normal—no white, no frills, and minimal glitter. She wore knee-high white boots, a short white denim skirt, and a white baseball-sleeve tee. As the kiss happened, her white clothes would burst into color, and the heavenly aura that surrounded Amelie's character (thank you, postproduction) would fade: Through true love, Class Angel would become human. Gary had told her that *Class Angel Goes to High School* was already in development, thanks to Amelie's idea. *If only getting the powers-that-be to let you actually go to high school were that easy,* Amelie thought.

Jake sat in his canvas chair, watching as the crew hoisted a boom mic out of shot range. He looked infinitely calmer than he had his first day on set, and it almost bothered her. When had he become Mr. Cool? And wasn't he a *little* nervous about their kiss?

"Places, please," Gary finally called. Amelie's stomach coiled like one of Shirley Temple's ringlets.

Amelie leaned against the stair railing, where Class Angel was supposed to lie in wait for Tommy. Jake took his time, thumbing out the last few words of a text message before finally sauntering over. He took his mark at the top of the staircase. His dark curls had been tamed with gel, and one stubborn lock of hair hung sweetly over his right eye. Amelie had almost forgotten how tall he was, and not just compared to petite Kady. Even at five foot six, Amelie would only reach his clavicle. But in heels, she'd be the perfect height to rest her head on Jake's toned shoulder.

"And, action," the AD called.

Action? No problem, Amelie thought, already feeling a frisson under her skin as Jake walked down the stairs, Tommy's letterman jacket slung over his shoulder.

Tommy stopped to ask if she needed help. Amelie nodded her head coyly.

"Yes," she said. "But not the help you think."

Tommy eyed her quizzically. "Are you new? Or waiting for someone?"

Amelie turned the full force of her aquamarine eyes on him. "Waiting for you, actually."

Tommy scrunched up his face in confusion. "I don't think we've met."

"We have, you've just never seen me," Class Angel said, leaning slinkily on the wall. She explained, in the same odd dialogue, who she was. Jake registered Tommy's reaction perfectly, going from skeptical to startled to intrigued.

"So if we kiss, you stay?" he asked, already lifting the ruffled halo from her head. For once, it hadn't been pinned down. Amelie almost melted as Jake's fingers brushed her scalp.

"Yeah, I think you're getting the idea," she said, parting her lips as Jake moved closer.

He leaned in and—with his fingers still woven through her hair—softly, gently placed his lips on hers. Amelie felt her nerve endings ignite, a hunger gnawing at her insides. Who knew Jake could kiss like this? His lips seemed made for hers as the kiss grew in force and intensity. Amelie reached for the back of his neck, lightly running her fingers over his hairline. She ran her other hand down his arm. It was like her lips were a pointillist painting, and every dot that made up her mouth was fizzing. If Jake was feeling half of what she was feeling, they'd have to head to one of their trailers to pick up where the scene left off.

"And, cut," Gary said, too soon. "That was perfect, you two."

Amelie took her time opening her eyes. But as soon as she did, she wished she'd kept them closed. Kady was bounding over to them without a care in the world. "You guys looked hot. I don't get this ending at all, but that kiss was spectacular."

Amelie forced a grin. She took a step back, hoping to give Jake a little privacy so he could tell Kady he'd just discovered his deep feelings for Amelie. Instead, Jake broke out in a relieved smile. Kady immediately gave him a long kiss, right in front of Amelie. The one-two punch knocked the wind out of her.

"You ready?" Kady asked him. "I put us on the list for the Vampire Weekend show at the Wiltern."

"Cool," Jake said, slinging his arm around her. He might as well have been slapping Amelie in the face. They were supposed to have tutoring today.

Amelie forced herself to smile. "You guys have fun. Jake, we'll do tutoring another time." That had been the knockout blow: He'd completely forgotten.

Jake could see the hurt in Amelie's eyes. He hadn't actually forgotten tutoring. But after seeing the pages of their new scene, he'd made plans with Kady so he wouldn't have to be alone with Amelie. He'd been terrified that the kiss would be bad, or worse, that by kissing him she'd somehow know exactly how badly he'd crushed on her when they'd first met.

The weird thing was, the kiss had been great. Like every fiber of his being had met its match in Amelie's being. And he could tell by the way Amelie couldn't quite look at him directly that she wasn't thrilled to see him ditching their session for another girl. But he couldn't imagine that she'd felt what he had felt when they kissed. She was a professional—she was probably just getting wrapped up in the energy of the scene. Plus,

Kady was his *girlfriend*, on- and off-camera. Kissing her meant something way bigger. Right?

"Yeah, definitely," Jake finally said.

"You're welcome to come," Kady said charitably.

Amelie felt even worse. Jake was acting like their kiss was no more of an event than splitting a craft services cupcake. And Kady was treating her like an unfortunate who needed a little TLC.

"No, thanks, I'm really tired, actually," she said. *Really tired of not living in the real world.* Maybe all those years in Fairy Princess's Enchanted Forest had gotten to her. She'd created an elaborate fantasy version of Hunter as the perfect guy who would one day fall in love with her. And now she'd believed Jake would fall head over heels after one kiss. A *scripted* kiss, no less.

Kady rapped Amelie on the arm. "Maybe *someday* you'll hang with me," she teased, guiding Jake out the door to their waiting car. For once, Amelie didn't care about being left alone. She had all her delusions to keep her company.

BABY'S GOT A BRAND NEW D-BAG

"So, should we do Nobu or Katsuya?" Kady's glimmering blue eyes looked up at Jake expectantly, waiting for him to make a decision.

"Nobu, definitely," Jake said, having no idea what cuisine was in store for him, but not caring. He was an actor. Going to dinner with his girlfriend. Who was also a star. Who used the word *we*. And who was too cool to be jealous over the fact he'd had to kiss another costar.

His mind did keep wandering over to the kiss with Amelie. But it was only nostalgia—his crush now seemed far in the past. Anyway, if they'd gotten together, the dynamic would have always been off. He'd always be the tutor and she the starlet. Now he and Kady were equals.

"That's what I was hoping you'd say," she cooed, standing on her tiptoes to kiss him right under his lips. Jake liked that they had a "thing"; Kady was tiny compared to him, but her chin kisses meant she was ready for the real deal. He leaned down and kissed her, still feeling the delightfully unfamiliar thrill of kissing a girl on school grounds. Jake never had expected to kiss a girl within a ten-mile radius of BHH, because no girl would want to be seen kissing PG. Since his paparazzi photo had emerged in the weeklies, though, Jake couldn't help but enjoy the new sets of female eyes sizing him up with interest.

A blaring car horn yanked Jake and Kady apart as a gleaming black Escalade pulled up next to them. It was a massive ESV with an evidently high-quality stereo—the Death Star theme was radiating out to the curb through the tinted glass windows.

The car clicked off, the door opened and Miles jumped out, practically vibrating with excitement. He stumbled slightly at the curb. With his huge Scott Pilgrim T-shirt and short, unevenly cut black hair, he looked like a little kid getting off a nausea-inducing amusement park ride. He tossed Jake a weighty Cadillac key chain.

"Dude, did I get it right or what?" He pointed backward at the car. "I texted you but didn't hear back, so I just said, 'This is Jake's ride.' I signed the papers ten minutes ago. It's so easy to get a car when you've got fat cash."

Jake nodded coolly, as embarrassed of Miles as he would be of his mom showing up to bring him clean underwear.

"This is yours?" Kady strode down the length of the vehicle and in through the passenger door. She opened the driver's side door and leaned out, her hand petting the dashboard. "Sweet ride. We should go. Is Miles coming?"

She gestured to Miles, whose smile had faded slightly at Jake's lack of enthusiasm.

"Hey, we've got a date," Jake said, already climbing

into the driver's side. "I'm sure Miles has manager stuff he wants to take care of. He's a busy dude." He shot Miles a look and winked. Miles didn't wink back.

Jake shrugged and started the car. He quickly spun the wheel on the iPod from the *Star Wars* sound track to a Hot Chip album. He shut the door, pulling away from the curb toward Nobu, and his new and improved life. If he'd looked back at Miles, he'd have seen his friend dumbstruck on the curb, stranded at school without a ride.

But Jake was a star now, so he didn't give it another thought.

Friday night, Jake dabbed some eye cream Kady had given him on his lower lids. He was tired after last night's Nobu date and a Sony promotional party at Citizen Smith. Even in his fatigued state, he felt like a new man. As he'd rolled up to the club in his Escalade, people had stared. He'd signed a few autographs and then been whisked to a private table. All summer, he'd dreamed of being a whole new Jake. And now he'd become that guy, and he was better than the version of himself he'd imagined.

Tired or not, Jake had to go out tonight. He was heading to the first party he'd been properly invited to in his whole high school career. Better yet, it was in his honor: All of BHH had been invited to a *Class Angel* wrap party at the Transnational lot.

"Jacob, come down for dinner before you go," Gigi hollered up the stairs. "I feel like we haven't seen you in weeks."

Jake rolled his now-depuffed eyes. It wasn't like he was partying *that* hard. The other night, he'd crept in past two after the Wiltern show. His mom had been sitting on the couch in her pajamas, staring at the door. Her hair was all messy, and she'd breathed a sigh of relief when he came in. He'd been so annoyed to see her sitting there, waiting to guilt-trip him—guilt was more her style than grounding. But couldn't she see his life was changing for the better? Instead of hanging out with Miles in his room, wishing they had something to do, he'd been out for a change. And with a girl. His girlfriend. Who happened to like nightlife. His mom should be proud, or at least understanding. Jake took the stairs slowly, estimating he could spend twenty-two minutes with his family before he absolutely had to leave.

His mom had gotten all his favorites from Tuk Tuk Thai—beef pad see ew, spicy basil-fried rice, and a few curries. He sat down at the table in a huff, not taking anything.

His brother, Brendan, shook his head annoyingly. "Dude, you got your period?"

Jonathan, Jake's rabbi dad, gave Brendan his *shut the hell up* look. "Bren, you haven't seen your brother all week. Let's have a little peace." Jake already felt ready to get out of there. The kitchen felt so small. And he'd wasted sixteen years of his life eating here every night, when there was a whole world outside his door where you didn't have to tell your old, uncool parents how your day had been, or eat the same food from the same neighborhood Thai restaurant all the time.

Brendan shoved a spring roll into his mouth. "Just

making conversation." It was the same response he gave every time Jonathan scolded him for insulting Jake. Jake rolled his eyes.

Gigi powered down her cell and stuck it in the no-calls-during-dinner bowl. She surveyed its contents and saw Jake's wasn't there. "Jake, phone in the bowl."

Jake shook his head. "Can't. I might get a call about tonight." Most of all, he wanted to keep his eye on the clock.

Gigi sighed heavily, sitting down to her plate of chicken lemongrass salad. "Fine, but if you do, step away from the table."

"I'd rather step away from the table now. I'm still not sure about this blazer," Jake said, petting the lapels of a Diesel jacket he'd bought with Kady. With her constant energy, Kady would be even more bored than Jake at the idea of sitting down for a family dinner. Her parents still lived in Connecticut, and Kady rented a suite at the Chateau Marmont.

Gigi and Jonathan exchanged a *what has come over him?* look, but let it pass. "You look handsome." Gigi reached out to ruffle Jake's hair, but he dodged her hand. Brendan laughed through a huge mouthful of curry.

"Handsome is for old guys," Jake protested. "I want to look hot."

"When you find the bassackwards place that calls you hot, send me a plane ticket," Brendan said. Gigi slapped his wrist. Jake, who usually shot Brendan dirty looks for his remarks, just poked at the plate his mom put in front of him. Arguing with your little brother was immature. He was past that.

"You're just nervous," Gigi said. "It's a big night for you. It's going to be awfully hard when the real world rears its ugly head again. I bet you've got loads of homework to do over the weekend." She affectionately tickled his elbow. Jake flinched away from her in irritation.

"Oh my God, Mom," Jake said. "I've been to events before." Since their first official date at the Polaroid House in Malibu, Jake and Kady had been seen at every new club to open in Hollywood. Anything older than six months was already over, Kady had told him. Before the movie, he'd barely realized so many clubs existed.

"Of course you're edgy," Jonathan piped up, patting Jake's shoulder. "Why else would you not be eating? It probably doesn't help that you've been staying out way past curfew. I know we gave you some leeway with the movie, but let's shoot for a reasonable hour tonight."

Jake shot a look of scorn around the room. "First, you seriously think I'm going to bloat myself on Thai takeout before getting my photo taken all night? And second, the party is for *me*. I can't leave just as it's getting started."

Gigi shoved her chair back violently from the table, grabbing one of the dumplings that were a no-no on her chicken-veggie diet. She bit into it, chewed, and swallowed angrily. Spying the keys to Jake's Escalade on the counter, she picked them up. "Are these the keys to that earth-destroying truck of yours? The one you're going to return first thing tomorrow?"

"It's called an Escalade," Jake said. "Don't insult it. And it's staying."

Gigi flipped the keys around on her finger. "You know what, Jacob? We have a word for people like you in this business." She leveled him with one of her scary stares, but Jake felt impenetrable. "Douche. Bag."

"Go, Mom," Brendan said, lifting a spring roll victoriously. "She just called you a douche bag, Jake!!"

"That's two words, Mom," Jake said, ignoring Brendan. He stood up, towering over his mom. He reached for his keys, which were looped around Gigi's index finger. "What can you do? Ground me? I have my own earth-destroying truck. Oh, wait, it's a *Cadillac*."

Gigi opened the oven, which made a creaking sound from lack of use. She tossed the Escalade keys inside and then slammed the stove shut. She leaned against it. "Not tonight, you don't. Go to your room."

Jake glared at her, his whole body trembling at the idea of missing the wrap party. "Fine," he said, storming up the stairs. There was no way he'd accept his punishment. He shouldn't have to suffer because his parents didn't understand his new life. For two people who claimed they wanted him to be happy, they sure weren't acting like it.

By the time he'd reached the top step, a plan had come to him. He still had his Corolla. It was no Escalade, but it would do.

He walked into his room, locked the door, and shoved a long box of comics against it. He could use his student ID to jimmy the lock when he got home, or he could always crash at Miles's. He arranged his pillows in a Jake-like shape under his comforter and eyed the window. He had no trees to aid his escape, and he didn't have time to tie a bunch of bedsheets together. It was only a twelve-foot drop, though. And if he climbed out and held on to the windowsill backward, it would only be a six-foot jump. Easy. He'd learned a lot from his *Class Angel* athletic and stunt work.

He opened the window, his jacket shoved into a pillowcase so it wouldn't get ruined. Pocketing the Corolla keys and clutching the pillowcase between his teeth, he backed out the window, gripping the sill, and extended his body down. He glanced at the ground and let go.

He landed perfectly on the balls of his feet. He crept around the house in the direction opposite the kitchen window, to his car, thankfully parked along the curb down the street—something he'd done to make room for the Escalade, which he now looked at wistfully. If only he could have pulled up in *that* car.

He slid into the Corolla's driver's seat, started it, and pulled away. So he had to drive the Corolla. He'd committed his first real act of teenage rebellion. And even a hand-me-down Toyota started to look hot when it had a driver like him.

GIRLS GONE AWRY

"Is that him, there? No, it's just Ed Westwick," Amelie said disappointedly.

The party was almost two hours in, and so far, Grant was a no-show. Looping a strand of red hair nervously around her finger, Amelie scanned the crowd gathered under the cast and crew tent, an open-air canopy with a ceiling of white mesh fabric and lined with golden twinkle lights. Not that she cared what Grant did, but Amelie could feel her already-tenuous grip on her BHH friends slipping. Talia's eyes darted back and forth like those on one of those cat clocks with the swinging tail. Billie tapped her gold Moschino crisscross sandal against the pavement. And Fortune made no effort at covertness as she checked the time on her BlackBerry Curve.

Grant had never shown up at last night's soup kitchen event, even though he'd been listed as a potential guest on the press materials. The girls had *not* been pleased at four hours of community service—dressed in skimpy white angel gear, no less—without Grant there as a reward, and seemed to think it was all Amelie's fault.

Tonight, they'd come to the *Class Angel* wrap party

with her, probably figuring that Grant would *have* to show up here and *have* to hang with the *Class Angel* people at least a little while. So far, they'd figured wrong.

Amelie searched the crowd in vain for Grant. "Isn't that Parker Pinelli, talking to Ed?"

The girls' eyes collectively shifted to follow Amelie's gaze. Parker, a recent BHH grad who'd gone on to land a bunch of big Hollywood roles, was a cross between James Franco and James Dean. He looked handsome tonight in a pair of jeans and a black blazer—classic L.A. male style. Talia smiled sympathetically, as if Amelie was a sad loser for thinking Parker could possibly substitute for Grant. "So Amelie, you're not coming to BHH?" Clearly apathetic about the answer, Talia plucked the maraschino cherry from her Seventh Heaven cocktail—Bombay Sapphire, grapefruit juice, and a sprig of mint—and popped it in her mouth.

"No, it doesn't sound like it," Amelie said sadly, toying with the ribbon trim along the neckline of her sleek, short black organza shift dress. "I'll probably be doing more *Fairy Princess* episodes, and I heard there might be a *Class Angel* sequel."

"At BHH?"

"With Grant?"

Billie and Fortune's necks seemed to lengthen with their excited questions.

"I don't know." Amelie shrugged, feeling more and more alone even as the tent grew more crowded. She'd known that her BHH friends' interest had been about Grant at first, but she'd really thought they'd started to like her. She'd hoped to stay friends after she returned to life as a sheltered, tutored teen star. But between last night's soup kitchen fiasco and this party, the chances of that were fading as fast as Tom Cruise's chance for an Oscar.

Amelie glanced around the tent again, praying for a Grant sighting. Instead, she saw Kady and Jake holding hands, getting their picture taken beneath a giant halo made of gold foil–wrapped Godiva chocolates. She quickly looked away, wishing she could be anywhere but here.

"What do you say we ditch this party? Maybe order takeout at my house?" Amelie asked hopefully. A big girly sleepover was exactly what she needed right now. "I got a screener of the new Keira Knightly movie."

"Oh, that sounds fun," Fortune said distractedly. She was staring off at something outside the tent, and Amelie followed her gaze. Myla Everhart, in a sleek green dress, pranced into a tent offering Spa 415 treatments and mani-pedis. Talia and Billie turned to look too. They eyed Bar-bar's daughter hopefully—like she was the cupcake they could have if they cleared their plates of brussels sprouts.

And Amelie was the brussels sprouts.

"The three of us just really need to go talk to Myla about something, and then we'll be right back. 'Kay?"

Amelie didn't bother responding, and didn't even have time to. The girls zipped from the tent, making a beeline for Myla.

Even Amelie's trusty delusions couldn't trick her into believing they'd be back.

Jojo was an insider. Plain and simple. How many other sixteen-year-old girls got exclusive invites to wrap parties held at the famous Transnational lot?

Okay, so it wasn't exactly exclusive: Everyone at BHH had been invited, as a thank-you for letting the film shoot at the school. Still, she was *here* and not hiding in a corner. The party was outdoors, and the lot had been decorated to look like a metropolitan version of heaven. Even the tawny golden Transnational gates bore a glittery sign that read, THANK HEAVEN FOR BEVERLY HILLS HIGH SCHOOL. Each wrought-iron spike was topped with a halo fashioned from twinkle lights. Down the lot's New York street, beneath their cover of a white, glittery sheen, Jojo recognized the brownstone steps where Anne Hathaway and Chris Evans had kissed over spilled groceries in the remake of *Barefoot in the Park*. Amelie Adams stood on the steps now, talking to BHH's principal, Dr. Nachez, who had the unfortunate nickname Dr. Nachos thanks to his slight paunch. He was oblivious to the fact all his students were carrying flutes of champagne in open violations of BHH's no-tolerance policy—perhaps on purpose.

Jojo debated snapping a photo of Amelie Adams wearing a chic taupe Zac Posen dress that she recognized from Myla's spring runway collection flash cards. She could send it to Willa. But Willa still wasn't speaking to her. Myla had suggested sending a basket of exotic apology treats, but instead Jojo had gone the *I fucked up big-time* route, admitting her lie and apologizing like crazy. All to no avail.

A waitress dressed as an angel, one who looked like she possibly stripped on the side, approached her with a tray of sweets. "Heavenly dessert?" Jojo scanned the tray of white chocolate ice cream scoops topped with white chocolate fudge in martini glasses, white brownies shaped like halos, and white frosted angel-wing sugar cookies.

Just as she was about to decide, Tucker appeared and grabbed two cookies in his fist. "Sweet," he said, handing Jojo a bottle of Corona, even though she'd asked for champagne.

"Thanks," Jojo said, immediately setting the beer down on a cloud-topped cafe table that had been set up outside the façade of a New York diner. Jojo was a little annoyed that Tucker didn't notice or apologize, but decided not to say anything. She'd attempted to ask Myla for advice on the Tucker front last night, but Myla had turned the conversation around, asking if Tucker had mentioned Ash. Jojo was able to repeat Tucker's lament that his "bro" had been babysitting Crazy Daisy a lot. Myla had been happy to hear that—happier than Jojo had seen her in days—and after that, Jojo hadn't wanted to ruin the mood by voicing her doubts about Tucker.

"No problem," Tucker said, guzzling his beer. "This party's kind of lame, huh?"

Jojo was thinking quite the opposite. Maybe it was touristy of her, but she loved being surrounded by the familiar backdrops of her favorite movies. "It's okay, I think."

Tucker nodded, looking around, his attention consumed by the barely dressed angels who passed with trays of food. His eyes landed on the long bar that stretched from the brownstone down to the old-fashioned fire department. Silver buckets of ice holding Moët champagne lined one side of the bar.

"Oh, hold on a sec," he said, touching Jojo's arm and jogging over to the bar. Jojo felt moderately better. He'd remembered the champagne. She watched as he sidled down the bar, peering into the buckets. He waggled his fingers at several of the waitresses, who flocked to him. Jojo hoped he wasn't going to make some big gesture and bring her the whole bottle of Moët. She just wanted a flute.

Tucker lifted one of the buckets from the table and carried it over to her, the waitresses following him like a flock of glittery birds. His face formed the mischievous grin that Jojo actually liked.

"I had an idea for how we can liven this place up," he said.

"Stealing an ice bucket?" Jojo chided. "Really?"

"No, Jo," he replied, and she winced at the dreaded nickname. "Wet T-shirt contest."

A horrified look crossed Jojo's face. She'd heard Tucker was a horndog, but this was a little too *Girls Gone Wild* even for him.

He hefted the bucket, which contained water from melted ice, onto his shoulder. "You wanna go first, since you're my girlfriend and everything?"

She stepped out of the way just as Tucker flung the cold water in her direction. The giant splash hit the waitress behind her. The girl shrieked, but giddily, as her near-sheer white negligee went from PG-13 to NC-17.

"What the hell, Tucker?" Jojo screamed, but Tucker was already running to the bar for more water, a trail of squealing waitresses behind him, yelling, "Me next!"

"Jojo, come here, this is awesome," Tucker yelled,

waving her over. He really thought she would be his cohort in an impromptu wet T-shirt contest?

She was so dumping him. At least she still had her sister.

"To us," Kady said, raising her champagne flute high.

"To us," Jake clinked her glass with his own, conscious of cameras firing away.

When he'd made his way into the party, he'd collected high fives and congrats from BHH classmates who'd only talked to him before to get homework help. Life as half of a superstar couple was treating him well. The only thing better was the way Kady looked tonight. She wore a short black sequined skirt with a red cotton racerback tank over it, a skinny blue scarf tossed around her neck. Her chin-length jet-black hair was pulled back on one side, enhancing her deep-set dark blue eyes and dewy olive skin. Sneaking out, even in the Corolla, had been worth it.

They were standing in a roped-off area reserved for principal cast and crew, studio execs, and BHH administrators. Jake was on full display—for the first time in his life, he was hanging out somewhere other people actually wanted to be. Other students looked at him with envy and admiration as they made their way past. Rod Stegerson and his buddies had even checked out Kady, her legs dusted with shimmer atop a pair of candy-apple red DSquared2 high heels that brought her closer to Jake's height. Rod had given Jake the "guy's nod" of acknowledgment.

If this was to be his life from here on out, he could definitely deal.

Kady took advantage of her added height and kissed Jake in the space behind his ear. Geoff Schaffer and Tucker Swanson, each carrying a bucket of melted ice, gave him the thumbs-up. Jake usually closed his eyes when Kady kissed him, but tonight he wanted to witness people seeing him as something other than the geek who could speak Japanese and Vulcan.

He glanced at Amelie, who was talking to his principal and one of the deans. She didn't look his way. Across the way, he saw Miles, Rush Baxter, an AV buddy who was a student PA on the movie, and a few other AV squad guys making their way to the PS3 tent. Miles wore a new jacket, a gray blazer that actually fit him. Rush half-smiled, but like he was afraid of Jake, not like they were friends. Jake waved at the guys. Rush's hand went halfway up, until Miles raised an eyebrow. Rush retracted his hand, and they all looked straight ahead and kept walking. So Miles was mad at him? A prickle of irritation tugged at Jake. This whole manager thing had been *Miles's* idea, not his.

Jake turned back to Kady. He had a special evening planned tomorrow night: He was going to take her to the Little Door. Last night at Citizen Smith, Brent Bolthouse, the club promoter, had recommended it. It was supposed to be an ultra-romantic restaurant, and really exclusive.

"I was thinking . . ." he started, holding Kady a little tighter. Just then, as eager photogs closed in, her Black-Berry beeped with an incoming e-mail.

"Hold on a sec," Kady said, squeezing his hand. She fished the device from inside the waistband of her skirt.

"Wow," she breathed. "I don't believe it."

"What's up?" Jake asked, snaking his arm around Kady's waist and pulling her close.

"I got a part in Ridley Scott's new World War II movie," she said, taking a deep breath and looking at Jake with a message behind her eyes. "Have you heard about it? The one about the time travelers from the present who go back to meet the Greatest Generation?"

Jake had heard about it, all right. The script was a collaboration between Ridley Scott and Christopher Nolan, and the cast so far included Christian Bale, Will Smith, and Eric Bana. And now his girlfriend. Jake was impressed as he catalogued all the awesome movies Ridley Scott had made: *Alien*, *Blade Runner*, *Gladiator*. . . . It was a habit from his geek days he couldn't quite break, but at least he didn't say the names out loud. "Congratulations," he said instead.

Kady kissed him happily. "I'm so excited. I auditioned months ago and never heard anything about it. It was such a long shot. But now I'm going to working with Ridley Scott." She shivered with happiness. Jake brushed his hands up and down her bare arms to warm her.

"I'm so happy for you. And for us," Jake said. And he was. If Kady was landing major roles in sci-fi historical epics, who knew what might be in store for him?

Kady gazed up at him, her long lashes half-shielding her dark blue eyes. "Well, that's the thing," she said, squeezing his hand. "It's filming in Prague. I leave next week."

He imagined himself visiting Kady in Prague. They'd stroll down cobblestone streets, tour all the castles and cathedrals, happen upon the shadowy nooks and crannies of the atmospheric city and steal kisses beneath the romantically dreary gray sky. "I've always wanted to go. Franz Kafka's from there. There's a museum for his work," he blurted. He winced at the involuntary emission of a nerd fact, and quickly backpedaled. "We wouldn't have to go or anything."

Kady's eyes popped, as if Jake just told her he was pregnant. "But Jake," she protested like she was talking to a child. "You have no idea how bad long-distance can be. I don't want to be a bitch, but it would just be impossible."

Jake took a step back, trying to remember to breathe. "But I thought . . ." he began, not knowing what words could bring her back to five minutes ago, when everything was still ahead of them. "We're Kake." Their couple name wilted in the air for a second. Jake wondered if he could have made a lamer argument.

Kady pushed a curl away from his forehead, looking at him pitifully, like he was in a full-body cast. "We'll always be Kake," she said, smiling dolefully.

Jake faced facts: She was dumping him. The movie was over, she had to leave town, and she was dumping him. Jake had never officially been dumped before, because he'd never had an official girlfriend before. But instead of the news hitting him like a shot to the gut, he processed it like a mathematical equation. There was only one possible outcome: Geek plus hot, famous girl equals geek getting dumped. He wanted to tell Miles, who was like a geek anthropologist when it came to this stuff. But he couldn't. He'd sent his buddy to do his dirty work, left him standing alone, and now Miles wouldn't talk to him.

His own *mom* had called him a douche bag. And she was right. He'd sold his soul for fame. As if fame could make your life everything you wanted it to be.

"Are you okay?" Kady said, squeezing his hands tightly, as if potentially breaking his metacarpus would distract him from the pain of abandonment. "We had so much fun, and if I was staying, there's no way this would happen. You're a great guy. You'll find a new girl in no time."

"Don't worry about it," Jake said, squeezing her hands back. He couldn't be mad at her. His status as dumpee was inevitable. He was lucky to even be in the position of getting dumped.

It had been fun. She was right on that. And maybe in some world, he was the kind of great guy who'd find a girl in no time. But without a new role coming up—and probably with a lifelong grounding and a pissed-off best friend—he somehow doubted his social life was going to be awesome from here on out.

CHARMED, I'M SURE

Myla held still as one of the *Class Angel* makeup artists carefully applied a dusting of highlighter to her cheekbones. She had to admit, the VIP tent for the party more than met her standards.

Guys in dark jeans with Reavis High jackets open to expose their chiseled, glitter-coated chests were giving neck and shoulder rubs, while the hair and makeup staff offered up their expertise. As a woman who looked twelve but had the voice of Kathleen Turner worked on her face, a flamboyant guy in a pink suit curled individual tendrils of Myla's hair, pinning them in a sexy, messy arrangement along her head. A lot of the BHH guys were in the tent next door, which was fully stocked with unreleased video games and girls in skimpy angel costumes offering massages and reflexology.

Myla was trying her best to relax, after no word from Ash since the beach party. She'd heard from Jojo via Tucker that Ash had been spending time with Daisy, which seemed to bode well. Of course, she had no solid reason to believe Ash would kiss Daisy and come running back to her. But she also had no reason to believe her plan *wouldn't* work. In one of her favorite scenarios, Ash, about to kiss Daisy, stopped just before contact, and realized that Myla had been telling the truth and that the kiss with Lewis had been less than meaningless.

Myla had taken extra care to look perfect when Ash arrived. She'd worn his favorite perfume, Harajuku Lovers Music, and his favorite color, green, in the form of an Alice + Olivia draped V-neck minidress. With her hair pulled up, her delicate neck and shoulder blades were exposed. She even had her Green Lantern ring, strung on a new gold chain, tucked into her violet Marc Jacobs clutch, for him to loop around her neck when they got back together. Her mom had received the clutch, covered in dozens of cutout hearts, today, and Myla took the hearts as a sign that tonight was her and Ash's night. It had to be.

"You have amazing bone structure," the makeup artist said in her husky voice. "So refined." Myla half-smiled in thanks, flicking her eyes to the mirror on the table next to her. Talia, Billie, and Fortune approached behind her. Even though they'd made no attempts to talk since she'd ditched them in the cafeteria, now all three girls looked as frightened as kindergartners left behind on a field trip. Clearly, Myla's closeness with Jojo had gotten to them, and they were worried their absence hadn't been missed.

"You really do," Talia said, her apologetic frown contrasting with the cheery retro print of her Juicy paisley silk dress. "I wish I had cheekbones like yours."

"I read that one of the most popular plastic surgeries with teens is to get Myla's cheekbones," Fortune said, trying to one-up Talia. "*Teen Vogue*, I think."

Billie bounced on the balls of her feet, looking ready to throw herself in Myla's arms for a hug. She nervously grabbed a handful of her short, gathered Thakoon skirt, printed with tiny pink petals. "We're so sorry for the last few weeks," Billie said, looking on the verge of tears. "And for not listening to you about Grant."

Myla shrugged. In a way, her friends' sudden ass-kissing for forgiveness was annoying. They were acting like they'd left *her* stranded. Which they had, right when she'd needed them. But she'd never have admitted that. Still, she felt warmed by their urgent need to apologize. "I could have helped you if you'd asked. Amelie's soup kitchen didn't work?"

"He didn't show. And he's not here tonight." Talia sighed heavily, flopping into the seat next to Myla's. "I can't believe Amelie lied to us and dragged us to that place," she said, wrinkling her nose. She picked up a makeup brush and swirled it absently into a container of powder. "I've never seen that many homeless people in one place, Myla. Even in Santa Monica. And then tonight Amelie tried to act all, 'Who cares if Grant's not here? We have each other.' Yeah, right. She was totally just using us."

Myla nodded triumphantly.

"Anyway, we really missed you," Fortune said. "Can I give you a hug?"

"Of course," Myla said, a sense of calm flowing through her body as Fortune smothered her in a hug and the other girls followed suit, a tangle of spray-tanned limbs, perfume, and hair products. But Myla drank it all in. She'd been feeling untethered in the weeks since her friends started drifting. Coupled with Ash's distance, she felt like everyone was abandoning her. Jojo didn't count. Because as much as Myla was starting to love her new sister, she knew Jojo would always be there. Jojo depended on Myla for everything—style, confidence, even a boyfriend. She wasn't going anywhere.

"Thanks guys," she said, drawing back from the hug. "Now, I was about to get a manicure. Do you want to join me?" She was careful to play the part of Old Myla, girl in charge. Showing too much emotion would be like displaying her weaknesses for the world to see.

The girls clapped and squealed with such enthusiasm, Myla thought they would break into an impromptu chorus of "Kumbaya."

The manicurist had just removed Myla's practically fresh violet coat of OPI Caffeine Fix when someone tapped her on the shoulder. Ash. He'd found her. Maybe all the pieces of her jigsawed life *were* going to be put back together tonight. She looked up, anxious to be staring into Ash's teddy bear eyes.

Instead, she got Jojo's violet eyes, peering down at her. Jojo's gaze shifted to Talia, seated in the manicure chair next to her. Talia smiled perkily but resumed giving orders to her manicurist. Jojo shrugged, and rolled up another manicure chair between Talia and Myla.

She plopped down, spinning the chair so she could have a private audience with Myla. All of Myla's fair-weather friends had returned, Jojo noticed. After all this time of having Myla all to herself, Jojo wasn't crazy about suddenly having to share her.

"You will never believe what just happened," Jojo

whispered, raising one eyebrow. She knew Myla would be surprised at first to hear that she'd dumped Tucker, but proud of Jojo for not putting up with a complete ass. "I dumped Tucker."

"You did what?" Myla's face was not the curious, bemused one Jojo was expecting. She just looked confused. "Why?"

Jojo shook her head as if to say, *Why not?* She looked seriously into Myla's eyes, ignoring Talia and the girls, who were already talking in hushed tones about Jojo and Tucker's split. "One, I don't know if he was ever really right for me. And two, about twenty minutes ago he decided this party needed a wet T-shirt contest. It almost cost me my Prada." Jojo gestured to her cream sundress.

"Is that seriously why you *dumped* the second-most popular guy in school? Why didn't you consult me first?"

"You're joking, right?" Jojo said, her eyes flicking to Talia, Billie, and Fortune. They watched with casual detachment, like Jojo was a minor character on a teen soap who was about to be killed off.

Myla rolled her eyes and patted Jojo's arm in faux sympathy. She wasn't planning to exile Jojo or anything, but she also didn't want her friends to see she'd formed a serious bond with Jojo in the short time they'd spent apart. Besides, for the girls to know she'd made a faulty Jojo-Tucker match was no good at all. To her friends, Myla's blessing a relationship was more powerful than the pope on Easter.

"Look, if you can't control your boyfriend, it's not

my problem," Myla said, turning back and extending a hand so the manicurist could keep working.

Jojo felt her whole body quake. She scanned the seats on either side of Myla, where Billie, Talia, and Fortune sat placidly, looking at her like they weren't sure what she was doing here now that the Fantastic Four had been reunited.

It dawned on Jojo that they knew better than she did. All the time, she had been nothing more than a project for Myla, a way to pass the time while her friends' attention was elsewhere.

Myla hadn't been helping Jojo. She'd been helping herself. She'd made Jojo dress like her, talk like her, walk like her. She'd made her squelch her feelings for a guy she actually liked—Jake—and pimped her out to a guy she didn't. And Jojo had gone along with it. Thinking about how willingly she'd gone along with Myla's scheme, Jojo hated herself almost as much as she hated Myla right now. She'd lied to Willa, her best friend in the world. The only true friend she'd ever had. Who didn't even want to be her friend anymore.

Jojo felt words pile up in her throat, like those last few moves on a Tetris game when the shapes are falling so fast you know you're going to lose.

"You know what? This is it. Thus endeth the lessons," Jojo said, hovering over Myla in the four-inch heels that were killing her. "I'm not some experiment. I'm not some robot you can dress like you and teach to talk like you and to act like you." Jojo cast a meaningful look at Talia, Billie, and Fortune, who looked like shelved marionette puppets with their mouths hanging open.

Myla sighed, as though bored, but wrenched her hand out from under the nail tech's cotton ball. She stood up, straightening her back so she was nearly Jojo's height, wishing Jojo were in flats.

"You know what? You're lucky—I took an interest in you," Myla sneered, already sick of Jojo's ungrateful tirade. "If it weren't for me, you'd still be Miss Sacrademento who can't hold her liquor. How could you be so ungrateful?"

Jojo cocked her head bitchily to the side, a move Myla recognized as one of her own. "Should I be *thanking* you?" Billie was texting wildly, probably live-blogging the showdown. "Shouldn't you be thanking *me?* I was fun for a while, right? A little project to keep you busy while you waited for your loyal subjects to come running back. 'Oh, Jojo will be so happy to have her life hijacked while I wait for my BFFs to get bored with Amelie Adams.'"

Myla took a step forward, so that she and Jojo were mere inches away. Jabbing her sister's chest with her polishless index finger, she spat out her words. "Whatever, BarfBarf. I didn't hear you complaining when I lent you my shoes, or took you shopping, or taught you how to walk upright instead of like some Central California cavewoman. Yakking on YouTube is about as entertaining as you'll get."

Jojo shook her head, willing herself not to stammer in front of the crowd that had gathered. Myla's friends, the manicurists, and dozens of other students were staring.

"You just don't get it, do you?" Jojo said. "You should appreciate all the people in this world who see enough in you that they're willing to put up with your shit. Instead, you think they're worthless unless you can make them do anything you want them to. As if having you pull the strings and call the shots makes them the luckiest people on earth. You know your rule, 'It's not you, it's them'? Myla, in your case, it's all *you*. You screw up the only things worth having, for, I don't know what, popularity? Power? You probably don't even know. But you can have it." Jojo yanked off the painful Stuart Weitzman platform heels Myla had lent her and dropped them at her sister's feet. "And you can have your shoes back."

Myla stared at the shoes like they were a pair of dead rats. She couldn't believe Jojo had the nerve to take her on in front of the entire school. And she couldn't believe she was letting it happen. But worst of all, what if what Jojo was saying was true? She pursed her lips and fanned her gaze around the nosy onlookers. Glaring at Jojo, she said, "You have no idea who you're messing with. You're over."

Myla expected tears. But instead, Jojo shook her head, looked over Myla's shoulder, and grinned.

"Okay, Myla," Jojo said, in a sincerely sweet voice. "Good luck with that. And good luck with Ash." Then she winked, and spun on her bare heel, striding out of the party.

Myla took a deep breath, hoping the oxygen would purify her. That was done, at least. For now. She should have known better than to reach out to Jojo. She'd created a monster.

But she didn't have the chance to breathe for long, because coming toward her was Ash.

With Daisy Morton. Holding hands.

Make that two monsters.

Ash caught her eye and whispered in Daisy's ear. Myla strode in their direction, too wobbly to look any of her friends or classmates in the eye. There was an explanation for this. There had to be. Maybe Daisy was wasted again, and the hand-holding was just a maneuver to keep her from passing out.

"Hi, Ash," Myla said, trying to control her shaky voice. She examined Daisy, expecting to find a trail of dry drool layered over caked-on makeup. She was a collage of *odd*: strands of hair dyed green and hot pink, shiny bright blue eye makeup, and a bizarre ruffled T-shirt dress worn over knee-high athletic socks and sequined Chuck Taylors. But Myla could tell she was pretty beneath the makeup, with silvery eyes and surprisingly clear skin. She glowed, even as she let go of Ash's hand and smiled faintly at Myla.

Ash seemed to glow, too. His shaggy hair was in its optimal default mode, a fringe of amber falling over his left eye. Right now, Myla was the center of attention, a position she'd never occupied as unwillingly as she did tonight.

"Can we talk?" Ash said, his voice more sympathetic than apologetic. Myla already knew what was coming. The void in her stomach was the same emptiness she'd felt when she was seven and Lailah had convinced her to give one of the poor kids in India her favorite American Girl doll, Izzy. She'd done it, hoping to feel good, but instead had felt Izzy's absence for months afterward. And now she'd given Ash away too. She'd hoped to put them on even ground, only to find that the ground had been ripped out from under her.

"You don't have to explain," Myla said, quietly at first, steeling herself to fight back the tears. All along, in some faint and ignored part of her, she'd known this was coming from the second she'd told him to kiss someone else. But she'd listened to the other part, the part that told her that having a plan was better than letting life keep you waiting. This was Ash's fault. If he had just believed her that the Lewis night was meaningless, she would have never had to make this idiotic bargain with him. And *he'd* been the one to tell her how disgusting Daisy was. With the world watching as hers fell apart, Myla summoned a memory.

"I thought you stood for something," she said, remembering what he'd told her on his birthday. She smirked into Ash's face, watching his eyes widen in panic as he recalled what came next. "Didn't you say you liked musicians who were about integrity?" She ticked off the words on her fingers, gleefully noticing Daisy's confused look. "Quality? Actual musical skills? So you cleaned her up, but is she talented enough for you? Or are you just like everyone else, captivated by a train wreck?"

She paused for a second. Everyone was silent. The perfect time for the knockout blow. "What else was it you said? You were stuck with her against your will? But look who's holding hands with a train wreck. Go ahead and ride that train all you want."

She took her eyes off Ash, raising an eyebrow at Daisy. She knew it was cruel. Daisy hadn't technically done anything wrong. But she wasn't going to let another girl take away her favorite thing without a fight.

Daisy's smile melted, her gray eyes narrowing—but

not at Myla. She stared at Ash like he was a stranger. And then she backed away from him.

Daisy stormed off, using the same beaten path as Jojo. Ash bit his lip, looking at Myla coldly. The way he'd looked when he saw her kissing Lewis had been bad, but this look . . . this look had *unforgivable* written all over it.

"If you think that just because she won't have me, you can, you're wrong," Ash said, as he moved in the direction Daisy had gone. "Maybe when we were going out, you could manage my life for me. But we're over, and if anyone's gonna screw my shit up, it's going to be me."

With that, he walked off too.

Myla tallied herself as 0-for-2 in the last words category. And 0-for-1,000,000 in the chance that she'd ever be happy again.

PLAY IT AGAIN, ASH

Jake trudged toward his car, feeling more tired than he had in days. Maybe it had been the movie, or having a girlfriend, or being the star of his own life for once that had made him impervious to fatigue. But now, with the movie over and Kady gone—really gone—he felt every ounce of energy draining out of him.

Maybe he just needed to eat some carbohydrates, though. Because, weirdly enough, he wasn't broken-hearted about Kady dumping him. If anything, he felt kind of like a normal guy for once—he'd actually been with a girl, and it hadn't worked out. It was like a badge of honor. He'd high-fived with football players, sneaked out of his house, and gotten dumped, all in the space of a day.

He arrived at the visitors' parking lot, seeing his Corolla crammed into a spot between two monster Escalades. Sitting on the curb near the valet turnaround was Ash Gilmour, his head in his hands, his hair tufted into spikes of frustration.

It was oddly quiet, the party noises muffled by the high hedges that surrounded the parking lot.

"Hey, dude," Jake said, looking down on his next-door neighbor. Ash looked like he'd lost his dog, his best friend, and a bet. Maybe he had.

Ash looked up at him, his face registering surprise. "Jake, hey, you're leaving early."

Jake chuckled. "Yeah, well, I have one weekend to catch up on two weeks of homework."

"Oh, the movie," Ash said, grateful to talk about anything but the fact that Daisy had run out on him. He'd followed her to the parking lot, but she was gone. He needed to go home and think. Hearing Myla say the awful things he'd said had made him feel like a shitty, judgmental prick. And it had cost him the girl he liked, one who made getting over Myla seem like a distinct possibility.

"Yeah, the movie," Jake said. "The teachers don't care if I'm Jake or Tommy Archer. Deadlines are deadlines. So, do you want a ride home? I'm going that way."

"Cool," Ash said, heaving himself off the curb. He walked toward one of the Escalades.

"Um, no, the Corolla is me," Jake said sheepishly, wondering if Ash would decide to just wait instead of going home in his powder blue Dorkmobile.

Ash grinned. "Keeping it real, Goldsmith," he said. "Nice."

Sinking into the passenger seat, Ash toyed with the tape deck as Jake pulled away from the lot. As they drove through the Transnational gates, Ash ran his hands over the tape deck controls. "Retro. Kinda cool. I sort of think iPods are killing albums. Well, I didn't think it. I read it in *Rolling Stone*. But still. Is it cool if I turn it on?"

"Yeah, sure," Jake said, praying he didn't have some lame Duran Duran cassette in there.

Ash punched play, and after a few seconds of silence the sound of Queen's "You're My Best Friend" poured out.

Even though the song was about a girlfriend, or one of Freddie Mercury's boyfriends, Ash smirked at the memory of him and Jacob singing along to the song together as kids.

"Remember how we thought this was, like, a best-friend song? And not a love song?" Ash said, staring at the looming semitruck rumbling up the freeway entrance in the next lane.

Jake laughed, merging into traffic. "Remember how when we hung out, we didn't like girls? I'm thinking that we should bring that back."

Ash sighed, his eyes on the hills misted with clouds far on the horizon. "Yeah, tell me about it."

"I know that was rhetorical, but I'll tell you anyway," Jake said, sighing. "Kady dumped me to go film a new movie overseas. I have no skills. I guess just because you play big man on campus doesn't mean you are one." He wondered if school would really be any different on Monday, or if he'd go back to being lame Jacob PG again. Or worse, lame Jacob PG who got dumped by Kady Parker.

"Hey, supposedly I'm some kind of big man on campus. Which actually sounds like a totally douche bag thing to be. And it didn't help me. The girl I liked just found out the asshole remark I made about her before I got to know her. And she ran off."

"Wow, we sound like an episode of *Dr. Phil*, huh?" Jake said.

"Next on *Dr. Phil*: 'How to Be a Douche Bag,' with Ash Gilmour and Jake Porter-Goldsmith," Ash said in an announcer's voice.

Jake laughed. "No, but seriously, that sucks, dude," he said, trying not to look up as he drove beneath a billboard for Kady's next horror movie, *The Unwanted*. "If it makes you feel any better, Kady's going to Prague. She better be in that movie, or I'm going to think she dumped me in the most elaborate way possible."

Ash smirked, opening the glove box to check for other tapes. "She wouldn't make that up. At least you can tell yourself she left because she had to, not because she thinks you're a total piece of shit." *And because your ex is a complete psycho who wants your life without her to be absolute misery,* Ash thought.

Jake squinted sideways at Ash. "A total piece of shit? Three-quarters, maybe, but not total." He worried for a split second that Ash would think the joke was lame. But Ash laughed.

"What's more than three-quarters?"

"Seven-eighths," Jake said automatically.

"Then I'm that," Ash said. "I said that I had to hang out with her against my will. Which was a little true, at first. But then I started to like her." Ash swallowed as he imagined what Daisy was doing now. He'd wanted so badly to protect her, and then he'd been the one to hurt her the worst, after all her ex-boyfriend drama with that punk musician. He just couldn't seem to get girls right these days.

"You can't not have first impressions," Jake said, pressing the brake as they got caught behind another snarl of traffic. He smiled at the memory of Kady calling him perfect. Not perfect enough to visit her in Prague, apparently. "I totally freaked Kady out. She says she's going to Prague, and I'm practically booking a honeymoon suite in some old castle. Who does that?" Jake quickly told Ash his unlikely story—that he'd crushed on Amelie, gotten in the movie, and wound up with Kady after getting lessons from Jojo. For some reason, he didn't feel weird telling Ash everything, even the Justin Klatch mantra.

"Well, you gotta try. And there's another girl out there," Ash said, laughing bitterly. He'd found his other girl, and look how that had turned out. "Just don't screw it up."

Jake moved the car through an opening in the sea of brake lights, winding down the exit to their street.

He pulled to a stop on the curb between their houses. Ash hopped out, while Jake remained in the driver's seat. A few steps onto his lawn, Ash stopped and turned back. "Hey, want to come inside, play some PS3?" He grinned. "The graphics are way better than that shit we used to play on Nintendo 64."

Jake chuckled. "Oh yeah? Was it the graphics' fault that I beat your ass at Mortal Kombat?"

Ash shook his head, laughing. "No, that was 'cause you're a total freak."

Jake tinkered with the keys hanging from the ignition. A friend would be nice right now. But he had a friend, one he had completely screwed over. One who had hunted high and low for the perfect car that now sat lonely in the driveway. One who had begged Jake to take him to the next big party, who never had a moment of disbelief or jealousy when Jake scored a date with Kady, one who'd pretty much do anything for him out of friendship, not because he wanted anything in return.

As Queen wound down the song with "You, you're my best friend," Jake knew what he had to do. As tired as he was, it was time to pay Miles a visit. To make an apology. And to grab a huge bag of In-N-Out burger with fries as both a peace offering and, thank God, the first starch to enter his system in days.

"You know, it sounds good, dude," Jake said. "But I have somewhere to be tonight. And I think you do too."

Ash nodded. "Yeah, I should probably do the whole find-her-and-tell-her-how-I-feel thing, huh?" he said, heading to his Camaro instead of his front door. "But anytime."

As Jake headed in the direction of Miles's house, he decided that "anytime" would be sometime soon.

PENCILS, BOOKS, AND DIRTY LOOKS

The day after the party, Amelie lugged her heavy Big Brown Bags through the corridors of the Beverly Center. After she wrapped filming a movie or a season of *Fairy Princess*, she and her mom always went on a shopping spree.

They passed a trio of girls about her age, all wearing nearly identical skinny jeans, high-top Vans, and tank tops—skater girl chic. Amelie eyed them jealously, watching their bright yellow Forever21 bags swing back and forth on their wrists. They'd probably just had more normal teenage fun in the fitting rooms than she'd had in her whole life.

"Are you getting too old to shop with your mom?" Helen said, shoving her Aveda receipt into her plaid Burberry tote. "Maybe you'd rather have called your girlfriends from Beverly Hills High, or Kady?"

Amelie grinned wanly. She didn't feel too old to shop with her mom at all, though she did sometimes wish she had a few girlfriends to call for these trips. Not only had Talia, Fortune, and Billie swarmed Myla the second they'd realized Grant wasn't coming, they'd left Amelie talking to the dullest adult in the room, the school principal, Dr. Nachez. They hadn't looked her way again all night.

Her other potential shopping buddy, Kady, was headed to Prague. But, Amelie had decided, she *was* a friend. Last night, Kady had pulled her aside just as Amelie was making her way out and told her that she'd broken up with Jake.

"I can't do the long-distance romance thing, Amelie," she'd said. "It's just not me. And Prague has an amazing club scene, tons of natives and backpackers just partying till dawn. If I'd hooked up with someone else while dating Jake, I would never forgive myself."

Amelie's face had borne a mixture of pleasure and surprise. Pleasure that he was free. Surprise that she'd be stupid enough to let Jake go. "Are you sure you want to do that?" she'd asked Kady.

"OMG. Do you like him?" Kady had slapped her forehead like she should have seen it coming. "I should have guessed. I'm usually good at those things. I saw your bliss face when you kissed him. That's the kind of face a girl only gets when she's getting a Balinese massage at the Four Seasons or is kissing a guy she's gaga for. But I guess I thought it was just acting. Still, you should have seen how dazed he was after that kiss."

The words had cheered Amelie exponentially. But what would she do? Call him? And she fretted about all the changes his recent fame had wrought. Would he ever like her if he became the Next Big Thing? What chance did they have for a normal relationship?

Instead of answering her mom, Amelie grabbed Helen's wrist and steered her into the Ben Sherman store. A song from the new Shout Out Louds' album was blaring, as salespeople milled around modeling the label's punk rock–meets–prep school aesthetic. It was all very Kady, and Amelie wanted a reminder of her friend after she left. She wanted to be as brave and as open as Kady. A little less wild, though "wild" was probably not in Amelie's makeup, but more willing to do things because she wanted to, and not because it was what someone else expected of her.

Amelie began scanning the racks of sweaters, jumpers, skirts, and dresses, picking out a gray miniskirt with angled zippers along the sides and a funky blouse with white cuffs and a tuxedo ruffle down the center. She could wear black eyeliner in the smudgy way Kady had taught her, and get blunt bangs cut. Bangs were the mark of courageous girls, Amelie had decided after her days of studying BHH's student body.

Helen came up at Amelie's side, a blazer draped over her arm. It was navy, very prep school style, with a Union Jack crest embroidered on the left pocket.

"Try this on," Helen said, holding out the hanger, blowing a wisp of hair out of her mascaraed lashes.

Amelie studied the coat. "I have so many jackets, though."

"Just try it. For me." Helen took the coat off the hanger and handed it to Amelie. Her mom's hazel eyes watched expectantly as Amelie slid out of her cardigan and threw the jacket on over her dress. It was cute, with a nipped-in waist, and double vents so it rested perfectly over her hips. Amelie turned side to side in the mirror, appeasing her mom.

"That looks great on you, love," called out a salesguy whose hair had been plastered with so much product his scalp might crack.

Helen nodded approvingly. "I think it would be perfect for your first day of school."

"What do you mean?" Was this a joke?

Helen took a step closer and put a hand on each of her daughter's shoulders. "I think I was too quick to turn you down," she said. "It was selfish of me. I got a call this morning, from Dr. Nachez."

Dr. Nachos, Amelie thought, suppressing a giggle.

"I guess he spoke to you last night and was really impressed," Helen said, beaming. "He said you're very levelheaded for a girl who's been in this business for so long, and said you expressed a real interest in academics."

She had? Amelie remembered listening politely—a skill acquired through tons of eternal chat sessions with the middle-aged at parties—as Dr. Nachez talked about test scores, student-to-teacher ratio, and the benefits of an education that covered the arts *and* sciences. Amelie barely remembered it now, but she'd probably rattled off some of the facts and viewpoints she'd learned at many an education fund-raiser.

"He said BHH could use a role model like you," Helen continued. "And promised me he'd do his best to help you maintain your career. You'd probably work a little less, or maybe just do *Fairy Princess*. Kidz Network said you could shoot full episodes on weekends."

Amelie couldn't believe all the details were already worked out. Apparently, Helen was a better momager, and mom, than she'd ever realized. "So you're going to let me go to school?" Amelie said, filled with pleasant jitters. She'd have real textbooks, not just tutoring worksheets. And an English class where she could answer questions about her favorite literature. She wondered if they'd read *Jane Eyre* yet. She'd have a locker. She pictured Jake leaning against it, waiting for her between classes.

Helen nodded. "I enrolled you this morning. You're now a BHH Knight. You even get a sweatshirt, because I made a booster club donation."

Amelie couldn't believe it. She was going to BHH. She was going to be *normal*. As normal as a girl could be at a school like Beverly Hills High, anyway. She stared at her face in the mirror. No bangs. She wanted to look studious. Maybe she'd trade contacts for glasses, the dark-framed kind that made her look smarter.

She squealed and spun around, grabbing her mom in a hug. "Thank you, thank you, thank you!"

Helen squeezed her tight. "You're welcome," she said. "But remember, this isn't something to take lightly. This is about education. Dr. Nachez said you seemed more levelheaded than the rest of the student body. So I don't want to hear that you're putting off homework to chase boys."

Amelie knew she wouldn't be chasing boys. Boys plural, anyway.

For her, there was only the one.

EX-DIVAS' SWAN SONGS

Jake stuffed the last of his textbooks into his straining backpack, each heavy addition bringing him more back down to earth.

It was amazing what a weekend could do. He was grounded, for his tantrum and for sneaking out. His Escalade had been returned and the lease canceled. The bulk of his *Class Angel* money had been placed in his college fund. He was single. But at least he and Miles were friends again, though he could tell Miles was still a little hurt. As soon as his grounding was up, Jake was going to take him comic shopping and buy him a little peace offering.

He was definitely out of the movie business. After Jake's little episode last week, his mom had put out an all-points bulletin to every agent she knew, telling them and their colleagues that Jacob Porter-Goldsmith was not allowed to have representation or any further film offers. He had been offered a one-episode gig on *Bromance*, as a clueless underling that Brody Jenner would take under his girl-groping wing, but his mom had picked up the phone and given MTV a stern talking-to. It had to be the first time in film history that a young star turned down a role because his mommy wouldn't let him take it.

It was fine with him, in a way. Plowing through a few weeks' worth of physics and math homework made him conscious of how much he actually missed school. And his English teacher was starting his "science fiction as literature" series, starting with Kurt Vonnegut's *Cat's Cradle*, followed by Philip K. Dick stories—they'd be comparing the original text to the film versions, and it didn't really get any better than that. If he'd gotten anything out of his stardom, it was that he now felt fairly comfortable with his geekdom. And that, he thought, was what Justin Klatch would do.

As if to prove things were really back to normal, the words *Now You're Really PG!* were scrawled in red on his locker. Someone had gone the extra mile and cut a pair of angel wings and a halo from construction paper and glued them to the door. A note poked through the vents. *From your friends at pep club! Congrats on the movie!* Okay, so it was embarrassing, but they'd come in peace for a change. *That* was the only perk of fame he'd like to keep.

As she headed to her Spanish class, Jojo realized things were quiet at BHH today. And not lazy, rainy Monday quiet. She was sure her classmates were talking about her. Or would be, as soon as Myla crafted a rumor to explain how Jojo had gone from Myla's closest confidante to the female equivalent of a No Fucking Way boy.

The weekend had been a lonely one for Jojo, since Willa still wasn't taking her calls—after tons of begging, Jojo had tried Myla's tactic. But apparently, an *I'm sorry* arrangement of designer baked goods and specialty candies from Dylan's Candy Bar in New York did not make up for lying to your best friend either. Jojo had spent the weekend pretending she had a ton of home-work. She'd had her first two-hour-long conversation with her dads, Fred and Bradley, in days—they'd gotten a Mac with a webcam. Both of them had horrible colds, and their noses were like Rudolph's on her screen. She'd gone to Saturday and Sunday night dinners with her parents and the kids, while Myla had gone out with her girlfriends.

The two days away from Myla had been good for her, though. She'd spent her first few weeks in L.A. desperately trying to make Myla like her and her second two weeks trying desperately to be like Myla. And she just wasn't that girl. She wasn't sure who she was, exactly, but she had a feeling the real Jojo resided somewhere between the soccer-playing, goofing-around-with-Willa version and the focus-on-my-fabulosity model.

She lugged her backpack, overloaded with books in true PM (pre-Myla) fashion, past classmates who seemed unsure whether to say hi, mock her, or hide from her. She turned down the hallway toward her Spanish class, and saw Jake Porter-Goldsmith struggling to cram another book in his backpack. Speaking of No Fucking Way boys . . .

Her heart sped up a little too fast for her liking. After all, this guy had been dating Kady Parker and shooting love scenes with Amelie Adams for the last few weeks. But it couldn't hurt to say hi.

"Don't you have someone to carry those for you?"

she joked, sidling up to Jake's locker just as he shut the door. She broke out in the half-smile she couldn't seem to give up. She felt like it had been her smile all along. There'd been some positives from the Myla makeover.

"Hey, Jojo," Jake said, blushing as Jojo looked at the girlish graffiti. "What's going on?"

Jojo shrugged, focusing her violet eyes intently on his hazel ones. She noticed a green, heart-shaped fleck on his left iris. "You tell me, Mr. Movie Star."

Jake laughed, looking sheepish. "Those days are past me already. I didn't even get to fade away. I did a supernova." He looked nervously down at his Chuck Taylors. "Um, that means exploded." *And it was kind of my fault*, Jake thought, still not believing that a week ago, he'd been wearing sunglasses indoors and letting himself be referred to as Kake. He must have subconsciously wanted to live out his superstar days in one heavily compacted burst, just so he could go back to normal.

Jojo ran her hand up and down her backpack strap, the nylon making a faint scratching noise. "I know. I had a field trip to the Griffith Observatory last week. When you were busy with the whole leading-man thing."

"Yeah, some leading man," Jake said, pushing one of his unruly curls from his face. "But in case I never said it, thanks. Your Justin Klatch advice really worked."

Jojo fake-punched Jake in the arm, wondering even as she did it why she was acting like such a dork. Her gaze fell on the red writing on Jake's locker. "What about your advice to me? Shouldn't you be scrubbing your locker?"

Jake bit his lip. "No, that's actually a good thing. From the pep club. It's just kind of weird, right?" He grinned goofily. Having his existence acknowledged at school actually felt pretty good.

"No, it's not," Jojo said, touching one of the angel wings. "It's about time you got some respect at this school, Porter-Goldsmith. Even if you kind of went over to the douche side."

Jake's face turned the same red as his backpack. "I did bag on my best friend," he said. He wanted to say it out loud, because he still hadn't fully forgiven himself for the shitty way he'd treated Miles.

"I was just teasing you," Jojo said, worrying she'd taken it too far. In her heart, she knew the movie star Jake of *Class Angel* hadn't been the real Jake who she'd come to know and like. "But it happens to the best of us." She shook her head, thinking of Willa and knowing exactly what he meant. Was best-friend ditchage a side effect of the charmed life? Couldn't you be fabulous *and* a decent person? Maybe she could try that next. "Anyway, I'll forgive you if you walk me to class." She looked up at him with her flirtiest stare.

Jake brightened. "You sure you want to be seen with PG?" He reached out, and adjusted her backpack so that it sat straight on her shoulder. Jojo felt a tickle dance along her collarbone.

"I'm sure."

NO PICNIC

Myla sat in her usual chair at the best table in the cafeteria, her boxy Prada bag on a chair of its own. Fortune had insisted she not let the buttery leather touch the table.

Things were back to normal. Or, back to two-weeks-ago normal. No signs of *Class Angel* remained, save for a crappy advance movie poster that hung outside Dr. Nachos's office. And her friends were still in full ass-kiss mode. This weekend, they'd taken her for a spa day at Bliss (their treat) and then rented a bunch of her favorite movies—*Vertigo*, *Clueless*, *Mean Girls*, and the BBC version of *Pride & Prejudice*—to watch in Fortune's family's screening room.

She hadn't seen Jojo all weekend. In fact, she'd carefully avoided her sister. Jojo was once again her mortal enemy, but Myla was stumped when it came to a suitable revenge plot. It had to be special, somehow, worthy of the terrible things Jojo had said. But nothing was coming. She'd passed Jojo in the lunch line, her tray loaded with Myla-forbidden fries. Even with the perfect opportunity to start a nasty round of whispers, Myla had come up blank.

She hadn't seen Ash, either. She kept glancing across the caf toward his table, but saw only Tucker, Geoff, and his other friends. Ash must have been eating in the music lab, a privilege he'd earned after Gordon donated an ungodly amount to the department. Last year, they'd had weekly picnics in the room, kissing and cuddling and having a hard time pulling away from each other once the bell for class rang.

Myla shuddered, picturing Daisy in her place on the plaid picnic blanket. She got what Ash had meant about being haunted. Everywhere she looked, anytime she saw a couple holding hands, she pictured Ash and Daisy, bound together. It was worse than if she'd seen them drunkenly making out. Or if she'd learned Ash had hooked up with some common skank, like Cassie "Easy" Eastman. To torture herself, Myla had played Daisy's songs on her iPod while she got her massage at Bliss. She couldn't compete. The masseuse had ended the session saying, "I work out a knot, it comes back. You have to learn to let go."

But she wouldn't let go. Her glimmer of hope lay in Daisy running from Ash at the party.

She picked at her honey-turkey-and-gouda panini, listening to the rain patter against the roof, an echo of the rhythmic downpour ringing in her ears. The rain was picking up speed, which meant every news station in L.A. would lead with a story called "Storm Watch." Thunder rumbled and then a crack of lightning erupted, casting a split-second flash of blue light over the entire cafeteria.

As if on cue, Myla's cell vibrated, quivering back and forth on her tray. Maybe she was being obsessive, but she'd set a Google Alert for "Daisy Morton." Her first one had arrived. The top headline, from TMZ, read *Crazy About Daisy*. She clicked it open.

Beneath it was a photo of Ash and Daisy leaving BLD, a cute, newish café near the Grove. The photo was a little out-of-focus, but she could clearly make out Ash's hair and Daisy's smile. They were holding hands again, and Myla felt like the lightning had struck her through the heart. Myla caught Fortune's eyes as they shifted to the story still on Myla's screen. She placed her phone, the picture still on-screen, in the center of the table. Her friends were jonesing for a gossip fix and fought each other to look at the story.

Myla felt her lip trembling and she fought back tears. *I did this to myself, didn't I?* she thought, stunned to even think it. It wasn't her style to take the blame. In a panic, she mentally scrolled through anyone else who could take the fall. Ash's dad, who had put Ash on Daisy detail in the first place. Her friends, for not being there when she needed them. Ash, for being so unwilling to trust her. Jojo, who could have told her the kiss-someone-else idea was bad from the get-go. But wouldn't she have told Jojo she was too untrained to know what she was talking about? Myla pushed her lunch tray away, unable to look at the food she hadn't touched anyway. She didn't even want to think about what she could have done differently. She needed to know what she could do next. And not "next" in her plot to get Ash back. Nope, "next" as in helping her survive the next few seconds. "What am I going to do?"

Talia shrugged, reading the story. "It says you should start dating someone else. Ooh! We should go to the Kress. It's sooo hot right now. Girls' night!"

Fortune clapped excitedly. "Omigod! Speaking of girls' nights, did you guys hear about Grant?" She whispered. "He got arrested with a prostitute in Hollywood."

Billie almost spit out her smoothie. "Eeew! Why would he get a hooker when he could have us?"

Myla deleted the TMZ post on her phone and shoved it into her bag. Her friends might be experts at spa sessions, clubbing, and all the other things girls with broken hearts were supposed to do to recover. But trying to actually *talk* to them only made her feel worse.

Myla hugged her bad-day sweater around her, collecting as much warmth as she could from the soft gray cashmere. But her whole body still felt cold. If Daisy could forgive Ash his nasty comments, Ash and Daisy must have something meaningful. "What if they're in love?" Myla said aloud, unable to stop herself from saying what she was thinking.

Fortune rolled her eyes. "Who cares, My? You guys have been broken up for weeks. Maybe now you'll finally start dating again. Single Myla is getting old, don't you think?"

Myla wanted to shove her plate away and storm off— but she couldn't. Without Ash, she *needed* her friends. A tinkling, familiar laugh wove around the now-faster rainfall. Myla cast a glance in the direction of the sound to see Jojo sitting with Miles Abelson and Jacob PG. For a second, their eyes met, but Jojo quickly looked away.

She would listen. *She* knew how to make Myla feel better. She'd probably see right through Myla, but in a good way. In the way she needed desperately to be seen right now. As a terrified, heartbroken, and lonely girl who never wanted anyone to see her terrified, heartbroken, or alone. She'd driven away Jojo the same way she had Ash. She was an expert at hurting people more than they could hurt her. She'd just never realized how badly she could hurt herself.

"Myla . . . hey, wake up," Talia snapped her fingers in front of Myla's face. "Did you hear me? We're going to hit Bebe and Bloomie's after school, to get new outfits for the Kress this weekend. Remember what you always say, 'The only things you need in this world are fabulous clothes and a place to be seen in them.'"

The words hit Myla like a blunt object as she realized that she'd asked for this, just like she'd asked for every nightmare of the last few weeks. Her friends were well trained. Being around her long enough had taught them to act like and treat her like the girl she thought she should be: cool, calm, purposeful, and never willing to let her guard down. They'd soaked up all her maxims, and Myla-isms. Probably too well. Jojo had been the only one smart enough to get out.

As a clap of thunder cracked her heart into even smaller pieces, Myla wished the rain would fall hard enough to wash away all the parts of her she didn't like. Because Jojo had been right.

It wasn't them. It was her.

Blair Waldorf, Serena van der Woodsen,

Nate Archibald, Dan Humphrey, and

Vanessa Abrams went off to live their lives.

Now, they're coming home for the holidays.

A lot can change in a few months . . .

but some things never do.

Turn the page for a sneak peek of

I will always love you

a new gossip girl hardcover
featuring the original cast

Disclaimer: All the real names of places, people, and events have been altered or abbreviated to protect the innocent. Namely, me.

Hey people!

The more things change, the more they stay the same.

For years, New York City—the center of the universe, the place where anything can happen—was our home. But we've moved beyond our uniform-required, single sex schools and into bastions of higher education around the country. Yes, it finally happened: we went to college. For the past few months, we've been surrounded by people who don't know who we've hooked up with, who don't remember the time we wet our pants on the playground in kindergarten. We've learned new things and made new friends and maybe even met the loves our lives. We've changed.

Or at least, *some* of us have. Others are just as fabulous as always. Take **B,** heading to Vermont to spend a perfect holiday with her perfect Yale boyfriend and his perfect family. That girl always had her eye on the prize. . . . And speaking of prizes, what's rumored SAG nominee **S** doing these days? Formerly worshipped by her Constance Billard class-mates, she's now followed by paparazzi and a posse of fellow movie starlets. No matter where she is or what she does, **S** will *always* be the center of attention.

Then there are the people who've tried their hardest to change: **N** is on a sailing trip around the world. But as we all know from reading Kant in our freshman seminars, no man is an island. He'll be back. Then there's **D,** scratching out poetry in his Moleskine notebook in the Pacific Northwest. It may look like a total lifestyle change, but he still insists on Folgers instead of French press in the coffee capital of the US. He also spends every waking moment attempting to Skype his shaven-headed, ultra independent filmmaker girlfriend, **V,** who's at NYU and seems to almost . . . have *hair.* And friends. Lastly there's **C,** last seen with a pack of flannel-wearing, very rugged boys. Is he into a new type, or has he gone through yet another reinvention? That man puts Madonna to shame.

Everyone's back in town for the holidays, and this winter break is guaranteed to be filled with makeups, breakups, and shakeups. Lucky for you, I'm going to report *everything* worth reporting. Let the reunion begin.

sightings:

B on a train from New Haven to Montpelier, VT, looking very out of place in a sea of flannel . . . **S** with three identical girls, on the red carpet for a premiere. . . . **V** and some friends from NYU, including her very young, very cute teaching assistant, at a film-screening party in Bushwick. Is someone trying to get extra credit? . . . **D** and his little sister, **J,** splitting a plate of chocolate-chip pancakes at one of those curiously packed diners on upper Broadway. . . . **C** and a group of cowboy-boot clad guys ordering sodas at the lounge at the **Tribeca Star**. Ride 'em, cowboy!

Break the rules

Remember, you don't technically live under your parents' roof anymore. You've already indulged them in holiday merry-making: Scrabble with the siblings, kissing Grandma, and decorating cookies that nobody's going to eat. Which means now is the time to use all your pent-up energy to party. Remember, you can always reform after January 1st—that's what resolutions are for. So go out, have fun, and most of all, show your former besties and former flames just how much *better* you've become.

Besides, now that you know I'm watching, aren't you just dying to put on a show? Thought so.

You know you love me,

gossip girl

All B wants for Christmas

"You awake, Scout?"

Blair Waldorf awoke from a nap to the sight of her boyfriend, Pete Carlson, gazing down at her. Pete smiled his adorable, lopsided smile. His eyes were a yellowish brown and reminded Blair of her cat, Kitty Minky.

She threw the plaid Black Watch duvet to the foot of the couch and discreetly checked for drool with her index finger. She *loved* being woken up by Pete, especially when he called her by an adorable nickname. Currently, it was Scout because she'd directed him and his three older brothers to the best Douglas fir Christmas tree, deep in the woods of the Carlsons' expansive Woodstock, Vermont, estate.

"Of course I am," Blair lied, sitting up and yawning. Why sleep when her waking life was so much *better*?

"Good." Pete settled next to her on the couch, pushing Blair's long bangs tenderly off her small, foxlike face. Her hair was a little shaggier then she'd like, but she simply didn't trust any of the hair salons in New Haven. Besides, what were unkempt bangs when she was with a guy who loved her?

"Have any dreams? You were making these little growls in your sleep. It was cute." Pete pulled the blanket off the floor and draped it over their legs.

"Oh." Blair frowned. She was *growling*?

In truth, she'd been having a lot of weird dreams lately. Last night, she'd woken up and thought she was at a sleepover at her old best friend Serena van der Woodsen's house, only to find herself all alone in the guest bedroom of the Carlsons'.

Maybe it was just homesickness. After all, she hadn't seen Serena since August, she didn't have a home in New York anymore, and no one in her family was even in the United States this week. Her father, Harold, was celebrating Christmas in France with his boyfriend and their adopted twins. Her step-brother Aaron was spending the break on a kibbutz in Israel. Her mother, stepfather, brother Tyler, and baby sister Yale had moved to LA back in August, to a gigantic, tacky Pacific Pal-isades mansion that they were making even bigger and more tacky. While the renovations were taking place, they were spend-ing the holidays in the South Pacific, visiting the islands that Eleanor Rose, in a fit of pregnancy-induced mania last spring, had bought for each member of the family. Blair had been some-what tempted to tag along, if only to see her baby sister, the least fucked-up member of her tragically absurd family.

Not to mention pay a visit to Blair Island.

But once she'd been invited to spend Christmas with the Carl-sons, she felt it was her duty as a girlfriend to go.

"I was just dreaming about you. Us. I'm just so happy." Blair sighed contentedly as she gazed into the orange fire roaring in the wood-burning stove across the room. Outside, a thin blanket of snow covered the ground.

"Me too." Pete ruffled her hair and pulled her face into his for a kiss.

"You taste nice," Blair breathed, letting her body relax into Pete's muscular arms.

It was funny how things worked out. When she arrived at Yale, Blair discovered that her roommate, Alana Hoffman, sang a cappella all the time. Blair would wake up to Alana singing "Son of a Preacher Man" to her collection of teddy bears. Avoiding her room, Blair spent a lot of time in the library, where Pete was writing a paper for his Magical Realism in the Caribbean class. They'd exchanged flirty glances, and finally Pete invited her for coffee.

It was amazing how *easy* everything could be with Pete. For the first time in Blair's nineteen years, her life felt like it made sense. She loved her classes, had an adoring, handsome boy-friend, and had even found a surrogate family in the Carlsons.

For the past few days, they'd spent every waking hour with the family: his former US senator dad, Chappy; his Boston debutante mom, Jane; his three older brothers, their wives, and assorted nephews and nieces Blair couldn't even try to keep straight. It sounded like a nightmare, but it was great. His dad was barrel-chested and red-faced and told bad jokes in a way that made everyone crack up, and his mom would randomly recite poetry at the dinner table without being drunk. The brothers were friendly and smart, their wives were nice, and even the kids were polite. So far, it had been a perfect holiday.

And it was about to get even better. To celebrate the New Year, Chappy had booked the entire family at an exclusive resort in Costa Rica. Obviously, Blair could do without the rainforest adventure part, but she'd heard the beaches were pristine, the sun was hot, and the villas had the most incredible mattresses.

Just then, there was a knock at the door. "You kids decent?" Pete's brother Jason called as he entered. He had the same lanky frame as Pete. Tall, blond, and handsome, all four of the Carlson brothers—Everett, Randy, Jason and Pete—looked like they could be quadruplets, even though there was a two-year age difference between them. A second-year law student at UPenn, Jason was the second youngest of the Carlson brothers. He was adorable, and Blair would've had a crush on him if she wasn't dating Pete.

At least she has a backup.

"We're playing charades. Your presence has been requested."

"Do we have to?" Blair suppressed a groan. It was cute in theory, but they'd played Charades, Pictionary, or Scrabble the last three nights.

Maybe they should shake it up with some Truth or Dare.

"And guess who's requested you on his team again?" Jason smirked, flashing Blair the trademark white-toothed Carlson smile. "Our dad loves you!"

"Aw, that's cute!" Blair said, mustering her enthusiasm. They'd be at the resort soon, so she might as well continue being as polite and friendly as possible to his family. She followed Pete through the wide, arching hallway that led to the kitchen. A large wood stove hunkered in the corner opposite two massive Sub-Zero refrigerators. Several overstuffed yellow chairs sat in front of a large dormer window, each one containing a different member of the family. Pete's father Chappy stood in front of the group.

"Scout!" He called happily as he spotted Blair and Pete.

"Hi, Mr. Carlson." Blair smiled warmly.

"I already claimed you, so back off, boys," Chappy said jovially to Pete's brothers, who all smiled politely back at her. "I'm telling you, Scout, I don't know how I'm going to manage without you next week," Chappy continued.

"Oh, well, I'm sure we can play on the beach or something," Blair said. She blushed. "Play charades on the beach," she clarified.

"Yeah, but what'll I do without my favorite teammate?" Chappy shook his head sorrowfully. "No offense, Jane." He cupped his hand over Blair's ear. "My wife cheats," he whispered, winking at his wife. Jane Carlson had wheat-blond hair cut in a sensible bob and was tall, with an athletic frame. Only the deep wrinkles in her forehead made her seem old enough to be Pete's mom, and they didn't make her look ancient so much as friendly.

"I do cheat, I'll be the first to admit it," Jane said merrily. "I'm glad you're on the straight and narrow." She winked at Blair.

But Blair was still stuck on the part of Chappy's sentence that implied she *wouldn't* be in Costa Rica with them. She'd bought five new Eres bikinis for the occasion. They made the most of the five pounds she'd gained from Yale's meal plan. "*Without me?*" Blair repeated stupidly.

"I mean, I'd bring you along, but we've got a saying in the Carlson family . . ." Chappy began, his eyes shining, as if he were about to deliver a stump speech. "I believe, when it comes to vacations, in the *no ring, no bring* rule."

"It's the Carlson curse." Jason sighed, elbowing Blair in the ribs sympathetically. Blair stepped away. While it was true she'd never *officially* been invited to Costa Rica, she'd been invited for Christmas, for God's sake. Wasn't that even more exclusive than a beach holiday? And why *not* invite her? After all, she'd brought Nate Archibald, her high school boyfriend, on her family vacations for years and it wasn't like she'd been married to him.

Except in her dreams.

"Blair, we love you and we want you in our family for years to come, but I need to be a stickler on this," Chappy explained sympathetically, as if she were one of his constituents, arguing over some impossible and arcane rule. "I've raised four boys, and while they've behaved around you, honestly, these gentlemen cause more theatrics when it comes to ladies than the Yale School of Drama," he finished.

"Maybe you could get together with your girlfriends and have a girl's adventure!" Pete's sister-in-law Sarah piped up from the corner of the room, stroking her eight-months-pregnant belly. "I remember when I heard the Carlson rule, I had a great time with the Theta girls. We went to Cancún!" A look of happy reminiscence crossed Sarah's heart-shaped face.

"You did?" Randy asked, shooting a look at Sarah. "I didn't know that."

"All I'm saying is that Blair should have her own fun." Sarah winked conspiratorially at Blair.

"More hot chocolate, anyone?" Pete's mother asked, excusing herself.

"Sorry, son!" Chappy said, genuinely sounding remorseful as he clapped Pete on the back. "Sorry, Scout!"

Blair narrowed her eyes at a painting that hung over the fireplace, of a ship in what looked like an exceptionally violent storm. What type of fucking art was that to hang in a house? And what the fuck was up with that stupid nickname? Scout?

Out would have been more appropriate.

"Blair, I'm sorry," Pete said simply. "I thought you understood . . ."

"What? I knew I wasn't coming," Blair lied, smiling fakely. Her stomach was churning wildly. For a brief second, she wanted to excuse herself, run to the second-floor bathroom, and puke everything she'd eaten for the past five days. But she didn't.

"Blair, darling, here's your hot chocolate. I made sure to put some extra marshmallows in there." Jane pushed the steaming mug into Blair's hands. "Won't you sit down?" She gestured to one of the comfortable overstuffed chairs.

"Thanks," Blair said. She squared her shoulders and turned to the waiting Carlson clan. "You all ready to play?" She forced herself to smile, a plan already forming.

"Maybe I *will* have a wild girls' weekend," she whispered to Pete. "I haven't been to New York all year." His face fell as he no doubt pictured all the fun she'd be having without him. Blair raised an eyebrow challengingly. After all, she was a woman. A Yale woman. She had places to go.

And games to play.

make new friends, but keep the old . . .

"This came from the man at the other end of the bar," the skinny bartender slash model said as he proffered a glass of champagne.

"Thanks." Serena van der Woodsen glanced down the long, dark oak bar of Saucebox, the new lounge in the just-opened hotel on Thompson Street. Breckin O'Dell, an actor she vaguely remembered meeting a few times, held up his own glass of champagne and saluted her. Serena nodded, brought the glass to her lips and took a sip, even though she preferred vodka.

"Oh my God, you should totally date him. His agent has ridiculous connections," Amanda Atkins said, pulling on the sleeve of Serena's The Row scoopneck jersey dress in excitement. "Can we get some shots down here?" she called to the bartender. Serena smiled indulgently. Amanda was an eighteen-year-old recent LA transplant best known for her role in a dorky sitcom about a girl from Paris who moves to a farm in Tennessee to live with her redneck uncle. Recently, though, she'd been cast in an indie film and was trying to break free from her good girl reputation.

Another shot and she's almost there.

"Maybe," Serena said unconvincingly. She stared at the bubbles fizzing to the top of her glass as if they held the secrets to the universe. If she looked around her, she'd see tons of Breckin O'Dell look-alikes, no doubt wishing *they'd* been the ones to buy Serena van der Woodsen—*the* Serena van der Woodsen—a drink. Instead, they buzzed around Amanda and her other two actress-friends, Alysia and Alison. They called themselves the three A's, even though Alysia's name was actually Jennifer.

The three A's were admittedly a little shallow, but they were also goofy and fun and never turned down a party. Usually, Serena had a blast hanging out with them, but tonight, she felt a little . . . off. Her parents had just left for St. Barts, while her brother, Eric, was spending the winter break in Australia with a girl who'd been a visiting student at Brown last year. It wasn't like she wanted to spend New Year's Eve with her family, but she also didn't like waking up in their huge Fifth Avenue apartment alone. Serena downed her champagne in one gulp, telling herself that she just needed to have fun.

And, after all, she is the expert.

"Hey, you're that farm chick!" one guy stuttered, not looking Amanda in the eye. His hair was gelled and he was wearing a pink and white striped button-down. It was clear that he'd had to bribe the bouncer to get into the bar.

"Yes," Amanda sighed. "But, actually, I have to stand over here now." Amanda took two steps away, as Alysia and Alison snorted in laughter. Serena offered the guy a sympathetic smile. Even though she was beautiful, Serena was never mean.

An infuriating combination.

"God, you'd think Knowledge would know to not to let guys like that in. Did you see his hair? It was, like, sprayed on." Amanda flipped her extensions over her shoulder as she named the beefy bouncer whose job was to keep Saucebox as exclusive as possible, even though, to Serena, it felt exactly the same as every other bar she'd been to recently.

"Serena?"

Serena whirled around, ready to have another one of those *so great to see you* conversations with someone she'd probably met once. Instead, she saw a familiar, smiling face that immediately took her back in time.

"Oh my God, Iz!" Serena squealed excitedly. She slid off the smooth bar stool and threw her arms around Isabel Coates, a fellow Constance Billard alum who'd gone to Rollins College down in Florida. She was super tan and had highlights in her shoulder-length blond hair. She automatically looked over Isabel's shoulder, sure she'd see Kati Farkas, Isabel's best friend and constant sidekick. Isabel and Kati had done everything together back in high school. Kati even turned down admission to Princeton so they wouldn't have to be separated. But instead of Kati, a girl with a ski-jump nose and straight brown hair stood next to Isabel.

"This is my girlfriend, Casey," Isabel announced proudly.

"Oh." Wait, did that mean *girlfriend* girlfriend? Serena noticed Isabel's hand intertwined with Casey's.

"We met in a women's studies class." Isabel smiled adoringly at Casey.

There's her answer.

"This is Serena van der Woodsen. We went to school together," she explained.

"Nice to meet you, Casey," Serena said, holding out her hand to the tall girl, who took it gingerly.

"Nice to meet you, too. I haven't seen any of your movies," Casey announced self-importantly.

"How's Kati?" Serena asked.

Isabel sighed and shook her head. "She has this, like, football player boyfriend and is pledging a sorority that wears pink sweatsuits to class. It's awful," she sighed disdainfully. "Casey and I pretty much do our own thing. But what about *you*? I saw your movie. You were pretty good," Isabel allowed.

"Thanks," Serena said, resisting the urge to roll her eyes. "Things are okay. Just working a lot. We're filming a sequel to *Breakfast at Fred's* that's coming out in summer, so that's fun . . ." Serena trailed off. Even though she'd been on the cover of the October issue of *Vanity Fair*, part of her felt stuck. After all, she'd come home from her big premiere to her same pink childhood bedroom in her parents' sprawling penthouse. If possible, she almost felt *less* grown up than she had last year, especially since she now had an agent and a publicist who told her exactly what to wear, what to say, and who to be seen with.

"Sounds great!" Isabel cooed. "Anyway, I was just showing Casey all the old places we used to go. Remember how we used to like, spend hours trying things on at Barneys? I just can't believe we were ever so *young*. Things have changed a lot," she mused, nuzzling her blond-highlighted head against Casey.

"Things *have* changed," Serena agreed. Less than a year ago, she and Blair and Kati and Isabel would meet before school to smoke Merits on the Met steps and imagine their lives in college. Now, Blair was a poli-sci major at Yale, Isabel was a lesbian, Kati was a sorority girl, and Serena was a movie star.

"So, have you seen anyone?" Isabel asked.

"No." Serena shook her head. For her, only two people really mattered: Blair and Nate. She and Blair had tried to keep in touch, and once Serena had sent Blair a package full of Wolford stockings and black and white cookies in a Barneys bag—all of Blair's favorite New York things. Blair had reciprocated with a stuffed bulldog wearing a Yale T-shirt. They'd send occasional e-mails and texts, but never anything long or involved. It was fine, though. Blair and Serena were the type of friends who could go weeks without speaking, then pick up right where they left off.

As for Nate . . . they hadn't talked since he left, to sail the world for a year. Serena wondered if she'd ever see him again. But she didn't want to think about that right now.

Or ever.

"Are you going to Chuck's New Year's party tomorrow night?" Isabel asked, draining the rest of her drink. "I mean, I know he's, like, such a misogynist, but I figured, you can only protest so much, you know? I prepared Casey."

"Wait, didn't Chuck go to military school?" She hadn't

thought about Chuck—with his sketchy history, his trademark monogrammed scarf, or his questionable sexuality—for months. But the last she'd heard, after getting rejected from all twelve schools he'd applied to, he'd gone to some underground, in-the-middle-of-nowhere academy. Of course her parents saw Chuck's parents socially, but they never mentioned him. It was an unspoken rule on the Upper East Side that parents didn't discuss their unsuccessful children.

"Who knows?" Isabel shrugged. "The party's on, though. I saw Laura Salmon at City Bakery this morning and she told me she spoke to Rain Hofstetter at some lame Constance alum tea party that Mrs. M organized. Thank god I missed that. But, anyway, I guess she talked to Chuck? I don't know. It's at the Tribeca Star. But I guess since you're a movie star and all, you probably have to host some MTV special or something, right?"

"Well . . ." Serena trailed off. In truth, she already had an invite to a party at Thaddeus Russell's Chelsea loft. Thaddeus had been her *Breakfast at Fred's* costar and was a true friend. But he wouldn't mind if she stopped by to say hi and then went off to Chuck's party.

"I'll be there," Serena chirped. She suddenly couldn't wait for New Year's Eve. How could she *not* go see her old high school crowd? While she may not have been thinking of them all that much recently, it wasn't like she'd forgotten them.

And they certainly haven't forgotten her.

I will always love you

a gossip girl novel

the secret is out 11.03.09

Spotted: **B, S, N, D** and **Little J**
on Limited Collector's Editions of the
#1 bestselling Gossip Girl novels
that inspired the CW's hit show.

Each edition includes an
exclusive poster on the
reverse side of the jacket
featuring a gorgeous,
frame-worthy image
from the show.

Add style and scandal
to your library.
Collect all twelve!

Welcome to Poppy.

A poppy is a beautiful blooming red flower
(like the one on the spine of this book). It is also
the name of the home of your favorite books.

Poppy takes the real world and makes it
a little funnier, a little more fabulous.

Poppy novels are wild, witty, and inspiring.
They were written just for you.

So sit back, get comfy, and pick a Poppy.

poppy

www.pickapoppy.com

THE A-LIST
HOLLYWOOD ROYALTY

gossip girl

THE CLIQUE

ALPHAS

SECRETS OF MY
HOLLYWOOD LIFE

the it girl

POSEUR

And introducing ALPHAS, the hawt new Clique spin-off series,
coming September 2009.